AFTER YESTERDAY

JACQUELINE HAYLEY

Copyright © 2022 by Jacqueline Hayley

All rights reserved.

No part of this book may be reproduced in any form or by any electronic or mechanical means, including information storage and retrieval systems, without written permission from the author, except for the use of brief quotations in a book review.

Editing by Kelly Rigby www.writewithkelly.com

JacquelineHayley

Romance ♥

Reader warning: This series is set at the end of the world, so you can expect violence, gratuitous swearing and sex scenes that will make you blush. *you're welcome*

*Dedicated to V.B. Law, who gave me
the motivation to get this book written.*

This novel was written on Wiradjuri Country in Central West NSW, Australia. I would like to acknowledge the Wiradjuri people who are the Traditional Custodians of the Land, and pay my respects to the Elders both past and present.

PROLOGUE

12 DAYS AGO

"You take one more step in this direction, and I can almost guarantee you a permanent disability."

Rachel Davenport wasn't exaggerating. The last person she wanted to see right now was James O'Connor—the high school sweetheart who'd destroyed her when he skipped town eight years ago. And now, apparently, the same man who wanted to make amends.

She wasn't sure that 'fuck off' was an emotion, but she felt that shit in her soul.

"Did you just quote *Dawson's Creek* at me?" James hiked an eyebrow.

Nope. Just, no.

He did not get to bring up the fact they had watched the whole six seasons of *Dawson's Creek* one rainy summer, limbs entwined and eyes tender.

There was *nothing* tender about her now.

So why, *why* did the sight of him unlock every fluttery-sweet memory that she'd worked so hard to lock away? In the eight years since he'd left, he'd filled into the promise of his youth—tall, broad and, damn it all to hell, gorgeous.

"What are you doing back in Sanford?" she demanded, crossing her arms over her chest then letting them swing free again when she realised she was still holding a basket of strawberries.

Her free hand landed on her hip, and she glanced around the supermarket to gauge exactly how quickly this "reunion" was going to make it onto her small town's gossip radar.

It was then she noticed how empty the place appeared. Tinny music, which normally couldn't be heard over the bustle of shoppers, echoed.

"Where is everyone?" Her best friend, Kat, barrelled into the produce section with their shopping cart. "This place is deserted. And I know you said no Doritos, but I got Doritos."

She careened to a stop. "Holy shitballs, look what the cat dragged in." She looked wildly between James and Rachel. "What are you doing back here, fuckboy?"

"That's what I'd like to know." Rachel resisted the urge to spit the words like an enraged feline. This man did not get to waltz back into her carefully curated life. Not after leaving the way he did.

"You two make one hell of a welcoming committee." James raised his palms in a placating gesture. "I'm the Operations and Logistics Manager for the Smythson Group. I'm here to overview the whiskey distillery and—"

"We don't care," Kat interrupted. "I want to know why you think Rach would have *anything* to say to you."

While Rachel appreciated Kat had her back, she hadn't developed a reputation for being a hardass for nothing. She could handle this.

"Do what you've got to do, James. Like Kat said, I don't care." Her voice was hard, clipped. And she registered the surprise that flared in his eyes. "Do your job, stay out of my way, and then get out of my town."

The sadness etched on his face made something twist in her chest, but she turned away.

"Did you get milk?" she asked Kat, silently urging her friend to let this go. Kat thrived on drama, but she was loyal to a fault.

She walked away, Kat trailing her with the cart.

"Your brand wasn't on the shelf. They were out of those muffins I like, too."

Margo Worthington, a neighbor to their friend Quinn, looked up from a list she was holding. "I heard the delivery truck is late." She choked out a phlegmy cough. "Sorry, this cough is knocking me around."

"You should be in bed," said Rachel.

And not spreading your germs to everyone else.

"Seems like it's going around," said Kat.

Rachel stilled, listening to various unseen people coughing in other aisles.

"Let's get out of here before we catch whatever it is they've got."

"So, you're good with Doritos?"

"I knew I shouldn't have agreed to you tagging along."

CHAPTER ONE

DAY 8

The world as Rachel knew it had changed irrevocably eight days ago. This morning, however, it had shattered beyond recognition.

With the outbreak of the Syrian Virus decimating the world's population, Rachel had watched in horror as her hometown of Sanford fell to the misogynist men running it; she'd known the town council was a ticking time bomb. And it had just exploded.

Forcing herself to focus, she surveyed Chloe's kitchen. What first?

"What do you need?" asked James, standing in the doorway.

"Ah, I need you to get out of Chloe's house. What are you even doing here?" Rachel glanced up from the kitchen drawer she'd begun ransacking. "Chlo, where are your sharp kitchen knives?"

"Rach, stop. You can't bring a knife to a gunfight," James said.

"Are you even kidding right now? Our town's Mayor

has turned into a psychopathic dictator and just trafficked Mackenzie, my best friend, to a motorcycle gang. You think *now* is the time to be cute?"

"You forgot Jake tore out of here to take on the gang practically single-handedly, and half the world is probably dead from Sy-V," Kat added through a mouthful of Doritos.

Chloe flinched at the mention of her brother.

"Not helping, Kat."

And it's a lot more than half.

The Syrian Virus—Sy-V—had been nothing more than rumours on the Internet. Until it wasn't. Until the United States military were bombing cities where the virus couldn't be contained, telecommunications ceased, and the population of Sanford—their hometown—now numbered in the hundreds, not thousands.

In just days, society had fallen.

And an inconvenient ex-boyfriend was the least of Rachel's worries.

"I get it. I'm not trying to make this harder for you, Rach. But we're in this together." James ran his hands through his hair.

"No, we're not," she replied flatly.

Mackenzie's dog, Dex, pressed himself against her leg and growled at James. It was just a warning, but the big German Shepherd was scary as shit.

James took a step backwards, and Rachel patted the big dog's head.

"Would you two drop it?" Quinn's growl was almost as low as Dex's. The big man was Chloe's cousin, and his bulk made the full kitchen appear even more crowded. "We need to pack up and get the fuck out of Sanford. The motorcycle gang was taking Mac to Dutton, and Jake and the others should be there by now. But they're going to need backup if they have any hope of rescuing her."

"Okay, what do we need?" Kat pushed the Doritos away and sat up straighter. "Jake and Jesse took all the weapons we had."

"Walkie talkies," Rachel said. "We should try to steal some from the council. We need to communicate."

"Good idea. But I think Quinn meant longer term. I'm assuming we're all in agreement we can't live in Sanford while the council is running things?" said James.

Sanford was the picture of an all-American small town. Until Sy-V had hit. The women of the town's council were away on retreat, leaving the men to consolidate power and install a totalitarian regime that saw them bartering Mackenzie and two other women to a brutal gang, in exchange for a promise the town was safe from attack.

"What? You mean leave for good?" Chloe's eyes darted from face to face. "We can't do that!"

Rachel hated the idea of leaving their hometown, too. But with the council finally showing their true colors, she didn't see they had much of a choice. It's not like they could bring Mackenzie back. None of them were safe here, knowledge that sat heavy on her chest.

"We can't stay here, Chlo. Who knows what Mayor Townsend will do next?" Rachel closed the kitchen drawer.

"No!" The pitch of Chloe's cry had them all swinging to face her.

"Are you worried about catching Sy-V outside?" asked Kat, pulling Chloe close with an arm around her waist. "Because you know what Jesse said; if we're still alive now, then we're immune."

As a veterinarian with a science background, Rachel agreed with Jesse's hypothesis. But it was still just that, a hypothesis. The government or military had yet to make an appearance with information. Or a vaccine or supplies or, *anything*.

They'd been living in the vacuum of Sanford since the start of the outbreak. Which Townsend had capitalised on, instilling fear and tightening his control. Rachel wanted to believe someone would arrive to save them, but her gut told her that wasn't happening anytime soon.

"No. I can't leave," Chloe's mouth set in a determined line. "I need to be here when Ash gets back."

The chances of Ash being alive and making it back to Sanford were close to zero. Rachel wasn't sure how to break that to Chloe without sounding too brutal. She caught Kat's gaze and bit back her response when she saw Kat's subtle head shake.

Now wasn't the time to tell Chloe her husband was most likely not making it back from his business trip.

"We can't stay, Chloe." She knew it sounded heartless, but Chloe and Kat were her family, and there was no chance she was leaving one of them behind. Even if she had to knock Chloe out and get Quinn to carry her over his shoulder.

"We could leave him a note," suggested Kat, grabbing for a shopping list notepad on the kitchen bench, "then he'll know where to find us."

"No," Chloe repeated. She was holding onto the back of a dining chair, her knuckles white.

Exasperation had Rachel's fists clenching. She didn't have the patience to explain to Chloe how she was putting them all in danger. She'd just force her into a vehicle when they were ready to leave.

Right now, they needed to prepare.

"Winter is coming. We've got maybe a week or two

before the snow starts," she said. "Quinn, do you know what Jake and Mackenzie did with those camping supplies they picked up?"

"I think they're still at my house."

"That's in the Evac Area." James stepped further into the kitchen.

"So?" Rachel snapped. "We pick them up on our way out."

"And how are we getting out, exactly?" asked James. "Because last I knew the council was patrolling the Safe Zone, and had guards on all entry and exit points to the town."

"That's keeping people out, not in. They'll let us leave. Townsend knows we're against him and will be happy to get rid of us. Plus, it's fewer mouths to feed." Rachel wasn't sure why she was explaining herself to James, and when had she just accepted that he was coming with them?

"Well, I say we just leave. We can scavenge what we need when we're out." James crossed his arms across his broad chest, as though he'd decided their course of action.

Rachel slammed closed the cupboard she'd just opened.

"Easy for you to say, when you're not leaving your home."

It was a bitter reminder that Sanford hadn't been his home for eight years.

"The only essentials right now are weapons, and Townsend has already confiscated everything," James reminded her. "We're better off getting out of here before—"

Dex let out a booming bark that felt like a physical assault, making both Chloe and Kat scream and Rachel drop the can of beans she was clutching. The dog raced to the front door on high alert.

James and Quinn moved to follow the dog, but Rachel pushed ahead of them. Had someone come with news of Mackenzie and Jake?

Dex was crouched low, growling at the closed door, the hair along his spine bristling. Rachel had the fleeting thought that without Mackenzie, could they even control this animal?

"Who's there?" she called out.

The door burst open, and Trent Gelbart stormed through, gun first and several men behind him. Time slowed as Dex reared back on his powerful haunches and launched at Trent's throat. Rachel watched, horrified, as the man's gun centred square on the advancing dog's chest. But Dex was frighteningly quick. And deadly. His jaws had clamped around the intruder's neck as Trent fell backwards. He was dead before anyone registered his ripped-out jugular. Before he even fell to the ground.

Rachel recoiled violently, crashing into James. The carnage splayed out before her had a flash of bile rising in her throat.

Dex, muzzle dripping red, backed off Trent's lifeless body and planted himself before Rachel, his growl reverberating through her as he faced the remaining men.

"What the fuck!" one shouted, stunned.

"Someone, shoot that fucking dog!"

Rachel reached a trembling hand to Dex as James pushed in front and slammed the door shut, locking it. "Get to the kitchen!"

Tugging on Dex's collar and shepherded by James, Rachel raced back to the others. Kat already had the back door open and was bundling Chloe into a jacket. She hadn't seen the men coming up the porch steps, weapons levelled and steady.

"Kat!" Rachel screamed.

"We need to get rid of the dog," James said, pulling Dex's collar from Rachel's grasp and hauling him towards the laundry.

"What are you *doing*?" Rachel hissed.

"Getting him out of here before they shoot him."

Rachel heard the external laundry door open and James yell at the dog to go. Hopefully, Dex was smart enough to get the hell out of here. If James was smart, he'd use this opportunity to get the hell out, too.

If Chloe and Kat couldn't run, Rachel wasn't either. It seemed Quinn was of the same mind. Together, the four of them backed into the middle of the kitchen, warily watching the advancing men.

"No one has to get hurt. Get on the ground," called out Gavin Turner, coming through the back door.

Rachel blanched. Gavin had been in Quinn's year at school, and his cruelty to younger students had become the stuff of legend. And nightmares.

"What's going on, Gav?" Quinn put his hands on his hips.

The sound of the front door being busted open preceded three men coming up on their rear.

"Hands in the air," demanded one of them, his trucker cap pulled low. "You, get with the others." He lifted his chin and Rachel realised he was speaking to James.

Not so smart, then.

"Gavin, what are you doing?" asked Rachel. "We've done nothing wrong."

"Where's that mutt?" asked Trucker Cap.

"Who cares about a dog? Secure them," Gavin demanded.

11

"You didn't see what the dog was capable of. It needs to be put down."

"Forget the damn dog. Townsend wants these five at Town Hall, stat."

"Gavin, what–" Gavin's palm cracked across Rachel's cheek, pain blooming sharp and hot, making her stagger from the force.

"You've always had a big mouth, Rachel Davenport. You need to learn to shut it," Gavin snarled.

"Get your hands off her!" James faced off the smirking Gavin, who casually waved the barrel of his gun.

"Or what, big man? Nothing you can do about shit."

"James, no," Rachel whispered, hand against her throbbing face. She wanted nothing more than to bitch-slap the smirk off Gavin's face, but she wasn't stupid.

In minutes they had their hands zip-tied behind their backs, and the men were marching them from the house and into the back of a truck.

Rachel flashed to this morning, when Mackenzie had also been escorted from the house with her hands tied. Instinctively, she pulled against her restraint, wincing as the plastic cut into her skin.

The gut churning fear for her friend surpassed her own predicament. Because no matter what, she'd survive. She always did.

———

DAY 12

James had had some bad days since he'd been back in Sanford, but today was hitting a new low. They'd known Mayor Townsend was getting out of control, but this was insane.

"This is the democratic United States of America, not a war-torn third world country," he muttered, pacing the length of the office within Town Hall that they'd been crammed into four days ago.

"Wrong. There is nothing democratic about the apocalypse," Rachel snapped at him, furiously scribbling on a piece of paper.

Snapping seemed to be her sole way of communicating with him and, after two weeks, it was wearing thin. He loved this woman. Loved her spark and her strength and her smarts. Loved that she insisted on doing everything for herself and loved that she *could* do everything for herself. But damn, could she cut him a break?

He knew he had a lot to make up for, and when he'd come back to Sanford, he hadn't thought it was going to be easy. But he also hadn't factored in the world as they knew it ending. It didn't help that she wouldn't give him a chance to explain.

"Rach–"

"Back off, James." Kat got up from her spot on the floor and attempted to intimidate him with her diminutive statue. "Don't make this worse."

Could it get worse? They'd been subsisting on whatever vending machine junk food their guards threw in twice a day and using a bucket behind a screened off desk as a toilet.

All of them, for four days.

The smell of human waste was thick. Bearable only because the temperature was dropping every day, and the council hadn't seen fit to heat their makeshift prison.

"I told you, any snark and it's twenty push-ups." Quinn hefted his bulk from the chair he'd been sitting on. "All of you, on the floor."

James readily joined him, relishing the pull across the back of his shoulders and the burn in his biceps. Quinn's constant efforts at keeping them moving, building their strength, was the only thing keeping him sane.

Out of the corner of his eye, he saw Rachel begin her own set, purely, he suspected, to prove she could do anything he could do. She was rapid and precise, and he pushed himself harder to distract from the small grunts she was making.

He wasn't sure how much longer he could take this proximity without taking *her*. Because when he finally acknowledged the truth—that it may have been first love with Rachel, but it was *true* love—he hadn't been able to take a full breath until he'd called off his engagement. Until he'd booked a flight back to Sanford.

Only then had his lungs eased.

And now. Now.

Now, he was in some kind of purgatory, attempting to atone for his past sins.

"Kat, lying on the floor does not constitute a push-up," said Quinn drily, having finished his set and rolled over to start on sit-ups.

"Fuck off," Kat mumbled into the carpet.

"Don't make me make you," the big man threatened.

James hid a grin.

It was obvious Quinn had a thing for the little fire-cracker, and James wished him well. Kat had always been a handful and, from what he could tell, nothing had changed in the years he'd been away.

Chloe remained huddled on one of the bare mattresses they'd been given, and no one forced her to join them. She wasn't doing so well. Envy had stabbed at his gut when he thought of all the years Chloe had had with Ash, her high school sweetheart. Years he had wasted.

But he didn't envy the grief that shrouded her now.

And not just for Ash.

Chloe's parents had been vacationing in Hawaii, so chances were she'd never know what happened to them. Even if they survived the virus, he doubted airlines would be up and running anytime soon. Then she'd discovered someone on the council had gone rogue and murdered a bunch of elderly folks—her grandmother among them. And now her brother, Jake, had taken off, looking for Mackenzie, a woman more like Chloe's sister than her friend.

They were all worried about Mackenzie's fate. Not knowing if Jake and the others had rescued her from the gang who'd taken her was a constant gnawing fear, overshadowed only by apprehension for their own predicament.

"Townsend can't be so concerned about our dissent that he'd keep us locked up for days," James said, rolling onto his stomach and speaking to the ceiling. "Why not just kick us out of town? We'd go willingly."

"He doesn't want to lose face. Can't have the rest of the townspeople see us losing faith. Deserting," Rachel said, having also flopped onto her stomach. "It's about control."

He mulled that over, closing his eyes against the harsh fluorescent lighting overhead.

Several gasps had his eyes popping open, to complete blackness.

"What's going on?" Chloe cried.

He blinked, trying to get accustomed to the dark. Not once in the four days they'd been locked in the windowless office had the lights gone off.

It had been becoming harder and harder to keep track of night and day.

"Do you think that was on purpose?" His thoughts raced. Was this a new kind of punishment, or had there been a power outage?

No one answered. In silence, they listened to the sounds in the hallway outside, amplified now without the incessant low-key buzz from the lights. Muffled footsteps appeared to be running, and a radio crackled to life with a muted voice.

"Did you hear that?" Rachel sat up, and James realised it wasn't as dark as he'd first thought. "Whoever was on that radio said electricity was down. Everywhere."

"It was only a matter of time," Quinn commented.

"What? Why?" Chloe squeaked, moving closer to Kat.

"No one to keep the power plants going." In truth, it surprised James how long the electricity grid had held up. Water would be the next utility to go.

Damn, he'd miss hot showers.

"Now. We should try to escape now!" Rachel had jumped to her feet and was pulling futilely on the door handle. "While they're distracted, maybe there's no guard on our door."

"You've forgotten we've already discussed how none of us can pick a lock," said James, even as he wished he weren't the one raining on her parade.

"You and Quinn are big enough. Can't you just bust the door down?" Rachel demanded.

James was pretty sure that only worked in the movies but, hearing the distress in Rachel's voice, he shut up.

"Quinn, can't you—" That was Kat.

"James is right," said Quinn. "We should stick to the original plan and attack when they get complacent bringing us food. The last thing we need is one of us getting shot."

James watched as Rachel took a deep breath and

stepped away from the door. What he wouldn't give to comfort her right now.

"James could take one for the team," she offered helpfully. "I wouldn't mind so much if he got shot."

He winced. "Harsh, Davenport."

IT WAS another twenty-four hours before their guards returned with food—waiting in almost complete darkness, with no knowledge of what was happening outside. Rachel wasn't the only one snapping now. They were all nearing the end of their endurance.

James' left leg was in a state of constant jitters. No matter what exercise or stretch he tried to ease the muscle tension. It was driving him insane.

He was the only one awake when the door opened, filtering in weak daylight and signalling it was early morning.

"Fuck! It reeks in here," Gavin said, throwing a handful of protein bars on the floor. "Get up, all of you. It's time to work for your rations."

"Gav, just let us go. We'll leave Sanford," said Quinn, rising from the floor and stepping forward.

"Back the fuck up, Big Q," Gavin warned, raising his AR-15. "Townsend needs workers and you, my friend, are gonna work."

James saw Rachel start forward in his periphery and instantly moved to block her. No way was Gavin laying another hand on her. The hot rage when he thought of the red stain Gavin had left across Rachel's face churned in his gut. His jaw cracked as he ground his teeth.

"Get your shit together and let's go." Gavin gestured

with his rifle. "Townsend is putting work teams together to clear the abandoned houses."

They found out over the next several days that "clearing" houses was a systemized process, with each work team involving a guard-driven truck. Two armed guards would sweep a house first, identifying dead bodies and shooting any pets that had been left behind. When James, anticipating Rachel's outrage, asked if they couldn't just release the pets and leave them to their own devices, he'd received a rifle butt between his shoulder blades. They all took that as a no.

A pair of "workers" would be dispatched to drag dead bodies—human and animal—into the backyard where they were burned, while several others would strip the house of anything useful. They were expected to leave each place a shell—Townsend even wanted doors unscrewed and loaded onto the waiting trucks.

He'd requisitioned the old Benson warehouse behind the distillery as a supplies store, and had teams working within it to catalogue, categorise and stock the pallet-lined shelves.

It was an enormous undertaking that would take weeks, if not months, to complete.

Logistics was part of his role with the Smythson Group, and James had to admire the lengths Townsend was going to build Sanford into what he assumed would be a trading powerhouse within the surrounding region.

James paused in hefting an armchair onto its side to watch through a back window as Quinn and a guy James didn't recognise poured gasoline onto a pile of three cats, and lit it.

The fact he was becoming immune to the stench of burning flesh would have been disturbing if he weren't so exhausted. They were worked fourteen hours a day, grateful they'd been assigned a bathroom block within Town Hall that housed a shower, and were finally being fed actual food.

There was a feverish impatience to the guards—no doubt transferred from Townsend—and James couldn't help wondering what their Mayor thought he was preparing for.

Quinn caught his eye, and they shared a grimace. James had offered to share in the gruesome work detail, and pushed his relief at Quinn's refusal down into the pit where his guilt and regret over Rachel lived.

Mercifully, there had been few dead human bodies in the houses they'd been through over the last couple of days. Had it already been days?

He watched Rachel—stoic and methodical—and despaired over the brittleness she exuded, fearing she was breaking inside. His heart ached, and his arms ached, and he was tired. So tired.

Minutes became hours, and the hours dragged, blurring into each other until days had passed and they were too weary, too disheartened, to think. To plan. To do anything but trudge to the next house.

CHAPTER TWO

DAY 20

The scent of decay pervaded their whole town. Even if they were clearing a house that didn't have decomposing bodies to dispose of and burn, there was the sweet rot of bananas left on a bench. The stench of spoiled food as you opened a refrigerator.

And, depending on the way the wind blew, the horrific reminder of the many, many bodies of their fellow townspeople, rotting at the town's hospital where they'd been sent for quarantine. Rachel shuddered at the thought of those left to die in undignified huddles.

The first snow of Winter couldn't come fast enough.

She surreptitiously glanced over her shoulder, checking the guard had gone back outside to smoke a cigarette against the waiting truck. She'd already found a loose square of linoleum on the kitchen floor, and now gathered up the pile of photographs she'd been collecting.

They'd been told to remove all personal effects from frames, and burn them with the bodies. Her small rebellion of secreting these memories away in the ceilings or floors of homes was the only way Rachel could stomach what they were doing.

What Townsend was making them do.

Their Mayor was walking a fine line keeping the community supporting him in his totalitarian regime, but so far, his fear tactics were working.

"What are you doing?" James came into the kitchen as she replaced the linoleum and stood, her foot smoothing over the edge of the flap.

Concern was etched on his handsome face and Rachel hated, *hated*, that she even noticed what the man looked like. It shouldn't matter that he had an attractively blunt jaw, that his shaggy hair fell into beautifully blue eyes, or that his lips... Jesus, his *lips*.

She shook her head. James O'Connor could be the Messiah for all she cared. The frustration she harboured over her untameable desire morphed into anger, and her eyes narrowed.

"None of your business."

"Whatever it is, stop." James' jaw ticked. "These guys aren't playing at guards, Rach. They're deadly serious."

As if she didn't know that. She'd been standing right beside him yesterday when a guard from a work group two houses over shot Jez Parker for hiding batteries in his jacket.

They killed him over *batteries*.

But it wasn't really over stolen goods. It was about "stealing from the greater good". It was about exerting absolute control. And if you had the guns, you had the control.

"Seriously, Rach..."

"I get it, O'Connor."

And she did.

A side-effect of Sy-V's annihilation of society was an anxiety that made you want to hoard. And the initial panic had given way to self-interest—an innate need for self-preservation that made people do things they never would have before. Like carrying weapons against neighbors and friends.

"I just want..." He stood close to her. Too close.

She took a step back, narrowing her eyes. For fuck's sake. Could the man ever finish a sentence? He wanted what? To apologise? Because it was going to take more than words to make amends for the bloody mess he'd made of her heart all those years ago.

"You want what, James?" she snapped, angered anew at her body's traitorous reaction to his presence.

"You feel it too," he accused softly.

"I don't feel anything."

"Well, I do. You feel like home."

His words were a whispered caress, a balm against the heavy ache she carried. An ache for the memory of what had been. Because they may have been young, but their love had been fierce. It had been the forever kind of love.

Until it wasn't.

She took a second step backwards.

"You two, move it. We're heading back to Town Hall. Snow's coming," said Shelton Morris, shouldering his rifle to pull on gloves.

Rachel shoved her hands into her pockets and braced for the icy air as she headed out to the truck. Kat and Chloe stood with their arms around each other, stamping their feet. Flakes of snow already caught in their hair.

"Would you rather," started Kat when she saw her, "be in jail for five years, or be in a coma for a decade?"

Playing 'would you rather' was how they spent the walk back to Town Hall each evening.

James and Quinn fell into step beside them as they began the trek back through the streets of Sanford, their breaths puffs of white in the air before them.

"Is this pre-apocalypse?" said James. "Because that's definitely going to affect my answer."

"Do I need medical care for my coma, or can I just chill in my bed and you'll feed me with an intravenous drip?" Rachel asked.

Chloe rolled her eyes. "You're the only one of us who knows how to do something like that, so that's not an option for your coma."

Rachel smiled, purely because Chloe had been so quiet lately, and it was nice to have her engaged in the conversation.

The truck they were following stopped suddenly, and the five of them halted. In the red taillights, the snow was swirling thicker.

"What's the holdup?" Quinn asked as Shelton jumped down from the truck's cab, radio in his hand.

"We need to be back at Town Hall *now*. Get in the back of the truck." Shelton opened the double back doors and waved them inside.

"There's not enough room." Rachel's fight-or-flight instinct engaged. Something was wrong.

"That gang is back, so hurry the fuck up, or I'll leave you here. With a bullet in your skull," said Shelton.

Dread fisted Rachel's gut. Did that mean they'd find out what happened to Mackenzie and Jake? She stumbled into the cramped interior of the truck, standing between a stack of boxes and the strong, warm chest of James. His size bracketed her, protecting her from the jolt of the truck starting forward.

She swallowed a suddenly dry throat, steadying herself against the boxes and leaning away from the comfort of his presence.

This is what irritated her. He kept pushing himself at her, apparently heedless of the *fucking apocalypse*. She did not have the mental capacity to deal with him. To deal with her stupid body and its stupid cravings.

"Do you think they'll have Jake and Mackenzie?" Chloe's gripped tight to Kat's hand.

"I hope not. Imagine if they've been captives this whole time," Rachel replied.

"If they got away, why haven't they come back for us?"

No one answered.

The truck shuddered to a stop and in the silence of the engine ticking over, they heard Shelton and Troy exit, slamming their doors. Everything was muffled. Distant.

Minutes passed.

"They're not going to leave us in here, are they?" said Kat, a catch in her voice.

"Can we open the door from the inside?" Rachel pushed against the immovable weight of James. He turned just as the doors flung open.

Gavin gestured at them to get out. "Big Q, get up here. We need you."

Rachel looked around wildly, taking in the men of Sanford's council standing on the steps to Town Hall, facing down a dozen gang members on motorcycles and several more in pickup trucks with attached snow-ploughs.

In the descending darkness, the scene was lit by the pickups' headlights, causing macabre shadows to dance across the footpath as Sanford residents rushed to stand behind their leader.

"Do I get a gun?" Quinn asked Gavin.

"Not a fucking chance."

Close enough now to hear the conversation between Townsend and a leggy brunette, Rachel, Kat and Chloe crouched behind a parked car. The brunette had no weapons, but was flanked by two seriously scary guys who carried the kind of guns Rachel imagined belonged in a war zone.

"I'm insulted you don't look happier to see me." The brunette laughed at Townsend.

"We had a deal, Gemma. We gave you the women, and you leave Sanford alone." Townsend appeared full of his usual bluster, but Rachel saw the telltale tremor of his hand.

"Those women you gave us ran off. So, it's time for a new deal." The brunette—Gemma—shrugged. "I want your whiskey distillery."

Chloe sagged against Rachel, and Kat reached for their hands, squeezing tight. Mackenzie had escaped.

"No. Absolutely not." The color was rising in Townsend's face. "I'm willing to offer you whiskey in return for protection, but you're not getting the distillery."

"I'm not asking, Mayor. We'll be back in twenty-four hours, and I want unrestricted access. That distillery is now mine." Gemma's smile was confident. Victorious. "And don't be stupid. I'm being reasonable and allowing you to stay here, but I'll slaughter every single one of you if there's any form of resistance. And you know we have the fire-power to do it. See you tomorrow, Mayor."

Gemma flipped her long hair as she turned on her heel, striding to an enormous motorcycle and swinging a leg over.

Kick-starting the beast, she tore out of the town square, followed by her gang of marauders.

The townsfolk erupted into a rabble of noise, and Rachel tugged Chloe and Kat with her further into the shadows. They had to get out of here, now.

A single gunshot burst into the night air, and they froze.

"Settle down!" Townsend bellowed. "Now is not the time to panic."

Rachel gasped at a hard hand on her shoulder. "Rachel fucking Davenport," sneered Gavin. "Where do you think you're going?"

RACHEL'S CHEEK was smarting from the new blow she'd received from Gavin, but it was nothing compared to the fury bubbling inside her. Not for the first time she cursed the empowerment retreat that had taken all the women from the council out of town, days before Sy-V had collapsed the world. Her mother among them.

Maree Davenport had been a prominent councilwoman for many years, and her discontent with Mayor Townsend was legendary. Maree's progressive attitude was a thorn in Townsend's side, and Rachel *knew* things would be different in Sanford right now if her mother were here.

If she framed Maree's absence in this way, she could ignore the ever-present pain of missing her as a mother. Rachel didn't cry as a rule, but every reminder of her mom had tears at the back of her eyes, just waiting to fall.

She grit her teeth. There would be no tears.

They had herded the five of them back to their prison within Town Hall, after listening to Townsend expound the dangers of leaving Sanford for the Sy-V ravaged world beyond. It was only then that Rachel realised he hadn't shared the knowledge of possible immunity with the rest of their community.

He needed their fear to maintain his control.

In this way, he'd convinced everyone that leaving wasn't an option, and neither was defeat. They would barricade themselves inside the distillery and the adjoining bar—The Strumpet—and fortify. Bunker down and defy Gemma's orders.

"We need to get the fuck out of this town." James paced before them as Rachel nestled on the floor with Kat and Chloe for warmth. "Did you see the artillery that gang was packing? They could blow this whole place to hell."

"Which makes you wonder why they're even negotiating," said Quinn, his large frame sitting atop a cleared-off desk.

"They're going to need our townspeople, at least the ones who know how to work the distillery," James answered.

Quinn nodded. "When everyone's moving into the distillery tomorrow, we look for a chance to run. Head to Dutton and see if we can meet up with Jake and Mackenzie."

"How? How are we going to achieve this, exactly?" Rachel's teeth were chattering. Jesus *Christ,* it was cold in this room.

The electricity provided by the generator Townsend had set up in Town Hall was not extended to their side of the building.

"If you see a chance to slip away, take it." James drilled her with his gaze. "Don't wait for all of us to leave at the same time. Even if only one or two of us get out, it's better than none."

Rachel nodded in agreement, even as she internally

scorned his stupidity. As if there was a chance in hell she'd leave without Kat and Chloe.

———

THE TEMPERATURE CONTINUED TO DROP, and James wondered how much snow was building up outside. Inside, it was frostier than Rachel's attitude.

Vivienne Oxley, a former classmate of theirs, had delivered their evening meal and furtively shoved two blankets through the door. It would barely keep the five of them warm, but James appreciated the thought. At school, Vivienne had given Rachel grief on a daily basis, and it was nice to think she hadn't stayed a bitch.

"We'll take one blanket, and you boys can share the other," said Rachel, shoving two of the single mattresses together.

"Nope. We all need to bunch together and make the most of body warmth." James realised his years as a reluctant Boy Scout might actually have some benefit. "Quinn and I lay with Chloe between us. You and Kat lie on top of us, and we spread the blankets over the top."

"Not going to happen." Rachel crossed her arms over her chest.

"I don't care, I'm too tired to argue. I need to lie down." Chloe fell onto the mattresses.

"Yeah, whatever. I want to sleep and be warm. If Quinn wants to be my bed, I'm not complaining," said Kat.

The three of them settled. Quinn's arms holding Kat sent a spike of jealousy through James. He wanted his arms around his woman, too.

Too bad she didn't want to *be* his woman.

"Come on Rach, you gonna die on this hill?" He lay

beside Chloe. "I want to be warm. I want to keep *you* warm. Let's just go to sleep."

Her reluctance and simmering resentment were clear, but she did lower herself, awkwardly laying atop him. He relished the weight of her, wrapping his arms around her stiff body and pulling their half of the blanket over them.

It wasn't about being close to her—okay, it was. But not in a sexual way. They were all still wearing their jackets and shoes, there was nothing sexy about it.

It was about holding her. Protecting her.

"You're the woman I want to go to war beside, not against," he whispered into her hair. She stilled her fidgeting, so he knew she'd heard him. "I'm sorry, Rach. For everything. And I'm sorry it took me so long to make it back to you."

DAY 21

James recalled the saying that everything looked better in the morning. Which was unfortunate because everything did not, in fact, look better this morning.

Mrs. White—a sixty-something widow who'd presided over the Sanford Women's Club forever—was assigning sleeping space for all one hundred and fifty of the remaining townspeople in Townsend's fortification process and, having been hustled to The Strumpet, James was under no illusions of their status when the door locked behind them.

Townsend and his cronies had set up base in the Benson warehouse, which left close to one hundred people to be housed within the rooms above The Strumpet, and the conference facilities at the distillery itself.

Thankful that at least the five of them hadn't been separated in the move, James watched from the window as Townsend fortified below.

Any vehicle within a ten-block radius that could be readily started was being driven to the compound to form a ring around the warehouse, distillery, and bar. So far, it was three vehicles deep. The constant rumble of the snow-plough, orders being shouted and vehicles revving, were background noise to the townspeople hurrying through the ankle-deep snow, bringing in provisions from the previously guarded supermarket.

"Notice that Townsend's set himself up in the ware-house, which has the added protection of a ten-foot chain-link fence?" Quinn commented from the other window.

"They're going to need more than a barrier of cars and a fence. I hope they've got the firepower to back this up." James agreed that, in theory, the whiskey distillery was too valuable an asset to lose. With the collapse of the world's economy, Sanford could use the whiskey to barter with whoever was still alive out there.

But it wasn't worth Gemma's wrath.

Sanford wasn't his town. He didn't have a connection to it and the only reason he was still here was Rachel.

He wanted to get the hell out, start over again some-where safe. He'd spent a lot of time thinking about it, and they didn't need to go far. This was good farming country. There were small properties with dairy cows and vegetable gardens.

They could find a secluded farm and become self-sustaining.

That said, he knew Rachel came with Mackenzie, Kat and Chloe; they were a package deal. Which meant Jake and Quinn, too.

He was good with that. They could start their own little community. They could make this new world work.

Providing he could convince Rachel to come with him.

The sound of their door unlocking preceded Shelton, who stomped inside and smiled.

"Big day, people. Your town needs you. Quinn, Gav needs your mechanic skills. And Chloe, you're a teacher, right? Choose either Kat or Rachel to come with you and get over to Spring Street. Apparently, there's a bunch of teenagers holed up playing video games and smoking weed. You need to bring them in."

This was the opportunity they were waiting for—a chance to escape. Glancing at Quinn, James knew the man wouldn't leave without Kat. And the chances of Kat leaving without Rachel were negligible. Which meant they needed to convince Shelton that Chloe needed both Kat and Rachel to help her.

"You go," Rachel said to Kat, looking at her meaningfully. "And look after Chloe."

"No! I'm not choosing between you two." Chloe glanced desperately between them.

"I'm not stupid," said Shelton. "One of you stays here so the other two don't run off. If you don't come back, it won't be pretty for the one left behind."

Well, fuck.

"In that case, I'm going," Kat declared. "They're at Lucas Hernández's house. They'll come with me."

Of course, Kat knew about the delinquents, she'd been one herself during their high school years.

James didn't think about the fact it would be just him and Rachel until the door had clicked shut and they were staring wordlessly at each other.

He swallowed, suddenly unsure.

This girl—*woman*—had been his entire world; he'd never since experienced the intimacy the two of them shared so easily. So why did it scare the shit out of him to be alone with her now?

"Your apology last night was rubbish," she finally said, leaning her butt against an armoire and glaring at him. "You need to do better."

"Well, it wasn't exactly an apology..."

"Now you're *not* apologising?"

Her raised eyebrow sent a rush of desire straight to his dick.

"I was admitting I was wrong, not apologising. My apology is going to be big. Grand. A lot of thought has gone into it, you can't rush it."

"But you admit leaving town without saying goodbye was a shitty thing to do?"

"Beyond shitty," he admitted, advancing on her slowly and noting the dilation of her pupils, the shortness of her breath.

He knew she didn't *want* to want him. But she did. There was magic between them, always had been.

He'd been young. Stupid. Thinking that the love they shared was common, and he'd find it again. But that kind of connection—intense, fierce—had evaded him his whole adult life, and Rachel's face still came to him in his dreams.

She was etched indelibly onto his soul, and he'd bet anything it was the same for her.

"You feel it too," he repeated his words from yesterday, coming to stand between her parted thighs, his palm cupping her face so his thumb could trace the delicate contour of her jaw.

"I feel attracted to you, but so what?" She gave a subtle

shake of her head. "I'm also attracted to the barista at Scotty's. Doesn't mean anything is going to happen."

He could shake her at how obstinate she was being. "Why not?"

"You and me? We don't get a second chance, O'Connor."

His thumb stroked in silent disagreement, the need to prove her wrong an urgent beat in his chest.

"Can I touch you like this?"

Her tongue flicked out to wet her lower lip, and he groaned. Low and guttural. "You don't have to forgive me. I get that's too much to ask right now. But I can make you feel good, Rach. Let me do that."

Her hands had settled on his hips, and he wondered if she knew she was clenching her fingers. Needy. As desperate as his pounding pulse.

He wanted to kiss her senseless, to drown in the sweet nirvana of her mouth. His head lowered, and he waited for her eyes to flutter closed. Instead, she pushed at him.

"No kissing."

"No kissing?"

"You want to fuck, right? Well, so do I. But that's all this is, O'Connor. So, no kissing."

He blinked.

She turned, bending over the armoire with her hands splayed across its surface.

"Fuck me, James."

His cock pulsed against the zipper of his jeans, and a grin tugged at his lips. He would take Rachel Davenport any way she wanted.

Grabbing at her hips, he kicked her legs wider, leaning forward to lick at the exposed crease where her neck and shoulder met. She shivered.

"You want it rough and dirty, baby doll?"

She moaned, and he closed his teeth over the smooth skin, biting the spot and then laving it with the flat of his tongue. Her head dipped forward and her ass pushed back in implicit invitation.

Pressing against her, he reached around and unzipped her jeans, roughly tugging them over her hips and then dropping back on his heels so he could pull them down, down.

She was wearing simple white panties that encased the perfection of her ass and he couldn't stop himself from kneeling, pulling the sides high so he could feast on the lushness.

The scent of her arousal made him dizzy. Made him remember that first time he'd ever tasted her sweetness and the way she'd bucked beneath him, sensitive and enthralled. As a girl, he'd known her body intimately. As a woman, she was unchartered.

And he was determined to conquer her.

His thumbs hooked the side of her panties and slid them down to tangle above her boots with her jeans, holding her captive. Spreading her ass cheeks, his head dove between her legs, seeking the remembered sweetness with single-minded determination.

Sighing, she obliged him, widening her stance and crying out when he tongued at the softness of her folds. He breathed deep, wanting to inhale her whole.

He ate at her as though she were his last meal, messy and insatiable. Her thighs were trembling under his onslaught and, although reluctant to stop his feasting, the driving need to bring her to orgasm surpassed all else.

She mewed a protest as he pulled away, only to gasp his name when he forced a finger through her wet heat. He added another digit and pumped them, fucking into her tightness.

"More. More!"

"Touch yourself," he ordered.

She didn't hesitate, her fingers circling at the sensitive nub of her clit.

"Good girl," he praised, crooking his own fingers to reach her sweet spot.

She was chanting fuck over and over, until it was a reverent prayer. Until, shuddering, she screamed his name.

CHAPTER THREE

As the last of her orgasm ebbed through boneless limbs, Rachel hid her face in the crook of her elbow. Was it embarrassment that she'd given in so easily? This man had *annihilated* her—body and soul—when he'd left. And she'd just let him back into her vagina without a second thought.

"This changes nothing," she muttered, registering the cool air on her exposed flesh. She turned, straightening up.

James was there, already pulling up her underwear and jeans, gently smoothing them into place. She batted away his hands when he reached for her zip, uncomfortable with him still being on his knees before her.

"That's okay. I've got hours to change things."

He was far too confident for her liking.

"And just to be safe..." He got to his feet and picked up the only chair in the room, wedging it beneath the door handle.

"And that's going to..." She raised an eyebrow.

"Give us a few minutes to get dressed if they come back sooner than we thought." He grinned. "The eyebrow raising is new. You didn't use to do that."

"What can I say? You bring out my inner bitch."

"It's hot."

She shrugged. "I'm not getting naked with you."

"Not even a little bit?"

"I want to hear about this grand apology you've been planning." She flopped sideways onto the bed, rolling onto her stomach and looking up at him.

He joined her, his bulk making the mattress dip and causing her to roll into his side.

"How about we talk about all the ways I wish I'd left differently?" He stared straight ahead at the blank wall. "You knew I wanted out of this town, Rach, but it wasn't fair to leave without telling you. I can't tell you how many times I've searched for you on social media..."

She changed her mind. She really *didn't* want to hear the apology. Or how sorry he was. Every word was pick, pick, picking at the scab crusted over her heart.

"We don't need to talk about this." She shifted, trying to get some space. "Just because I let you finger fuck me doesn't mean I want to know about you or your life. What just happened then? Wasn't anything more than two people wanting to get off."

Rachel bit the inside of her cheek, pretending her body wasn't humming at the proximity to James. Pretending she hadn't loved every moment of the rough release he'd wrung from her.

They'd been seventeen when they lost their virginity, and that was after *months* of experimenting with everything but. They had consumed each other. The sex had consumed them. They'd been young and impatient, willing to be vulnerable—everything had been a discovery and no question was unanswered.

Rachel had never since experienced that kind of open

intimacy. After James had left so suddenly, she'd hardened her heart against further hurt, unable to bring herself to expose the soft parts of her soul. Her deepest desires.

Not like she had with James. He'd cracked her open and seen what was inside her, and then left. She wasn't risking that again.

"Rach, what are you thinking?"

His hand brushed over her head, tucking stray hairs behind her ear.

It was tender. Knowing. And she *hated* it.

She hated that she craved it. That she wanted him so badly. It had been *so long* since she'd been intimate with a man, and even longer since it had been satisfying.

What would happen if she just... gave in? It didn't have to mean anything.

"Quit with the touching. We can fuck, I *want* to fuck. But that's all this is, James." She flipped onto her back, fingers deftly unbuttoning her jeans and tugging them down to her knees. "Have you got a condom?"

He stared at her, and she was struck anew by the years that had passed. She'd never have guessed there would come a time when she couldn't decipher his expression.

"What? Changed your mind?" she taunted, unnerved at the niggle of uncertainty that crept over her.

"Not a chance." His eyes flashed. "I'll take you any way I can, Davenport."

In seconds, he had manhandled her back onto her stomach, shoving a pillow beneath her hips so her ass jutted high. She sighed, relaxing into the mattress and closing her eyes. This is what she needed. What she craved. For control to be abandoned and power relinquished.

This was what she'd been unable to articulate to past lovers—the need for domination. Because that wasn't what she wanted in any other area of her life, and she judged herself harshly for it.

But not here. Not with him.

"I know what you need, baby doll." He kneaded the cheeks of her ass, rough enough for wetness to flood her pussy. Rough enough to leave fingerprints.

She moaned into a pillow, hands clenching the sheet beneath her.

It had been unwitting, that first time the sex had changed. She'd held her arms above her head, eyes pleading with him for *something*. And he'd just known. One hand had held her wrists—tight, immobile. And she'd seen stars.

"Hands up high, Davenport," he demanded now, straddling her body and bringing one of those big hands to the nape of her neck, squeezing.

She complied immediately, giving over to him both a relief and a kindling to the desire banked deep inside. Her nipples were tight, pressing against unyielding fabric, and she ached to spread herself wide for him, both hating and loving the restriction of her jeans halfway down her legs.

"My girl doesn't like it slow and sweet." His breath was hot against her ear. "She likes it fast and dirty." He bit her earlobe and the sharp pain had a corresponding throb pulsing through her pussy.

It wouldn't take much to send her over the edge.

His fingers were in her mouth, pressing beyond her teeth and stroking against her tongue. "Suck me deep, baby doll. Get those fingers nice and wet."

She sucked, wanting to choke on him.

He withdrew, and she whimpered, swiftly followed by a gasp as those same fingers plunged between her thighs and high into her soaked center. Deftly he stroked her sweet spot and within seconds she was combusting, screaming his name into the pillow.

"That's how I like you, baby doll," he said, fingers still working her. "With your legs shaking and your cunt so tight around me. Are you ready for me? You want my cock in you?"

She nodded, unable to turn her head and meet his eye.

"Uh uh. Tell me what you want, baby. What you need," he scolded, withdrawing his fingers and smacking her ass sharply. The hot burn had her thighs clenching, the need to be filled with him unbearable.

"I want your cock," she mumbled, almost incoherent with need. She would beg if he asked her.

Instead, she heard the unmistakable tearing of foil and then, because she couldn't help herself—she *had* to see his cock—she turned her head and opened her eyes. Watched him roll on the condom with practiced ease.

Jesus, he had a beautiful dick. Long and thick and perfectly shaped.

She hadn't realized he was watching her watching him, until a low, sensuous chuckle had her raising her gaze to his.

"Like what you see?"

"I've had better."

"Liar."

His weight settled over her, one hand fisting her pony-tail and the other guiding his thick length into her, agonizingly slowly. After two orgasms, her pussy was deliciously over-sensitized, and she moaned, wanting the pleasure and needing the pain.

"James! Stop teasing."

She pushed her ass back into him, forcing his cock to seat fully within her. The penetration was intense and so perfect, tears came to her eyes.

"Naughty girl," he grunted, tugging on her ponytail. "Are you going to misbehave again?"

"No. No, I promise. Just fuck me, *please*."

"I like it when you beg." He groaned, bringing both his hands to grip her waist. "You feel like home, Rach."

She didn't have time to process his words as he began pumping forcefully, drilling her body into the mattress with each thrust of his hips. His rhythm was punishing, unwavering. This was an immolation of self as she lost herself to the desire that had been clawing at them since he'd returned—her need made more savage for having denied it.

Even as she shuddered her release, he kept on, driving into her body with relentless determination. Claiming her.

"I'm back, baby. And you're mine."

IT WAS hours before the others returned, and Rachel pretended to sleep to pass the time. There was no way she was having a conversation with James after—*that*.

She wasn't even sure what *that* had been. Mind blowing sex, yes. But was James going to think she'd forgiven him? Was it going to happen again? Did she *want* it to happen again? She tossed beneath the covers. She was behaving like an angsty teenager.

She sat up from the covers when Chloe and Kat were returned to the room, glad she'd told James to open the window so the scent of their fucking couldn't be detected. The last thing she needed was Kat knowing.

"It is *freezing* in here," Chloe spluttered, holding mittened hands up to her red cheeks. "Why on earth do you have the window open?"

"What's happening out there?" asked James.

"What's happening in *here*?" shot back Kat, her eyes darting between Rachel and James.

"Nothing," Rachel answered, too quickly, running her hands through her tangled hair.

"What did fuckboy do now?" Kat swung the door closed, and they all startled when it was pushed back open.

Vivienne Oxley stood in the doorway; her usual look of disdain marred by a purplish bruise dominating the left side of her face.

"What happened to you?" Rachel climbed off the bed and, against her better judgment, made towards Vivienne. She might not be a doctor, but as a veterinarian, she was the closest thing Sanford had to medical help.

Vivienne's eyes narrowed. "I'd be much more concerned about yourself, if I were you," she sneered.

Seems even the apocalypse wasn't going to change their mutual dislike. Or stop Vivienne from being an A-grade bitch.

"Suit yourself." Rachel shrugged. "Why are you here, then?"

"I wanted to give you the heads up that Townsend is willing to negotiate with that biker bitch, and you three are his bargaining chips." Her self-satisfied smile told Rachel she wasn't imparting this information to be helpful.

"You fucking asshole!" Kat launched herself at Vivienne, who stepped neatly back through the door and slammed it shut. "It's not like he could bargain with you, because no one would want you!" Kat screamed.

"No one is taking you. Any of you," James said firmly, pulling Kat away from the door and standing before it.

"You're right, because we're getting out of here." Rachel picked up her backpack. "Keep your jackets on. We're going out the window."

"You've seen how high up we are, right?" Chloe's eyes were wide.

"Not to mention we're at the front of the building, and everyone is on the street waiting for Gemma to come back." James ran his hands through his hair.

Rachel had done a lot of planning while she'd fake-slept, and while she wished Quinn had also returned, they didn't have time to wait for him.

"It's the perfect time to sneak out," she said. "Everyone is distracted, and it's started snowing again, which means they'll have their head down. No one is going to be looking up at us."

"And the fact we're at least twenty feet from the ground?" asked James.

"Worth the risk." Rachel stared at him, a silent dare to challenge her. When he said nothing, she continued. "We don't go out and down, we go out and *up*. If we can get onto and across the roof, there should be a fire escape we can use to get down."

"*Should* be," James repeated.

Rachel ground her teeth together.

"I don't know about you, but the possibility of broken bones from a fall beats the possibility of Vivienne being right. I'm not into being a sex slave." Kat moved to the window and opened the sash, letting in a gust of freezing air.

"I'm in," agreed Chloe.

Rachel was already stuffing her bright red jacket into her backpack. While it was going to be freaking cold and she would like nothing better than to wrap herself up in it, the color was too eye-catching.

"Wear mine." James was holding out his black jacket to her.

The thought of being cocooned in the warmth and scent of James was tempting, which meant it was a bad idea. Also, it was far too big. She shook her head.

"Davenport, take it."

She smiled at his annoyance. It was almost worth the chill she was in for. "It'll get in the way. The sleeves are too long. I can't risk it."

He huffed, but must have seen her sense, and shrugged the jacket on.

"At least wear another sweater." Chloe passed her a navy one and hefted her pack onto her back.

"Actually, we should ditch the backpacks." Rachel held up her hands at Chloe's screwed-up face. "They'll only slow us down, and none of this is ours anyway, right? It's just stuff we scavenged, and we can pick up more when we get out of here."

"That's not a terrible idea," said James, ignoring Rachel's eye roll. "We don't want to be wearing anything that could put our balance off. The snow is going to make the roof hella slippery."

"We can go via Quinn's house," interjected Kat. "Remember when Mac and Jake came back from the city? They hit up a camping store and had heaps of supplies, and they're still at Quinn's." said Kat. "We should probably try to wait there a bit, to see if Quinn can get away as well."

The four of them fell silent, and Rachel knew they felt as bad as she did about leaving without Quinn. But it's what he'd want.

And Mackenzie was out there, somewhere. Missing her friend was like a toothache, painful and constant.

They didn't have time to waste.

JAMES INSISTED ON GOING LAST, so he could boost the girls from the windowsill onto the roof. The guttering held firm as each of them pulled themselves up and the snow was making for near white-out conditions.

Rachel was right, no one from below was going to see them.

The cold, however, was merciless. Snow burned his cheeks, and his nose and throat were instantly raw from inhaling the freezing air. He wished Rachel had taken his fucking coat.

After hoisting himself onto the roof, he followed the girls in their laborious crouched shuffle along the edge, keeping a hand on the sloping roof to steady his steps.

Ice made his footsteps treacherous, and his heart was lodged somewhere in his throat, hindering his breathing. As much as he wanted to keep an eye on Rachel, it took all his concentration to stay upright.

A muted gunshot boomed through the falling snow and ahead of him, Kat slipped, her arms pinwheeling madly for purchase. James leapt forward and grabbed for her waist, causing them to crash against the roof and then slide towards the edge.

Kat screamed and at the last moment, James wedged his boot against the guttering, his ankle twisting painfully as their fall halted.

"Are you two okay?" Chloe's worried voice came from the swirling snow, her form just a shadow ahead of them.

No. No, James was definitely not okay. He was light-headed from the pain shooting from his ankle. Now was the worst possible time for a sprain. But he had to keep going.

"Define okay," Kat muttered, bracing against him to regain her footing. "Thanks O'Connor. I saw my life flash before my eyes."

Her brow crinkled when he stood, sucking in a sharp breath of pain.

"You okay?"

"My ankle. It'll be fine. We've got to keep moving."

It was fine. He could walk on it. But *Jesus fuck,* it was like a high voltage wire electrifying him. The pain, along with this exertion, caused him to sweat, making his body clammy beneath the layers of clothing. If he wasn't careful, the ruthless cold would turn the dampness into a killer weapon.

Not that he could do anything about that now.

One foot in front of another. Try not to stumble. Don't think about the excruciating pressure radiating with each step forward.

Time slowed; the roof seemed endless, like he was never getting down. Never escaping. He couldn't see the girls ahead of him. He was alone, wandering hopelessly in a snow globe of his own imagining.

The pain was making his thoughts take on a red tinge, blackening his vision.

And then he stumbled into the girls, huddled together and facing him. Waiting for him.

"What took you so long?" said Rachel, a crust of ice coating her eyebrows.

"How bad is your ankle?" asked Kat.

"You hurt yourself?" He wasn't so far gone that he didn't detect the concern in Rachel's voice. Pushing back on the pain radiating from his throbbing joint, he tried to keep it together, even as he sweated through his clothing and shook with uncontrollable shivers.

"Fire escape?" He wanted to get the attention off him. They had to keep moving.

"Just here." Rachel somehow wedged herself under his

armpit, taking some of the weight from his injury. "Are you going to manage it?"

He grunted in reply, hoping he was right. It had to be a sprain, he wouldn't be walking on it at all if it were broken.

Kat and Chloe started down, cautious on the iced-over steps.

"How bad are you hurt?" Rachel's hand was cupping his cheek, her woolen gloves wet and her eyes wide. Frightened.

"I can do it, but stay behind me. In case I... in case I fall and knock you off."

"You won't fall," she said, her determination bleeding all over him.

Her concern—her belief — bolstered him.

"I promise I won't fall, if you promise you'll stay behind me."

"Don't break your promise, O'Connor."

The descent was torturous, his shoulders and forearms carrying most of his weight as he lowered himself, step by step. The burn from his muscles competed to override the stabbing pain of his ankle, and the nausea threatened to swamp him.

He was exhausted, and he couldn't stop the shivers racking his body.

"You're close enough to jump," Chloe called from below.

His fall could in no way be classified as a jump, but he landed in inches of snow that cushioned the landing and rolled onto his back, lightheaded with relief to have the pressure taken off his body.

"I know what you're thinking, Rach, and no, we don't have time for you to look at it," he said as her face hovered over his. "Help me up and let's get the fuck out of here."

The snow had stopped falling, leaving behind a muted world that camouflaged any activity happening around them.

"You're going to have to climb over the barricade they've made with all the cars..." Kat looked at him doubtfully, biting her lip.

"We'll help him. It'll be fine," Rachel said, already grabbing his hands to pull him to his feet. "Jesus, you're big. Chlo, help me."

Together, the two of them got him to his feet and, with one under each arm, they hobbled to the far corner wall of The Strumpet. There was a fifty-foot space between the back of the bar and the wall of vehicles.

"No guards," puffed Kat, who'd stalked ahead to scout the area. "Make a run for it?"

James hid his grimace.

At Rachel's and Chloe's nods of affirmation, the four of them made a dash for the barricade, falling into a gasping pile at the rear wheel of an SUV. With their own breathing so loud, they almost missed the crunching of boots on snow. The telltale slide of a bolt as a cartridge was loaded.

Almost.

James raised his head slowly.

Gav issued a low whistle, a malicious grin spreading across his face.

Oh fuck.

"Well, look what we have here, Big Q. Looks like your friends are trying to make a run for it without you." Gav strode closer, and James realized Quinn was behind him.

"Don't do anything stupid, Gav." Quinn's voice was low and strained.

"You know what would be fun?" Gav lowered his AR-

15 and walked over to them, kicking snow into their faces. "We could let them run. See how far they got."

"You want to *hunt* us?" Rachel was shaking in outrage.

"I'm thinking of something a little more... *explosive.*" Gav winked.

Impotent fury flashed through James. If only he hadn't slowed them down. If only he could stand on his own two feet. A movement by Quinn distracted James from his frustration.

With his attention on his quarry, Gav didn't see Quinn's leather belt loop over his head, snapping tight against his neck with the force of every pushup and pullup Quinn had ever done. Stunned, James watched as Gav's rifle fell, and his hands clutched uselessly at his neck—his face had barely reddened before Quinn made a ruthless twisting motion and they heard an audible *crack.*

The smell of urine washed over them as Gav's body went limp, falling forward into the snow.

Shock at the deliberate violence was quickly replaced with a wash of relief as James swallowed against the taste of his own powerlessness.

"Oh my god, Quinn. What have you done?" whispered Chloe.

"Saved our asses." Kat got to her feet. "Good riddance to the sack of shit."

"What's wrong with you?" Quinn looked at James as Rachel and Chloe struggled to haul him to his feet. He strode over and gently pushed them aside, his massive hands gripping under James' armpits and pulling him to his feet.

"Ankle," James muttered.

"And I think he has the beginnings of hypothermia," Rachel added, a panicked edge to her voice.

"We need to move." Quinn re-adjusted his hold on

James. "Get over the vehicles but don't move even a *step* away from them on the other side. Do you hear me? Not a step. There are explosives rigged fucking *everywhere* out there."

"How long until Gemma gets here?" James asked Quinn, as the girls clambered over the hood of the SUV.

"Not sure. They were expecting her a while ago. Everyone is strung out and trigger-happy, so we need to get out of here fast."

"And the explosives?"

"We hope like fuck I remember where they all are, and we don't get blown to smithereens."

Without Quinn's muscle to assist him, James would never have made it through the barricade of tightly packed vehicles. As it was, it took long minutes to make it to the other side, his hands fumbling and his gait unsteady. He was so tired.

"What now?" Rachel asked, hands on hips. "How far out are the explosives?"

"What was that? I saw something move out there." Kat clutched at Quinn's arm.

"There shouldn't be anyone out here. Everyone's on standby for Gemma." Quinn stared out into the encroaching darkness.

"Could Gemma be coming in from behind?" James suggested.

They stared into the parking lot before them, alert for movement among the snow-covered mounds. A short bark drew James' attention to a pack of prowling dogs, muzzles pointed their way.

"They don't look so domesticated anymore." James was shivering convulsively now they had stopped moving.

"Surely they're not going to attack us?" Chloe asked incredulously. "They're not wild animals."

"Not wild. Hungry," said Rachel.

"They're going straight—" Quinn threw his hands up. "On the ground!"

An explosion ripped through the air, rocking James off his feet and pounding into his eardrums.

James was tangled in limbs and hair and someone was repeating "shit, shit, shit" over and over. Where was Rachel?

"Get up! Get up, we need to move." Quinn was lifting him fireman-style over his shoulders. "Follow me. Single file. Stay in my footsteps."

Pumping his legs, Quinn charged straight for the canine carnage ahead, trusting the way was clear. Jame gave in to the exhaustion. His vision swam and went dark.

"HE'S GOT HYPOTHERMIA, and it's essential we maintain his core body temperature. We need to get these wet clothes off him. Quinn, does that fancy fake fireplace run on gas?" Rachel's efficiency cut through the haze that fogged James' head, but he didn't have the energy to open his eyes.

"I'm okay," he slurred. He was tired, so tired.

Were they at Quinn's? How did he get there?

Multiple sets of hands were fumbling with his clothing, and he wanted to joke with Rachel that if she wanted him naked, all she had to do was ask.

He couldn't feel his ankle, which was nice. But the violent shivering racking his body was a pain in the ass. He just wanted to go to sleep.

"How did he get so wet?" asked Chloe.

"He fell in the snow. Also, I think he's been sweating with the pain, and it's made his clothing damp." Rachel leant over him, her warm breath on his face was nice. So nice.

"Here, I'll start the fire."

There was a sudden silence and, even in his confusion, James registered this was an unfamiliar voice. He struggled to open his eyes, fighting past the insistent lethargy.

"Who're you?" he mumbled, and then blackness claimed him.

CHAPTER FOUR

Rachel's head was spinning. James had blacked out, and now they had company?

"Stephen Worthington?" Quinn asked.

"Cassie Blackley?" Rachel looked between the two teenagers standing at the door to Quinn's living room. "You're Sami's friend, right? I saw you at the vet clinic the morning after this all started?"

"What are you two doing here?" Of course. As the local high school guidance counselor, Chloe was sure to know them.

Rachel remembered back to the beginning of the end, when she'd dropped the two of them back to Stephen's home—a few doors down from Quinn's. Stephen was Quinn's neighbor. But what were they doing *here*?

"Have you been in the Evac Area this whole time?" Chloe asked, gesturing them inside the room.

"Uh, Miss Brent-Maxwell. Hi. We've kind of been using this house as our base. I hope you don't mind?" Stephen looked at Quinn. "We couldn't... it was hard to stay in our own homes."

"And Dex was here," added Cassie.

"Dex?" Mackenzie's adopted pooch?

"Ah, the dog? He's kind of taken up residence in the main bedroom. Sorry about that." Stephen grimaced. "He loses his shit if he's not allowed to sleep on the bed."

Rachel laughed; it sounded almost hysterical, even to her own ears. The damn dog was alive and camped out in the bed that Mackenzie had slept in.

"Guys, James is turning blue. I think we need to do something." Chloe reclaimed their attention. "Rach?"

"Get that fire going, and we need dry clothes. I'm going to need snow to pack his ankle, but there's no use doing that if he..." she paused, reality sinking deep into her weary body. Hypothermia could be serious if it wasn't treated soon enough. Dread tightened her stomach.

She shook herself; "He's going into hypothermic shock. We need to get him warm. Fast."

Stephen started the gas fireplace, and Quinn dumped an armful of towels and blankets beside Rachel. When she had James completely naked, she wrapped him up, instructing Chloe and Kat to each rub one of his feet.

"No, do it harder," she snapped. "He's not going to break. They need vigorous rubbing, or the blood circulation will stop."

"What can I do?" It was Cassie, and Rachel had a moment to take in how forlorn the kid looked. Lost.

"Grab a hand and concentrate on his fingers."

Rachel took his other hand, threading their fingers and chaffing them together.

She wanted heat packs. She wanted one of those foil blankets that paramedics gave to shock victims. She wanted electricity, damn it.

"Quinn!" she blurted. "Bring Dex downstairs. We'll get him to lie against James' side; he can act as a heat pack."

"On it."

"Rach, I'm not being a smartass, but if he needs body heat, don't you think you should maybe, like, get naked and lie with him?" Kat tilted her head in question.

Rachel glared at her.

"I swear I'm not trying to be a dick. But, you know, isn't that the best way to get someone warm again? They use it enough in the movies."

"She's right," said Chloe. "And if anyone's going to get naked with him..."

"It sure as hell isn't going to be me," Quinn interjected.

Dex nosed into Rachel's side, whuffing a welcome as he licked at the side of her face.

"Hey, boy. You remember James, right? I want you to lie down here, okay?" Rachel rubbed his ears and urged him down, pushing the compliant German Shepard against James' side. "Good boy."

Darkness had fallen since they'd arrived, and Cassie lit a candle for them to see by.

"We've used cardboard to cover the windows, so you can't see our lights from outside," she explained. "But we're running really low on food, sorry. We can't offer you much."

"I ate not long ago," said Quinn.

"I'm not hungry. I need sleep," Kat declared as Chloe yawned.

The adrenaline dump from their escape was hitting and, with nothing else to be done for James, Rachel watched as one by one they filed away to find somewhere to rest.

Alone with James, Rachel acknowledged that if it were anyone but him, human body heat would have been the first thing she'd have thought of. But there was a reason she'd fucked him today with her clothes on, and it hadn't been the temperature. She needed the barrier of clothing. The protection. The idea of skin on skin made her teeth ache.

But he was hardly conscious, so it didn't count, right?

She glanced around the empty room and then, before she could second guess herself, stripped down to her panties and bra, pulling aside the blankets to lie down. On the other side of James, Dex raised his head, and she swore he smiled, his tongue lolling.

"You have terrible breath," she muttered to the animal, arranging the blankets to cover all her exposed skin.

Sleep wouldn't come, even when she registered James' warming temperature and healthier skin tone. She didn't think she'd ever been this exhausted. Mentally and physically. With her defenses down, her mind wandered to her family, and a tear tracked down her cheek.

At least she knew where her mother was. Or had been. Her father had left the state after the divorce years before, and her older brother Marty had probably been dead before Sy-V.

Marty was the reason she was still in Sanford. At eighteen-months older than her, they'd been close. Until he'd fallen down the rabbit hole of amphetamines. It had ravaged their family, inadvertently forcing Rachel to hold her mother together.

There had been no way she could leave for college after high school. Her mother wouldn't have coped. So instead, she'd studied vet science by distance and commuted to a nearby community college for pracs. It had taken longer than normal—years longer—but she'd graduated a certified professional and when Marty had skipped town for good, her mother had rebuilt.

They both had.

Rachel had had her job, her mom, and her best friends.

Unbidden, a memory of seventeen-year-old James surfaced, long hair brushed back from his face, that cheeky head tilt promising all kinds of trouble. He used to flash a smile that had every girl in town dying to lock that shit down.

And she'd had him.

"You were what I needed, but I was only what you wanted. Until you didn't." The words fell from her lips and she immediately wanted to push them back inside. Back down deep where they should have stayed.

Everything came at a price, but Rachel wasn't prepared to pay the consequences for her transgressions this afternoon. She was over James O'Connor, and she was never falling in love with him again.

DAY 22

Rachel woke in the frigid dawn light, the fire having gone out—they must be out of gas. Both James and Dex were snoring, which she took as a good sign. As much as she didn't want to lose the warmth between their bodies, she also didn't want him to wake up with her in her underwear. She'd rather have clothes on, thank you very much.

But he was all hard, smooth male beside her, the dusting of hair across his well-defined chest a revelation. Damn, the boy had filled out nicely.

She wished she were waking up beside him in a different reality, where he'd never left and they'd spent a thousand mornings like this. She wished she could snuggle into him, relishing the comfort his closeness brought.

But wishing was for fools.

Taking a deep breath, she tensed her leg that was

thrown over his muscled thigh, preparing to lift it free. At her movement, he stirred. The arm she was lying on pulling her closer.

Her breasts pushed against his side, nipples aching and needy, and she froze, waiting to see if he would wake. He *could not* find her in this condition. When his breathing evened out, she slipped from his warmth and jumped to her feet, rushing to get clothes onto her already shivering body. Why did the damn apocalypse have to happen in winter?

Blowing into her hands, she made for the kitchen, where she swore she could smell coffee brewing. Surely the world wouldn't be so cruel as to let her hallucinate coffee?

"It's only decaf, but it's better than nothing," Cassie was saying to Chloe, the two of them sitting in the weak morning sunlight at the kitchen table, sipping from steaming mugs.

"You know that decaf only works if you throw it at people, right?" Rachel stomped in, her hopes of real caffeine dashed.

"There's not much of anything now that Townsend's crews are looting the houses in the Evac Area," Cassie explained. "We knew they were clearing out the homes in the Safe Zone, but we didn't think they'd get out here as quick as they did. We should have stockpiled more."

"Why *are* you out here?" Chloe sipped at her decaf. "I just saw a whole bunch of your classmates at Lucas Hernández's house. Why weren't you with them?"

Cassie straightened, her eyes shining with hope. "Was he okay? Was he with Jimmy and Sami?"

"Hang on," Rachel interrupted. "Weren't Lucas and Jimmy the kids who got caught selling toilet paper they'd scavenged from the Evac Area? The ones that Townsend tied to stakes as punishment?"

"What?" Cassie gasped. "We haven't seen them since they went back into the Safe Zone to check on their families. That was weeks ago."

"They're fine," Chloe assured her, shooting Rachel a dirty look.

"Miss Brent-Maxwell, do you think—"

"Cass, you've got to stop calling me that. It's just Chloe, okay?"

"We have to get them out too," said Stephen, who'd been standing in the doorway to the kitchen. He walked to Cassie and dropped a kiss to her forehead before turning to make himself a coffee. "Want one?" he asked Rachel.

"You two are a couple?" Rachel looked between the two of them as an odd maternal instinct kicked in. "Because you're a little young to be shacked up alone together."

"I'm almost eighteen," Stephen replied defensively. "And, you know, the world ended. So, there's that."

It was on the tip of her tongue to ask if they were having sex. If they were using protection. She felt like her mother. But seriously, someone needed to be looking out for these kids. They'd been out here, alone, for weeks.

The last thing anyone needed right now was a teenage pregnancy.

"Your parents?" Rachel asked, carefully.

"Mine were away on business and never made it back." Cassie fidgeted with her coffee mug. "Stephen's... died."

No one was untouched by tragedy in this new world.

Rachel was surprised at the visceral urge to comfort Cassie. Since when did she go around hugging virtual strangers? Since never, that's when.

"Apart from decaf coffee, what kind of supplies have you got?" Chloe asked, breaking the weighted silence.

"We were next door when Quinn dropped off that

couple, Jake and Mackenzie?" Cassie looked between Rachel and Chloe. "We didn't know if we should let them know we were here, and then by the time we decided they were safe, they'd gone."

"But they left behind some seriously cool stuff." Stephen sat beside Cassie with his coffee. "Flashlights, first aid kits, a survival knife, sleeping bags. Even a solar generator and a water purification system."

"We couldn't believe they'd just left it all here." Cassie shrugged. "But it's come in useful. We've been using bicycles to get around the streets, but it's getting harder now we have to dodge the looting crews."

"Lucky Cass runs track, or they'd have caught her at least twice by now," Stephen added, nudging Cassie. "We've been thinking we needed to move on, maybe to Dutton, to find somewhere with more food. People who aren't living under a dictator like Townsend." His scowl furrowed his forehead, making him appear years older.

A sharp yip from Dex came from the living room, and Rachel jolted, having forgotten about her patient. She'd make a terrible nurse.

"James?" she called, heading into the next room. James was groaning as he tried to sit up in a tangle of blankets and towels.

"Why did I wake up naked, spooning a dog?"

———

JAMES WAS CONFUSED. And hungry. And the pain radiating from his ankle made everything hazy. God, he hoped he didn't throw up in front of Rachel.

As though from a distance, he heard Rachel telling someone to get snow from outside, but he didn't have the strength to stay upright. He lay back in the nest of blankets and looked at the dog. Dex.

"Hey buddy," he murmured, and then closed his eyes. Maybe he'd just go back to sleep.

The shock of cold-packed snow on his elevated ankle had him snapping back to consciousness, and he moaned, long and loud.

"Just cut it off at the knee. Whatever you do, don't touch my ankle again," he pleaded, sweat breaking out on his brow. "Davenport, I mean it. Back off."

She sighed.

"You don't have any pain meds in your supplies?" she asked someone in his periphery. That's right, there were a couple of kids here.

"Just Tylenol," came the answer.

"Better than nothing." Rachel scowled when James protested again. "Stop being a baby. You've probably just torn ligaments, but until I get the swelling down, I won't know for sure."

"Here." Quinn was holding a whiskey bottle under his nose. "Take a swig."

James grabbed at the bottle and drank deeply, concentrating on the alcohol burning down his throat and not on whatever devil's work Rachel was doing on his tortured limb.

"This really fucking sucks," he said, to no one in particular.

"Sorry, fuckboy. I feel this is my fault," Kat called from the sofa. "You hurt yourself saving me from certain death."

"S'kay." He took another swig.

"Well, since we've got that out of the way," Kat nudged his arm with her foot, "want to share that whiskey with me?"

"Kat! It's barely seven in the morning," Chloe admonished.

A kid, tall and gangly, dropped a Tylenol packet into Rachel's hands and she popped four pills from their tabs. He swallowed them with another mouthful of whiskey and then passed the bottle to Kat.

"Have at it."

"What's the plan now?" Quinn's gaze didn't leave Kat, as she sipped the whiskey.

"We're going to need a vehicle to move James, and we shouldn't do that until it's dark," said Rachel, finishing with the compression bandage. "We stay low until then, see if we hear anything from the Safe Zone... explosions or gunfire."

"There's been nothing so far. Do you think Gemma didn't show?" said Chloe.

"I'd rather not stick around to find out," said Kat.

"Cassie and Stephen, have you earmarked any vehicles with keys and gas?" Rachel turned to the teenagers. "I'm thinking I can take that solar generator you mentioned and get James to the vet clinic. It's only a couple of blocks from the hospital and still in the Evac Area. I can do an x-ray on him and get proper pain meds."

"Nothing about that plan sounds like staying low," said Chloe.

"I'm onboard with proper pain meds," James contributed, finally feeling a buzz from the alcohol.

"No more of that, in case I need to operate." Rachel intercepted the bottle that Kat was passing him.

"Wait just a hot second. We were talking about drugs, not *surgery*."

"I'm talking about ensuring you're not maimed for life, O'Connor," Rachel retorted. "I think you've snapped at the lateral joint, but if I have to set the bone, it'll be a straight-forward procedure."

"Will you knock him out?" Kat asked with interest.

"She's *not* operating on me!"

IT HAD TAKEN a while for Quinn and Rachel to figure out how to use the solar generator to get the x-ray machine working, and in that time, the magic of the whiskey was wearing thin.

James studied the set-up of the vet clinic—which had clearly been ransacked—as he distracted himself from the insufferable agony of his injury. The idea of amputating at the knee was disturbingly appealing.

"We're good to go. Quinn, can you get him up onto the examination table?"

James wished he were back at Quinn's with Kat and Chloe and the kids. He *did not* want to get onto that stainless steel table. He trusted Rachel, he did. But she was a *vet*. And he was a *human*. And the thought of her operating on him was scary as hell.

When he was settled on the table and Quinn had backed away, Rachel unwrapped the bandage and he made the mistake of looking down at the swollen, black lump she was revealing.

He swallowed down bile.

"Okay, Quinn, go stand in the other room." Rachel pulled on protective gear, her face serious. James relished seeing her confidence in what was clearly her domain. He knew she was smart, but this kind of authority was seriously sexy.

"You're going to anesthetize him, right?"

"I am right here. Why is no one talking to me?" James demanded.

"O'Connor, if it's broken, of course I'm going to put you under. I've got some horse tranquilizer that should work perfectly."

"You're not joking, are you?" He waved his hands. "You know what? It doesn't matter. I'm going to lie here, and close my eyes, and you work your Frankenstein magic and fix me. Deal?"

"Deal."

EVERYTHING WAS light and deliciously cottony. He was floating. He couldn't stop thinking about his mouth on Rachel. On her neck, her belly, her thighs. Oh Jesus, those thighs.

He wanted those thighs wrapped around his face...

"I think he's coming around." Rachel's voice pierced his dream-like state, and he swallowed against a metallic taste in his mouth. He was thirsty.

There was no pain, though. Maybe she had amputated?

"Do I get a prosthetic limb?" His tongue was thick and unwieldy.

"What? It's just a bad sprain. You've had some pain meds and you're going to be fine."

"You didn't cut my leg off?"

"I didn't cut your leg off."

Her hand was warm on his arm, squeezing, and he fell back into the soft cottony oblivion.

WHEN HE CAME TO AGAIN, he was lying on Quinn's sofa, with everyone sitting around the living room. How long had he been out?

"Some bedside manner you've got," he accused Rachel. "I wasn't even conscious, and you were shipping me out of theatre."

"You weren't in theatre, you big baby. You fainted while I was performing the x-ray and I injected some pain relief." Her tone was dismissive, but he saw the way she bit her lip to keep from smiling.

"We heard gunshots coming from the Safe Zone. Thought we better get out of there," added Quinn.

"And you got all the meds?" asked Kat, still sipping at the same whiskey. Or was that a new bottle?

"Everything from the emergency stash that wasn't found when they looted the place." Rachel knelt on the floor beside the sofa to peer into his eyes. "You feeling okay? Woozy? Nauseous?"

"Hungry," he replied.

The teenager, Cassie, passed him a plate with crackers and he nodded his thanks.

"So now that we know Gemma still hasn't turned up, what's our plan?" Chloe asked, looking around at the group.

"Wait, how do we know that?" James said through a mouthful.

"Because Cassie and Stephen snuck off and scoped out the situation." The disapproving set to Chloe's mouth told him how she felt about that.

He noted Chloe was more animated than she'd been in days. Maybe it was the teenagers, reminding her of how she used to be?

"Hang on!" He looked up. "Why would that change

anything? As soon as it gets dark, we get the hell out of Sanford."

Rachel made a sound of non-committal and he stopped chewing to look at her.

"What does that mean?"

"Just that maybe we don't leave. Maybe we overthrow the council and reclaim our town."

James could hear a clock ticking somewhere in the house.

No one said a thing.

Had they talked about this while he was still unconscious?

"Hell no. We're leaving," he repeated. "Right?" He looked around at the others, and no one met his eye.

"Oh, come on! You can't actually think this is a good idea? How exactly do you plan to *overthrow* the council?"

"We poison them," Rachel replied simply.

James realized he was staring at Rachel with an open mouth. Like a damn cartoon character.

"We *poison* them?"

"They don't let anyone else drink the whiskey, so we'll put antifreeze into it and, you know..."

"Kill them?"

"Yes, James. We kill them. This is a different world, and—"

"Can you even hear yourself right now?" he demanded, sitting up fast enough to make his head spin. "We don't have to kill them. We just *leave.*"

"Because that's what you're good at, right? Leaving."

Her words punched through his lungs, making it difficult to take a deep breath.

"Low blow, Davenport."

Cassie silently passed him a bottle of water, and he gulped at it.

"What about finding Mackenzie and Jake?" he finally asked.

"They're going to be impossible to find without telecommunications. But if we make Sanford safe, they can come back to us," said Rachel.

"And Ash will know where I am," Chloe added, her face brightening.

James winced internally. Did Chloe really still believe her husband was alive and making his way home?

Everything about this situation was fucked up.

"We can't leave our friends in there," added Stephen.

"Aren't your friends the ones who were hanging out smoking weed? I'm pretty sure they're fine," James muttered.

He slumped back against the sofa cushion, closing his eyes. They all wanted to stay, and he wasn't getting anywhere without their help. He sighed.

"So, we stay."

CHAPTER FIVE

DAY 23

Poisoning people didn't seem so bad until Rachel saw the abject horror in James' expression. I mean, yes, she was contemplating mass murder, but it didn't actually have to come to that.

They could wait until the men on the council had consumed the antifreeze and were debilitated from the effect and then move in to take all the weapons and offer them the anti-dote—ethanol—if they left.

Or they could load them onto a truck and dump them out of state. What could go wrong with a group of misogynistic nutjobs—carrying a vendetta and with nothing to lose —roaming free?

Okay, so maybe they couldn't let them leave. Rachel didn't want to live her life looking over her shoulder.

Disgruntled, she tossed and turned in the bed she was sharing with Kat. It was almost morning, and her stomach was rumbling.

Chloe was asleep on a mattress on the floor at the foot of their bed, and Rachel had heard her stomach grumbling most of the night. Cassie and Stephen hadn't been kidding about their lack of food, and finding some was going to have to be a priority. They needed to eat. Everyone was already thinner, a hollowing of their cheeks betraying the continued lack of sustenance.

She flipped onto her back.

"Would you quit?" Kat mumbled sleepily.

"Sorry."

Quinn and Dex's snores could be heard from the master bedroom. Rachel waited a beat and knew she wasn't going back to sleep. She should check on James and start making plans for how they were going to eat today.

After throwing on another sweater and going to the toilet—resolutely pushing aside the thought of what they were going to do when the water stopped—she made her way downstairs to where James lay on the sofa with his leg elevated.

It was still unnerving how completely dark the nights were without the illumination of streetlights, but the moon was full and her eyes had adjusted. She could make out James' bulk beneath the heap of blankets.

She faltered.

The way he'd looked at her yesterday. Disgusted. Disappointed.

There was a heavy rock in her gut, and she didn't like it. She was the daughter who was always there. The friend who did the right thing. The colleague who was reliable.

But someone had to make the tough decisions.

Vivienne didn't get a black eye from running into a door, and Mackenzie wasn't off on some jaunt. They had *trafficked her* as a *sex slave*.

"Rach?"

She startled. She hadn't realized he'd been watching her as she'd been watching him.

"Hi." She moved closer, reached out to feel his forehead. "How are you feeling?"

"Great. Those pain meds you've been giving me are great. Awesome. Fucking amazing."

"Mmm, I might need to adjust the dose."

"Don't you dare. I feel like I could run a marathon."

She'd given him canine prednisone but, having never prescribed it for a human, was guessing at the dose. Splinting damaged ligaments was one thing, but playing around with pharmaceuticals was something else altogether.

"Hungry?" she asked.

"Starving."

"Me too. We might need to make that run to Dutton for supplies, like the kids were thinking."

"Crazy that all the nearby food is already gone." He shifted on the sofa and peered through the darkness at her. "It's freezing, I can see your breath. Want to get under the covers with me?"

She hesitated, but it really was freaking cold. And she really needed some reassuring warmth at the moment. Proof that she wasn't a monster. She only wanted to keep them safe and save her town.

Careful not to bump his ankle, she slid in beside him, settling her head against his bicep as though she'd been doing it every day of her life. Familiar. Easy.

He pulled the blankets up high to cover her.

"It's been weeks. I guess it's not a surprise that food is running out," she murmured into his arm.

"Let's stop talking about food. It's just making me hungrier."

They lay in companionable silence, listening to the birds waking up outside.

"Thanks for fixing my ankle."

"Thanks for saving Kat."

"You're really set on the idea of staying?" James began rubbing circles on her back. "I bet we could find a little farm, set ourselves up and live happily ever after."

"I don't think we get a happily ever after, O'Connor. We've just got to make the most of what we have here. Now."

She paused at her own words. Did she believe that?

"Here and now, I have a stubborn, smart, incredibly beautiful woman in my arms." He tightened his hold. "And I want her. I want *you*, Rach. If all we have is this moment, then let's make the most of it." He shifted so his face was against hers. "I know I ruined us. And I will regret our years apart for the rest of my life. But I came back, Davenport. I came back because I couldn't live my life without you."

They were breathing shared air, their lips almost touching.

Could she do it? Was she brave enough to open her heart to him again?

The vulnerability that came with softening towards him was terrifying. But so, *so* tempting.

"You can't leave again," she whispered.

"Not without you," he promised, moving infinitesimally closer, so she felt the shape of his words against her mouth.

His lips were warm and firm and *God, she wanted him to kiss her*. The need to taste him was a heavy throb between her legs. She wanted this, she *did*. But years of obstinate resistance held her immobile; she didn't know how to open herself again. How to accept his love.

But this man knew her. Before, and now.

71

"Rach? I'm going to kiss you, okay?"

She acquiesced on a sigh, body melting in anticipation as he angled his head to slant his lips over hers, capturing her body and soul.

It was heady and new, but familiar and sweet, all at the same time.

It was her past and her present and her future.

He nipped at her bottom lip and she opened for him, his tongue dominant and thorough. There was a possession to his movements, to the hand that ran down her back to her ass, pulling her closer. She lost herself to their urgency, gasping when he pulled away to suck on her neck, his lips trailing to the shell of her ear.

"Jesus, Rach. I want to *inhale* you," he moaned.

"Less talking, more kissing." She grasped the side of his face and forced his mouth back to hers, her teeth pulling at his lower lip in reprimand.

They kissed until she was dizzy. Until the sun was streaming through the window and Dex was nosing at her elbow.

"Get a room, you two. You're gross," Kat said, coming down the stairs. "Come on, Dex, I'll let you outside."

Laughing, Rachel buried her face in James' shoulder. When had she last laughed? She was light and bubbly and *happy*. Her lips were swollen and her face was sensitive from the rub of James' facial hair.

"I like this," she commented, running her fingers through his soft beard.

"Lucky. Haven't had much of a chance for personal grooming lately," he said dryly.

"The inconveniences of the apocalypse." She laughed.

"Are you *laughing*?" asked Kat, coming back into the

room. "Who are you, and what have you done with Rachel?"

"Bugger off, Kat." Beneath their blanket, James was sliding his hand up the front of Rachel's sweater, cupping her heavy breast.

"No can do. The teenagers are on their way downstairs, so I suggest you two quit fucking around and pretend to be some kind of role model."

"As if they haven't been fucking around." His thumb brushed Rachel's tightly puckered nipple.

That caused Rachel to snap out of her sexual haze.

"They've probably been fucking like rabbits. We need to have a safe sex talk with them." Kat was right. The kids couldn't catch them. She pushed James' hand away and sat up.

"We're not doing anything you weren't doing at seventeen." Stephen was standing in the doorway with Cassie hugged against his side.

Grimacing, Rachel and James looked at each other.

"Can we *not* talk about this?" Cassie asked, her face bright red.

The teenagers made their way into the room, curling into a single armchair together. They reminded Rachel of her and James in their youth and, instead of a rising bitterness, all she felt was fondness.

Huh, seemed all she'd needed to stop being such a hardass bitch was to be kissed senseless.

"So, let's get to the important stuff. Food," Kat plopped into the other armchair, "how're we gonna get some?"

"Dutton?" Rachel asked.

"Dutton," James confirmed.

. . .

THE TEENAGERS HAD a family-sized mini-van parked across the street, belonging to the family of their friend, Jimmy. And having slept in their clothes and with nothing else to do, the seven of them were on their way to Dutton in no time.

They left Sanford via a back field belonging to Todd Berryman, one of Townsend's cronies. The dirt roads were familiar, as it had been the place for tailgate parties since Berryman was a senior.

Rachel knew it was the first time any of them had left town since Sy-V had ravaged the world, and she wondered if the others were as terrified and hopeful as she was. The roads were empty, save for drifts of snow. With no snow-ploughs operating, they were relying on the vehicle's snow chains and Quinn's careful driving.

Despite their grim circumstances, the landscape was pristine, unnerving in its untouched state. Like the natural world did not care about the problems of mere humans.

Well, Rachel did.

"After we get food, I'd like to see how close we can get to the Prestige Plaza, where Gemma and her gang are based. I know Mac and Jake aren't there, but it's a starting point." The longing for her friend tugged sharply. *Where are you, Mac?*

"If we could pick up some crutches from somewhere, that would be good," James added.

"And, uh, a drugstore?" came Cassie's small voice.

Rachel whipped around to face her. Jesus Christ, they needed a pregnancy test!

"No! It's not what you think." Cassie read Rachel's expression correctly. "I need tampons."

"Oh." Rachel slumped back around.

"Give the kids a break." Chloe elbowed her in the side, laughing.

"I take offense to being called a kid," Stephen called out.

They lapsed into silence, Rachel's mind whirring through a list of supplies they were going to need.

"What about Sam's Roadhouse? It's only a couple more miles down the road," said Quinn, breaking the quiet. "We could see if there's food there before heading on?"

There was a chorus of unanimous agreement, and James' hand tightened around Rachel's. Something fluttered in her chest, something very much like hope.

Which, considering their current predicament, was insane.

James raised the inside of her wrist to his lips, kissing the sensitive skin, and that hope bloomed.

"Quinn, would you rather..." started Kat. "Have sex with an ex, or sex with J-Lo? But if you choose J-Lo, your mom is watching."

———

QUINN PULLED their mini-van into the parking lot of the roadhouse and James' stomach clenched with hunger. God*damn,* he hoped there was still food in the kitchen or the adjacent gas station. He hated beef jerky with a passion, but right now he'd happily consume a box of that shit.

As everyone piled out into the ankle-deep snow, their faces shrouded in clouds of their own breath, James realised he wasn't going anywhere. Not without help.

The frustration of his immobility bit deep and he slammed a hand down on the seat in front of him, cursing.

"I got you, bro." Quinn stood at the open door.

"I fucking hate this," James muttered, reaching for his outstretched hand.

"You had Kat's back. I've got yours."

"Does she know you have a thing for her?" James was genuinely curious, but let it drop at Quinn's hard stare.

They both jerked around at a cry from Chloe as the roadhouse door swung open and several people ran outside.

"What the fuck?" James' heart jumped into his throat. Chloe was waving her arms and struggling forward through the snow to be enveloped by the people from inside. Squealing, Rachel and Kat joined them, causing the bunch of them to fall to the ground.

"It's Mac and Jake." A rare grin lit up Quinn's face.

James recognized Caroline and Maggie, who had been trafficked with Mackenzie, along with Caroline's husband Jim, Buddy, and Jesse—the pharmacist Jake had befriended earlier. And there was another kid hanging at the edges, watching the reunion with interest.

How were they here? That the universe aligned so perfectly for them to cross paths like this; what were the chances?

Quinn's big strides ate up the distance, dragging James with him, until he was wrapping Jake in a one-armed hug, thumping at the other man's back.

"Uh, hi," James said to Jake, struggling to maintain his balance.

"What are you doing here?" Jake asked.

"What are *you* doing here?" James threw back.

"Babe, this is our three!" Jake called to Mackenzie, who was in danger of being smothered by Rachel, Chloe and Kat.

"Three?" said Quinn.

"We're on a winning streak," Jake explained. "The

women got away from the Plaza, then we blew the Plaza the fuck up, and now we've found you."

"You *blew up* the Plaza?" Rachel separated herself from her friends and got to her feet, shaking snow from her jacket.

"Can we take this inside?" Maggie interrupted. "It's colder than a witch's tits out here."

THE ROADHOUSE HAD a generator and was humming with electricity and warmth. Maggie and the kid—Zed—stirred a pot of porridge in the industrial kitchen.

James forgot his hunger in the face of Rachel's elation—the pure joy shining from her. There was no intimacy like that between women who had chosen to be sisters.

Bundled into the restaurant's booths, everyone was talking and no one was listening. James was content to sit back with Rachel curled into his side, gratefully accepting the protein bars that Jake tossed them.

"Okay, okay. Enough!" Jim called out. "Let's do this one at a time, so we can actually hear what's what."

"My kids, have you seen them?" Caroline was the only one who didn't look like it was Christmas morning. She had dark circles under frantic eyes, and James got the impression she was close to breaking point. "Is someone looking after them?"

"They're okay, Caroline," Chloe reassured. "I saw them with Delaney Greene, your neighbor. She's taken them in and they're fine, I promise."

Caroline slumped into her husband, sobbing.

"Thank you." Jim's eyes were wet. "We've been worried sick, not knowing what was happening and how they were."

James had barely registered children or teenagers in

Sanford, and it wasn't just because there hadn't been many. They just weren't something he considered. It was surreal to imagine how the last few weeks had been for Caroline and Jim. He hadn't even known they *had* kids.

"Vivienne Oxley and Mrs White have set up a creche system to make sure no one falls through the cracks," Chloe said.

"Vivienne?" sniffed Caroline doubtfully.

"See? It's not just me," Rachel muttered to James under her breath.

"What happened at the Plaza?" Quinn asked through a mouthful of protein bar. "Gemma was in Sanford a couple of days ago, so we knew you'd escaped. But she said nothing about it being blown up."

"We only did it yesterday," said Mackenzie. "We'd been staked out watching them, and knew they were planning to go back to Sanford. So, when they left, we snuck in and rigged up a *tonne* of explosives."

"And when they got back, we let it go bang," Jake chimed in.

"Which would explain why they haven't made it back to Sanford." James was beginning to see that Rachel wasn't the only slightly homicidal one.

"You... got them all? They're dead?" Chloe asked.

"We don't know for sure, but we definitely got the majority." Mackenzie passed Quinn another protein bar.

"Since when do you know about explosives?" Rachel asked, almost snatching at the steaming bowl of oats that Maggie passed her.

"We call it Apocalyptic Upskilling." Jake grinned.

Rachel cocked her head, but James realized she was too busy eating to say anything.

"We hit up the Dutton town library," Mackenzie

explained. "We did our research and gathered our supplies and waited for the right time."

"Can you believe there was a book in the library on lock picking?" Jake said to Quinn, shaking his head. "Who needs the internet when you have books?"

"Not something I ever thought I'd hear you say, little brother," said Chloe.

Over the next few hours, they shared news and plans. They had been using the roadhouse as a base for a week, stocking it with supplies and splitting into two groups to watch both Dutton and Sanford.

"We didn't realize how bad things had gotten in Sanford until we saw Townsend moving everyone into the distillery and The Strumpet." Jake twirled a salt shaker on the table. "We've been trying to work out a way in to get Caroline and Jim's kids out, and we hadn't seen any of you."

"It was like you'd disappeared," Mackenzie added, snuggling closer into Chloe's side.

"We've got a way back in, but we needed food." Rachel scraped a spoon around her almost empty bowl. "We're going to take Sanford back."

Her conviction rubbed the shine from James' contentment. If they could get Jim and Caroline's kids out, and Cassie and Stephen's friends, then why fight? Why get the blood of dozens of men on their hands? They'd found Jake and Mackenzie and the others. They didn't need Sanford.

The porridge settled, heavy, in his stomach.

"And we don't have to go searching for food now," Rachel continued. "We could literally put our plan in motion today."

"Woah up there." James squeezed her shoulder. "The plan is extreme and only made sense because we hoped it would enable these guys to come back. Now, we can just sneak out who we need and get away. Start fresh."

Rachel turned to him, boxing him into the corner of the booth with her stubbornness. "Townsend doesn't get to keep Sanford. There is no starting fresh while he's doing what he's doing and getting away with it."

"Townsend needs to go," James conceded. "But everyone on the council? All the guards? Quinn was a guard. So was Buddy. We don't know how many of them are willingly going along with him, or if they're being coerced."

"Everyone has a choice, O'Connor."

Annoyance flashed through James. Why was she being so obstinate about this?

"What choice is it if they get thrown out of town if they don't comply? If their families don't get food rations?" He tried to keep his voice level, conscious they weren't alone.

"I know who the bad apples are." Quinn drew everyone's attention. "We get all our targets in the one spot and do it then."

"We take out fifty men, and we save a whole town." Rachel turned away from James to address the group. "What we're going to do will be hard, because it's not a nameless enemy we're facing. They're our neighbors, our friends. But it *has* to be done."

James' jaw ticked, but he swallowed his words. There was no point arguing. He was already the outsider in this group. Even Jesse cared more about saving Sanford than he did.

He knew that in this new apocalyptic world, the rules had changed. Consequences were different and people were behaving in unimaginable ways. But could they live with themselves after what they were about to do?

CHAPTER SIX

Rachel was not a crier. Never had been. But as the hot water from the shower sluiced over her weary body and greasy hair, washing away the worry and fear, she gave in to heaving sobs. Doubling over, she curled into herself, letting the water pummel her back as she gulped at air. They'd found Mackenzie. They were safe.

She was tired, sure. But she wasn't cold or hungry. While she was still heartsick with grief for her mother, the reunion with Mackenzie and the knowledge that Gemma's gang were no longer a threat brought considerable relief.

So, under the drumming water and alone for the first time in weeks, she let the tears fall unchecked.

And when she finally stepped from the bathroom, with braided hair and determined steps, she was ready for what came next.

"Feel better?" Mackenzie was sitting on the edge of the bed in one of the rooms the roadhouse offered as accommodation.

"I haven't been this clean in months." Rachel sighed, relishing the scent of the cheap hotel soap. "It's heaven."

"Rach, you know I'm one hundred percent onboard with your plan. But I need to know you've thought it through. All the way."

Rachel sat beside her best friend, leaning her head against Mackenzie's shoulder. "I don't see another way."

"I agree. I don't either. But... I had to kill two men. And I don't regret it, because they were sorry excuses for humans, but it plays on me, you know?"

"They were the ones who took you?"

"Yeah. I shot them." Mackenzie's voice was quiet, but steady. "They didn't deserve to live, but I'll never get that moment out of my head. Sometimes, when I'm trying to sleep, it just plays on repeat and I want to get bleach and scrub it from my mind. But it doesn't work like that. I have to live with what I did. Like we'll have to live with what we're going to do."

Rachel drew Mackenzie into her arms, hating that her friend had gone through this. Wishing she could take the memories away and carry them herself.

"I want my dog," Mackenzie whispered.

"He wants you, too. He's made himself at home in Quinn's bed, because it smells like you. Except now it smells like him. It's disgusting." Rachel screwed up her nose. "Quinn's gonna have to burn the house down."

"My dog does not smell."

"Honey, we *all* smell."

JIM HAD TOLD them all to take the day to rest and refresh. Think. And Rachel had to admit it was smart. They'd been exhausted for weeks, and the last forty-eight hours had been brutal.

The roadhouse had a fully stocked kitchen, electricity, and heated accommodation. All of which were not-so-small miracles in this new post-apocalyptic reality.

Having left Mackenzie in the room she and Jake had claimed, Rachel went in search of James. She had a rush of guilt that her desire for a hot shower had obliterated any thought of him, and how he was faring with his ankle. Could he even get into a shower without help?

Cassie emerged from a room, fresh-faced and so young.

"You okay?" Rachel asked.

"Uh huh. Hot water is the seventh wonder of the world."

Rachel smiled. "Do you still need tampons?"

"Caroline fixed me up. Have you seen the stockpile of supplies they've got? It's like their own drugstore, but without the fancy shelves. Jake has a thing for asthma inhalers. They have about thirty of them."

"I still can't believe we found them, and this place. It's like..."

"A sanctuary."

"Yeah, exactly." Rachel paused. Now seemed as good a time as any. "I don't need to have a sex safe talk with you, do I?"

"No." Cassie rolled her eyes. "Are you looking for James? He's in room six." She gestured towards a room a few doors down. "Do I need to have a safe sex talk with *you?*"

"Brat." Rachel swatted her arm as she walked past. Her cheeks hurt from all the smiling she'd been subjecting them to lately.

She knocked softly on the door of room six.

"It's unlocked," James called from inside.

Slipping into the warmth, Rachel closed the door behind her. Locking it.

James was lying on the bed, propped against the headboard with one arm bent behind his head. His hair was still wet from the shower and his ankle was elevated on a pillow.

"I didn't know if you'd come." He patted the mattress beside him.

"I'm just using you for your body." She climbed onto the bed, resting her head on his chest. "Urgh. Now that we're clean, I can smell how filthy our clothes are."

"Well, that's an easy fix." James grinned, unbuttoning his shirt.

"You're not mad at me?" She realized how desperately she needed him on her side. Her eyes tracked his fingers, which started unbuckling his belt.

"We can agree to disagree. Later. Right now..." He dislodged her as he sat up, pulling his shirt over his head and lifting his hips to pull his jeans down and off. "Right now, there are better things we could be doing."

Rachel's eyes widened, and she licked her lips. He wasn't wearing underwear. His hand swept up the length of his cock and she shifted onto her side, her hand joining his as he leisurely stroked the impressive length.

His abs contracted and released as he lay back, and Rachel was momentarily distracted by just how much of a *man* he was now. He was broad and defined, and she itched to pull her fingers through his dusting of chest hair.

She'd missed seeing him become this man, and it made her sad. Sad they'd lost that time. Because her memories had *nothing* on this reality.

She swallowed.

"You're going to suck my dick, baby doll." James smiled wickedly when she nodded.

His thumb ran across her lower lip, pushing inside as his palm cupped her chin. Holding his gaze, she sucked, moaning.

His grin was slightly feral as he pushed her head down, both hands now gripping the sides of her face to guide her as she moved down the bed until she was between his thickly muscled thighs.

One of his hands gripped the base of his cock and the other the nape of neck. Yes. *Yes. This* is how she wanted it. She was willing to be submissive, to be led. She wanted it.

And there would be no tentative exploration. No licking or sucking. She opened her mouth wide and lowered onto him, accepting the fullness of him as she slid her lips down his cock, reveling in the moment as his fist tightened on her hair and his hips pumped up, pushing him further to the back of her throat.

She gagged, tears forming and then falling.

She closed her lips, bobbing her head in rhythm with his thrusts, a pulse of pure pleasure flashing through her. *God,* she'd missed this.

She gasped in disappointment when he lifted her head, his cock bouncing against his stomach when she released it.

"I need you, Rachel. Now."

He was tearing open a condom and rolling it on, and she didn't move. Couldn't.

"Come on, baby. Ride me." He stilled, watching her and then nodding. "You don't want to be on top." It wasn't a question. He knew.

She liked sex when her partner was above her, over her. Being on top felt too exposed, and she'd never been comfortable setting the pace. Being dominant.

She knew it was his ankle that was determining his request. And she wanted to fuck. So badly.

"I've got you." He sat up, leaning against the bedhead and pulling her to straddle his lap until they were chest to chest. "I'm doing the fucking, baby doll."

Why did that make her want to cry? How did he *know her*, even after all this time?

And then he was tugging her sweater and t-shirt off, kissing at the tears sliding down her cheeks, murmuring reassurances as he unfastened and discarded her bra.

"You're even more beautiful than I remembered," he said, worshipping her breasts with his hands and his tongue. She arched into him, thrilling as his teeth latched onto her nipple, pinching just enough to hurt. He let go, soothing the aching point with a sucking kiss before moving to the other one.

"Do you remember..."

"Sitting in the back seat of my old SUV?" He laughed. "I couldn't get enough of your tits. I went to sleep dreaming about them and woke up hard every morning."

He plumped her in his big hands, licking into her cleavage.

"Remember your marching band uniform?" He groaned. "The way your tits used to bounce in that thing. The number of times Coach smacked my ear to get my head back in the game..."

"Let's not talk about Coach."

"Agreed. Let's get you out of these jeans, instead."

She wriggled out of them, taking her panties too.

"I'm keeping my socks on," she told him.

"You do you, baby doll. Just get on my cock."

Sliding a leg over his thigh, she settled back into his lap, submitting to his mouth as he kissed her senseless. And then he was holding her ass, lowering her until he breached her slick wetness, sliding to the hilt and grinding her down.

"James!"

She threw her head back, stretching her thighs wider to accommodate his girth. Her fingers were digging into his biceps as he gripped her ass and moved her up and down along his cock, a slow, delicious torture that made her scream again.

She was going to *die* if she didn't orgasm soon.

"I need.... I need..."

"I know what you need, baby doll."

Holding her immobile, he began a punishing assault, each forceful drive of his hips destroying another chink in the armor she'd erected around her heart.

She was panting. Out of breath and out of her mind.

The building tension was tearing her apart.

James plunged his cock high into her and held, just as his finger pushed inside the tight pucker of her ass. She exploded. The intensity of her release blackening her vision and stealing her strength.

She slumped against his sweat-slicked chest as he pumped a final time before reaching his own climax, groaning and burying his face into her hair.

"Every time, Rachel Davenport."

"Every time what?"

"Feels as good as the first."

———

"THIS ALL FEELS SO SURREAL." Rachel's head was on his chest, her fingers trailing over his chest.

James didn't open his eyes, just hummed in agreement.

They'd found a pocket of peace in a world gone mad—a sanctuary away from the ambient PTSD that permeated Sanford. A place with food and warmth and friends.

And Rachel was back in his arms.

"What do you think it's like, out there?" she whispered.

James didn't want to think about 'out there'. Because then he'd have to think about his parents living in an independent senior living community halfway across the country, or his brother and his three-year-old nephew.

Or Leah, his ex-fiancé, who was sweet and funny and hadn't deserved a broken heart. She'd been asking whether he thought they should have a vanilla or chocolate wedding cake, and he'd said neither, because he couldn't marry her.

"James?"

He stifled a sigh. "Jake said they'd run into other people, but mostly they were just in small groups, families and neighbors staying together."

"They haven't banded together like in Sanford?"

He shook his head. "And they're running out of food. Gemma's gang has ransacked Dutton. Jake said most of them were thinking about moving on. Trying to find somewhere else."

"We could take them in, when Sanford's safe again."

He opened his eyes wearily. He didn't want to have this argument.

He wanted to fall into a sated sleep with the woman he loved, safe.

"Rach..."

She turned in his arms, raising herself until their heads were level. There was a stubborn set to her features that didn't bode well.

"I see where you're coming from, I do," she said, quieter than he was expecting. She was determined, but not angry. "It's safe to say nothing is *ever* going to be the same again. Ever. And even if we get a cure, even if FEMA appears or the government steps up... the world has changed. And in the meantime, it's on *us* to make the future."

He started to speak, but she shook her head.

"Listen to me, James. We can choose to do the smart thing, or the right thing. And they won't always be the same. I *know* taking on Townsend isn't the smart thing. Don't think I haven't considered running away, starting new. But the *right* thing to do is to help our community. To liberate them from Townsend."

"It's on us to be doing right," he said slowly. There was something about her conviction that was testing his moral compass. Did he believe that the end justified the means?

"Exactly," she breathed, eyes ablaze.

"Tell me again how you think this is going to go down." He tamped down his judgement, wanting to understand.

"Cassie and Stephen are our key. No one has been paying any attention to the teenagers in Sanford, so they'll be able to assimilate without anyone asking questions."

"And if they do get asked questions?"

"They say they were at Spring Street when Chloe and Kat went to get everyone, but were asleep in a back room and were missed. Quinn has put together a list of people we think could be allies, and it'll probably take them a few days to feel them out, to see if they are willing to help. Because they're going to have to get to Jake and Quinn's mechanic shop to pick up the chemical. We have to assume Mrs. White will check their backpacks, so we can't send them in there with it."

"Does it have to be antifreeze? Any chance you've got animal tranquilizers in that stash you picked up from the clinic? They could say it's insulin, that Cassie has diabetes..."

"I don't have any, and besides, it would be impossible to inject everyone at once."

James thought about the fact they were asking teenagers to kill for them. At least with poisoning, they had some distance from the end result.

"And you think Cassie and Stephen are up to doing this?"

"They're smart. Resourceful. We'd have been capable at their age. I think they're good."

"At their age, all I was thinking about was pulling you into an empty classroom between bells so I could cop a feel." His humor disappeared when he realized Cassie and Stephen would probably never again enjoy a carefree youth.

"We can't send them in until they're fully prepared," he said. "It's going to take time, and we can't rush it. Their lives are at stake."

He could get onboard with Rachel's plan, but that didn't mean he wouldn't pull her back when she was getting reckless.

"You don't think I know that?" Rachel rolled onto her back, staring at the ceiling. "I hate that we have to send them in to do our dirty work."

"Okay, so they get together people they can trust, and they get the antifreeze. Then what?"

"They need to somehow poison the whiskey—"

"Or." James sat up, animated. "They poison food. The guards ate from the school kitchen, so it'd be a similar set-up now they've moved. It would be easier for the kids to infiltrate the kitchen than it would be for them to get near whiskey."

"You're right. They'd just need to make sure it was only the guards getting that food..."

"How long does it take for the antifreeze to work? Are they going to be debilitated enough for us to move in on them?" This was what made James uneasy. How much chemical did each person need to consume? What would the effects actually be? "Is antifreeze our only option? What about rat bait?"

Had he just said that? Instant remorse washed over him in a hot wave. What was he thinking?

"Arsenic is virtually undetectable. But with antifreeze, we can reverse the symptoms with ethanol, which the distillery has plenty of. I don't know how to treat arsenic poisoning in humans."

"And we want to reverse the symptoms?" he asked carefully.

"You were the one concerned about being a mass murderer!" Rachel exclaimed, shoving his shoulder. "I guess we need to take that to the group and vote on it. I don't like the idea of having to worry about whether they'll return, but we have to make a decision that everyone is comfortable with."

"Well, look at you, Davenport. What have you done with the unreasonable woman I know and love?"

She raised an eyebrow, and his dick jumped. Fuck, she was sexy.

"Let's not use the l-word, O'Connor."

"Why, I –"

A loud thumping on the room's door had them jumping from the bed.

"What is it?" James called.

A voice called for them to open up.

"Is that Jesse? Buddy?" Rachel asked, hurriedly pulling on her clothes.

"I don't know, but I've got a bad feeling about this."

James, finished dressing, stood awkwardly. "You think we could make finding some crutches a priority?"

"You'll be able to bear weight on it in a couple of days."

"That's not helping me now," he grumbled as Rachel came to stand beside him, waiting for him to sling an arm over her shoulder. "So much for Jim saying we got a day of rest."

Together, they approached the door, an uneasy feeling dogging James. What could have happened that would cause Jesse or Buddy to come knocking?

Unlatching the deadbolt, he stepped back to swing the door open, and was met by the barrel of a Remington 870 levelled at his head.

"What the fuck?"

He shoved Rachel behind him and tried to slam the door shut, but he lacked balance and didn't have the evenly distributed weight to push against the intrusion. Stumbling back, he shielded Rachel with his body, acutely aware of his own panting breaths.

It was one man, his face obscured by a black balaclava. Without saying a word, he held a finger to his mouth, and then crooked that finger in a 'come here' motion.

"Not a fucking chan–"

James was cut off by the barrel of the Remington smashing into his cheek. Pain rocketed into his skull and his nose gushed blood, but he still had the presence of mind to spin to Rachel and slap a hand over her mouth, muffling her scream.

Their assailant cocked his head and raised his finger in a shushing gesture again before stepping back and waving them forward.

Dripping blood, James and Rachel were shepherded into the diner of the roadhouse where they found the rest of their group sitting on the ground, guarded by another balaclava-clad man.

In the absolute silence, James heard the squeak of the door behind them, and Jake and Mackenzie stumbled through followed by a man nonchalantly smoking a cigarette.

No one said a word.

Jim's arm was around a rocking Caroline, her hand stuffed into her mouth and tears tracking down her face. Quinn sat with Kat on one side and Chloe on the other, their expressions terrified.

"Sit." The one herding Jake and Mackenzie pulled off his balaclava to reveal a medium-sized man with slicked back hair and seedy smirk. "Now that we've got the whole gang together, we can get the party started."

Rachel led them to sit with Cassie and Stephen, throwing her arms around the young girl. James half sat, half fell, the throb of his ankle overshadowed by the obnoxious ache in his face. He used the bottom of his sweater to wipe at the drying blood while cataloguing the weapons their enemies were brandishing. All three had guns, and the one who'd spoken also had a pistol in his belt.

A pile of weapons was heaped at the edge of the room, and James suspected they were the ones Jake and the others had brought with them.

"Let's start with introductions, shall we? I'm West, and my esteemed colleagues here are Terrance and Smithy." At West's words, the other two removed their balaclavas to reveal tobacco-stained teeth and bushy beards. "As luck would have it, I've already met these three ladies..." He flicked a cigarette butt into Maggie's face. "And while we could have just kicked you out into the snow and taken over the sweet digs you've got for

93

yourselves here, unfortunately, there are amends to be made."

"We can go. You don't need to resort to violence," said Jim.

West sighed. "It's not that I *want* to resort to violence, but that little lady you've got there made violence inevitable, didn't you, honey? Which one of you sluts killed Leon and Mickey?"

James blinked as the pieces fell into place. These men were part of Gemma's gang, and had been involved in the abduction of Mackenzie, Caroline and Maggie. He hadn't yet heard the full story about their escape from the Prestige Plaza, but it didn't surprise him that men had fallen.

And he wasn't sorry, either.

The question was, did these men realize who blew up their base?

West tutted into the silence. "No one's going to own up to their bad deeds? Well..." He shrugged. "I guess I'll just kill all three of you."

"Bring 'em back to Gemma," offered Terrance. "Kill the men, take the supplies and let's get the fuck back to the Plaza. I'm sick of being on the road."

Mackenzie laughed in a slightly crazed, hysterical way.

West's Remington swung in her direction, and Jake jumped to his feet.

"Mac!" James leant around Stephen to hiss at her. "Now is not the time!"

Their situation was already all kinds of fucked up. There was no telling what would happen if these men discovered the Plaza was no longer standing and Gemma was no doubt dead.

"Hey, this damn kid is a traitor!" said Smithy, standing

over Zed. "Weren't he the one feedin' us in the kitchen? The one who went missin'?"

"He's just a kid," Jesse growled.

"A kid who must have helped these bitches escape," West mused.

"I'm not sorry for it!" yelled Zed, struggling to get out of Jesse's hold so he could stand.

"Me neither," said West, as he pumped a bullet that tore through the middle of Zed's forehead.

CHAPTER SEVEN

Zed's blood spattered across Rachel's face. She wiped at it frantically, but only smeared it further. The boy had fallen across her feet, and the back of his head was missing.

She threw up in her lap.

Chloe and Caroline were screaming.

Buddy was restraining Jesse, who was on his feet trying to charge West.

Everything sounded tinny and far away, the gunshot still reverberating in Rachel's eardrums. She registered James at her side, holding her as she shook uncontrollably.

She spat bile onto the floor, tears obscuring her vision.

Two more gunshots boomed through the room and James dove across her, pushing her down and into Zed's lifeless body. She screamed into the back of Zed's jacket, the thick metallic scent of his blood invading her nostrils.

"Drop your weapon!" yelled an unknown man.

A gun was kicked across the floor, and everyone was talking at once.

James' weight eased from Rachel and she sat up, eyes tracking the spinning weapon until it came to rest against the leg of a table. In a split second, James was diving after it, snatching it up and raising it unwaveringly.

There was a man at the front of the diner, one hand raised in supplication and a rifle hanging loosely at his side. "Put the weapon down, son. I just saved your ass," he called to James.

Quinn was kneeling on Terrance's back, using his belt to secure the man's arms behind his back. West and Smithy were lying on the floor. Shot dead.

"You bastard!" Jake had leapt to his feet and launched himself onto their savior, tackling him to the floor and punching the man repeatedly in the face. Rachel watched, uncomprehending; her stomach turning at the wet, crunching sounds of Jake's fists smacking into the man's flesh.

The man's hunting cap was knocked off, and she recognized him at the same time that Chloe gasped, "Jefferies!"

Now, Rachel understood.

"Jake, back off!" Jim demanded, struggling to pull Jake away. Buddy and Jesse moved to assist him.

"What the ever-loving hell is going on here?" cried Maggie. "Why are you beating the shit out of John Jefferies, when he just saved us?"

Jefferies was the owner of Sanford's car dealership and a longtime town councilor. He was also the man who had slaughtered several older members of their community, Jake and Chloe's grandmother among them.

Chloe was keening, rocking backwards and forwards in Kat's arms.

The older woman was using napkins to staunch the bleeding from Jefferies' face while loudly demanding answers. "You're attacking one of our own? We don't got enough problems with being held at gunpoint?"

"He killed Grams!" Jake shouted, spittle flying from his mouth. "That bastard killed her in cold blood."

"He what?" Maggie stopped her ministrations. "You what?" she said to Jefferies.

"I can explain," he mumbled through his injuries. "Townsend used me as a scapegoat."

"Buddy, Jesse, tie him up," Jim instructed.

"Let me—" said Jefferies.

"Gag him, too," Jim growled.

James helped Rachel to her feet, tugging her into a tight embrace. She willingly buried her face into his chest, forgetting she should be the one supporting him.

What the hell had just happened?

Everyone appeared dazed, in shock. They settled at the tables, pulling them into a rough semi-circle with their captives on the floor before them.

"Cass, help me get some glasses of water." Rachel headed to the kitchen and cleaned the vomit from herself, before reaching for glasses.

"Bottles are easier," Cassie said, gathering an armful.

"Right. Right." Rachel shook herself. "You okay?"

"I'm still alive."

Rachel touched the teenager's cheek fleetingly before filling her own arms with bottles of water.

They passed out the water and then Rachel sat with James, his arm automatically going around her shoulders. A weak smile crossed Rachel's lips when she saw the look of surprise on Mackenzie. They had a lot to catch up on.

"Here's the state of play," Jim started. "We have one biker asshole who was ready to kill us all. And one Sanford resident, who's already killed some of our own. However, he rescued us from aforementioned killing. So..." He looked around at them all. "What do we do with them?"

"Shoot them both." Chloe's voice was clear and steady.

Rachel swung in her direction, stunned.

"Chlo..."

"What? You don't think they need to die?" Chloe's mouth was tight, her eyes hard.

It wasn't that Rachel thought they deserved to live. Quite the opposite. It was just shocking coming from sweet, generous Chloe.

Rachel was getting increasingly worried about her friend's mental health.

Terrance had no reaction, hanging his head and staring at his boots. Jefferies was vigorously shaking his head, trying to speak through his gag.

Everyone began talking at once.

"Hold up," James called above the noise. "Why don't we go around the group and everyone voice their opinion. And then we vote on it?"

"Good idea, fuckboy," said Kat, without menace. Rachel wasn't sure how James was going to feel about that insult becoming his nickname.

Caroline slapped her palm onto the table, drawing all eyes.

"We use Jefferies. Trade him back to Townsend in exchange for my kids."

Rachel furrowed her brow, considering. "What if Townsend doesn't want him? He already threw him out. And if Townsend is aware we're all out here together, we lose the element of surprise."

"He didn't throw him out," Caroline argued. "Jefferies defected before Townsend could make an example of him."

"Are we sure that Jefferies was the one responsible for killing those old folks?" James held up his hand when furious faces swung his way. "I'm just asking."

"So what? We give him a trial?" spat Jake. "No way. We shoot the bastard, just like he did to Grams."

"All I'm saying is that Townsend isn't the most trustworthy of sources, and Jefferies did just come to our aid," James continued. "Are you willing to kill him in cold blood?"

"Damn straight I am," Jake snarled.

"I worked guard detail with Jefferies, and I believe he killed those people at the Travel Lodge." Buddy nodded, short and sharp.

"I saw him blow up the church on the corner, back at the beginning," said Cassie. "And there were people..." Her voice hitched. "There were people in there. They wanted to stay in their congregation instead of going to Town Hall. I saw him running away from the explosion."

"I was following orders!" Jefferies had spat out his gag. "You don't know what Townsend was capable of!"

Jim stood abruptly, pushing back his chair so hard it toppled over. "We know *exactly* what he's capable of." He kicked Jefferies viciously in his ribs. "He bartered my wife as a sex slave, so don't tell us what he's *capable* of."

Jake pushed to his feet also, advancing on Jefferies' huddled form.

"We all need to speak our mind and then vote, Jake." James didn't look like he was dealing with the escalating tension very well. "This isn't some kind of *Lord of the Flies* situation."

"Isn't it, though?" Rachel questioned quietly.

And why didn't that thought terrify her more?

James looked at her sharply before directing his attention back to the group.

"I understand that the old-world rules don't apply. But what you want is revenge, not justice. Rachel said something earlier that I think we need to consider. We can choose to do the smart thing, or the right thing."

The reminder of her words was like gentle rain on the swirling dust of Rachel's thoughts. Clarity settled, and she stood, steeling herself.

"The right thing is to protect ourselves. And the smart thing is to use these two to accomplish that." She looked around at the group. "We talked a little about my antifreeze idea, but we don't *really* know how it would work. I say we use these two to finesse our plan."

"You want to *experiment* on them?"

"They can die for the greater good."

Rachel avoided James' horrified expression. He wasn't ready to accept the full implications of the world changing, and she wasn't prepared to waste time in explaining. There was no police station they could go to, there was no army coming. If they wanted to save Sanford, it was on them.

Her back straightened. James could think about her what he liked, it didn't change what had to be done. Because while he was judging her, who knew what Townsend was doing to the residents of Sanford?

AN ALMOST-MANIC HIGH kept Rachel scribbling on a notepad, even when her fingers were cramping. She had to get everything down. Potential doses, the best way to administer, causes and effects...

"Davenport, I think you misinterpreted what I was saying." James came up behind her. Not turning to face him, she straightened from her hunched position over the diner's counter, shaking out her shoulders and rolling her neck.

James's big hands settled on her shoulders, massaging,

and his breath whispered over her ear as he leant in. "In this situation, the right thing and the smart thing are two very different things."

"I'm sorry this is a moral dilemma for you, but it's not for me." She stiffened, refusing to relax into him. She didn't need his advice or his judgement. There was no doubt in her mind they were doing the right thing.

His hands stopped their circular movements.

"I'm not comfortable with the way things are going, and I want to talk about it," he said. "If you could just turn around..."

"O'Connor, I don't have time for this. Every hour between now and when the teens get back into Sanford decreases their credibility."

She turned around then, and immediately regretted it. His too-long hair was disheveled, and the lines bracketing his eyes were pronounced. There was still a smudge of blood on his chin from the blow he'd received, and the confusion in his eyes tore at her defenses.

But those defenses were hard won over the years he'd been gone, and a handful of sweet moments with him now didn't change who she was. What she believed.

She raised her chin, steeling herself.

They had to make the most of what they had here. Now. The future was not promised to them, not unless they fought for it.

"Those men cannot live, but they can be useful before they die."

"Do you hear yourself?" His eyes searched hers, but she refused to show any vulnerability. There was no indecision.

"Rachel, you're letting this turn you into someone you won't ever come back from." His hands gripped her upper arms. "If you do this, *you* may be able to live with it. But I don't know that I can."

"What exactly does that mean?" she spat.

His ultimatum stung, a knife cutting between her ribs.

She would not wince.

"There is a difference between killing someone in the heat of the moment and killing them in cold blood." His hands tightened on her.

"And what would you like to do with them, O'Connor? Set them up in Sanford's country jail and feed them three square meals a day? Because we can't even feed *ourselves* three meals a day. You're going to guard them twenty-four-seven, and empty their bedpans? Because that's the reality of this situation."

James sighed, his hands falling away.

"Can we at least discuss that option with the group? I'm not even sure that keeping them alive is what I want, but I know I don't want to be conducting experiments on them." His lip curled in disgust.

"Right. You're better than that," she mocked.

"I came back to Sanford desperate to have you forgive me. But I don't know if I'll be able to forgive *you*."

Rachel stumbled back, that knife in her ribs twisting. Drawing blood.

She was going to lose him, before she'd even properly got him back.

———

JAMES HOBBLED his way through the freezing evening back to room six, needing to get away from everyone. He was alone even when he was surrounded.

As a teenager living in Sanford, he'd never felt like he

belonged. He'd always wanted out. The close-knit community was stifling, the lack of opportunity depressing.

In his heart of hearts, he could acknowledge he'd come back to his childhood home harboring the hope Rachel would forgive him and they would start fresh, away from Sanford. He didn't know which was more stupid; thinking she would forgive him, or thinking she would move away.

Facing himself in the bathroom's small vanity mirror, he swallowed down two Tylenol dry, and admitted he'd made a mistake. Not in calling off his engagement—he could never have gone through with the wedding, knowing his feelings for Leah were a poor facsimile of real love. True love.

But the girl he'd come back to was a woman he didn't recognize. They were too different now. He braced his elbows on the sink, dropping his head.

He was in love with the memory of them. Even without the apocalypse, the reality would never have measured up to the golden moments of their youth—the heady rush of discovery and the intimate tenderness. The willful surety that nothing would ever separate them.

But he had, and now he had to live with the consequences.

The knowledge gutted him, leaving a hollow ache. When his ankle was better, he would cut his losses and leave. It should only take one day, two at the most, to drive to his brother. He'd start over.

Yelling from outside caught his attention, and adrenalin spiked his fatigue. What now?

"James! Bro, is Caroline here?" Quinn called through the closed door.

"Why would Caroline be in here?" James opened the door with a scowl.

All around him doors were being flung open, and Caroline's name was being shouted.

"Fuck!" Jim roared, spinning in a circle.

James swore under his breath. Had they not been through enough in one day?

"Caroline's missing?"

Quinn nodded grimly. "Our vehicle is gone. We think she's taken it back to Sanford."

"Her kids?"

"Yeah. Jim said she hasn't been coping. Keeps talking about getting back to them. I guess she's taking her chances with Townsend in the hope he'll let her back in."

"We have to go after her." James was shocked at his own declaration. He'd just been planning to leave these people, and now he was willing to chase after one of them?

Closing his eyes, he leaned heavily against the doorframe. Damn him and his conscience.

"It's dark, and the roads were practically impassable in the daylight. The chances she'll make it to Sanford are slim."

"You're right. But fuck, I was looking forward to an early night in a warm bed." Quinn sighed.

James grabbed his jacket and gratefully accepted Quinn's help as they walked back to the roadhouse.

"Before we head out, we need to find out from Terrance how they found us here." James mentally kicked himself. "Are there others from their group who'll come looking for them? Because I don't like the idea of leaving if that's the case. We should put people on lookout."

Why hadn't he thought of that earlier?

Buddy and Jesse were guarding the prisoners who'd been shoved into an over-sized broom closet. When James explained what they needed to know, Jesse shook his head.

"Terrance has been chatty since we didn't shoot him outright and gave him something to eat. He and the others found us by chance. They were driving past and saw lights on." Jesse interpreted James's panicked expression and held up a hand. "It's okay. Maggie and Kat have been covering up all the windows from the inside. Terrance said they'd been out on a recon mission for a couple of days, and their radio wasn't working, so they haven't been in contact with anyone from their group."

"He doesn't know about the Plaza?" Quinn asked quietly.

"Doesn't seem like it." Buddy shrugged.

James caught a furtive movement in his periphery and turned to step forward into the makeshift holding cell.

"What's that in your hand?" He reached down to grab at Terrance, who was shoving something behind him.

"Why aren't their hands tied?" he bellowed. This closet was full of cleaning chemicals that could be flung into eyes, and long-handled objects that would make handy weapons.

"We untied them to eat," Buddy protested.

James emerged holding a small black radio handset.

"Why wasn't he searched, and that confiscated?" Quinn demanded, taking it from James and switching it on. "It's working," he said flatly.

James closed his eyes, the implications exploding in a flash of violent images through his mind of marauding bikers with malevolent intent.

"I searched him! I did!" Buddy said.

"Not well enough," James snarled. He spun back to Terrance and stepped onto his outstretched leg, putting pressure on the tibia with enough force to crack the bone.

Terrance shrieked, sweat beading on his forehead.

"Who have you been talking to? Do they know where we are?" James asked through gritted teeth. Fear for their safety, for Rachel's safety, had him grinding his heel down harder.

"Stop! Stop," Terrance begged. "We haven't spoken to anyone since the day before yesterday."

Terrance began sobbing as James stepped back to face the crowd that had gathered at the door, which, he noticed, didn't include Rachel.

"We can't trust him. He took it for a reason. We need to assume that anyone who survived the Plaza could come here." There was a desperate fear coursing through James that had his jaw clenching.

"No one survived that blast," Jake said confidently.

"We staked it out for twelve hours. No one came out of the rubble," Mackenzie confirmed.

"What about others who were out scavenging or on recon?" James argued.

"They're coming or they're not. We can't change that," Jim cut in. "But Caroline's out there, and I can change that. I'm going after her."

James stared around at these people, *his* people, if the sense of responsibility that weighed on his chest was any indication. He was conflicted. It made sense that he and Quinn go with Jim, in case he ran into trouble out there. But he was loath to leave Rachel and the others, even knowing they had weapons to protect themselves.

"How many vehicles did you bring here?" he asked Jake. "Caroline took ours, and I don't want to leave you here without a transport option if we take yours."

"You're coming?" Jim looked surprised.

"We both are," Quinn answered.

"We brought a pickup and an SUV," said Jake. "The

SUV's tires had more bite and handled the snow better, but the pickup has better ground clearance."

James looked at Jim.

"We'll take the pickup," Jim said. "If we take two of the guns, that'll leave you with seven, so you'll all be armed in case..."

As much as James knew he needed distance from Rachel right now, the thought of leaving her behind tore at his heart.

"It's okay, fuckboy. I'll tell her you said goodbye." Kat lay a hand on his arm and it felt strangely reassuring despite her words. "Just make sure you come back to her. I don't want to have to start hating you again."

"Thanks, Kat."

Jim led the way through the front door, not even pausing at the sight of Zed lying outside. Someone had covered his lifeless body with a white towel, and in the light spilling through the door, James could see that blood had seeped through it in a macabre pattern.

"Jim, no disrespect, but I think I should drive." Quinn crunched over the snow to the driver's door of the pickup without waiting for an answer.

Jim grunted his acknowledgment and began scraping at the snow iced over the windshield. James didn't have to know the temperature to know it was below freezing. Way below. He wasn't even sure the vehicle would start.

He started scraping at the side windows, surprised at how much weight his ankle was handling. Although, considering the weather, it was probably just numb.

When they finally piled in and the engine started straight away, James actually laughed. He'd been expecting yet another obstacle.

Sitting in the front passenger seat, Jim turned around to glare at him.

"Something funny?"

"Just glad the engine turned over." James leaned forward from the back seat, stretching his hands toward the heat blasting from the dash. "How much of a start do you think she has on us?"

"Twenty minutes, maybe thirty." Jim's mouth was bracketed with worry lines and he bounced his leg, impatient to get going.

As Quinn carefully pulled out of the parking lot, they could see in the light of the headlights the tire tracks Caroline had made.

In fair weather, they were an easy fifteen-minute drive from Sanford. Who knew how long it would take with the road still covered in snow?

Jim's impatience manifested itself in a grim-lipped silence, while Quinn's tight shoulders betrayed his tense concentration. They were surrounded by endless blackness, their headlights creating a tunnel of light on the snow-covered road.

It was only another mile or two when Quinn swore, slamming on the brakes. The wheels locked up, but the truck's forward momentum didn't slow and James saw what they were sliding towards—the mini-van Caroline had been driving.

In slow motion, their pickup skated forward on a collision path to the van that was stranded in the middle of the road, facing them.

Its lights were off.

CHAPTER EIGHT

Rachel had watched the taillights of the pickup leave, and impulsively kicked the wall beneath the window. She wasn't hurt that James had left. Again.

She was pissed.

Pissed at her own stupid feelings, and at the world they'd found themselves in. Pissed that Chloe was retreating into herself more and more each day, pining for Ash, and pissed that Kat had been steadily drinking a bottle of vodka all day and was now a hot mess.

Pacing in front of the diner's windows that Kat and Maggie had covered with newspapers, Rachel ignored the warmed stew that Jesse brought over. Her stomach was churning with fury, not hunger.

So okay, yeah, James had hurt her. What gave him the right to judge her? To act all high and mighty, and then *leave*?

"Girlie, would you sit down?" Maggie leaned back in her chair. "He'll be back."

Rachel flushed, incensed the other woman had noticed her feelings about James.

"I know what I bring to the table. So trust me when I say I'm not afraid to eat alone," she snapped. "He's left before, and he'll leave again. I don't care."

She caught Chloe and Mackenzie sharing a look and hated they knew she was lying. Hell, maybe everyone knew she was lying.

"But you're right. We should talk about what needs to be done." She reluctantly allowed Kat to drag her into the booth seat. "It's too cold for anyone to keep watch outside, so we should probably bring mattresses in here and stay together, with someone at each of the exits."

"Jake and Buddy are already on it, and they've strung some empty tin cans up outside, so we can get warning of anything approaching," said Mackenzie, sliding in beside her and throwing her arms around Rachel's stiff shoulders. "You know he wasn't leaving you, right?" she continued softly. "He went to help Jim bring Caroline back."

Logically, Rachel knew that. But it didn't stop the crushing waves of abandonment that were assailing her. She *hated* that James had the capacity to affect her like this.

Chloe, Maggie, and Jesse joined them in the booth.

"Well, what do you want to talk about?" Maggie reached across the table to take Kat's bottle of vodka and took a swig herself.

"The *biiiiig* moral dilemma," Kat declared, snatching back the vodka. "Are we going to poison those two assholes in the cupboard, or are we going to, like, keep them in the cupboard forever?"

"They both need to die," said Mackenzie, void of emotion. "Jake, Chloe and I vote to kill them. We don't care how it's done."

Rachel took a moment to acknowledge how truly fucked up this situation was. That they could be so calmly and callously talking about taking human life. Her conviction didn't waver that these men should die, but at what point would this apocalypse change them beyond recognition?

"Maggie?"

"Terrence dies," Maggie agreed. "Jefferies... I don't know. We know him. He was one of us. I went to school with him." She shrugged. "And he saved us."

"He killed Grams," spat Chloe, showing more spirit than she had in a long time.

"We don't know that," Maggie argued. "That's what Townsend told Jake, but since when is he a trustworthy source of information?"

"So what? We give him a trial?" Rachel raised an eyebrow in disbelief. "Because we're fresh out of any type of credible judicial system right now."

"So, we're judge, jury, and executioner?" shot back Maggie, hands on her bony hips. "Because I'm sure as hell not comfortable with that."

"Buddy believed it," said Chloe. "And Cassie said she saw Jefferies blow up the church."

"Where *is* Cassie?" Rachel looked around. "I haven't seen her or Stephen in ages."

"Probably in one of the rooms, fucking like it's the end of the world," offered Kat airily.

"Not helping, Kat." Rachel rolled her eyes and pushed her way out of the booth. This odd maternal instinct was inconvenient and unwelcome.

Had Cassie been in room four? She pushed open the door when she found it unlocked, to an interior that was bathed in a soft glow from a lamp. Cassie and Stephen were curled together like a couple of kittens, asleep.

Staring at them, a lump came to Rachel's throat. What kind of future were these kids going to have? It was for

Mackenzie that Rachel wanted Terrence killed, but it was for Chloe and these kids that she believed Jefferies needed to go, as well. Life was going to be hard enough now. No one needed men like Townsend and Jefferies running the world.

"Hey, Cass." She shook the girl's shoulder softly. "Wake up, honey."

The teenagers stirred, and Stephen threw himself over Cassie as he came awake with a shout, protecting her. His action melted some of the lump in Rachel's throat. They were good kids, and they had each other.

They had her, too.

"Everything's okay," she reassured. "Come on back to the diner. You can bring the mattress, get some more sleep. But we need to stay together."

Buddy opened the diner door for them when they returned, and he tipped his chin at Rachel. "For what it's worth, I think Jefferies is guilty. My vote is for them both to die."

Rachel nodded and headed back to the booth, trailed by Cassie and Stephen.

"Do we get a vote, too?" Stephen asked, an edge of defiance in his voice.

"Yep, this impacts you as much as anyone," said Rachel.

"Anyone else feel like fries?" Kat asked, spinning a ketchup bottle.

"Seriously?" Rachel wondered how her friend could think of food during a conversation like this.

"I bet if I checked the cool room, I could find..."

"No!" Jesse yelled, grimacing when everyone focused on him. "Sorry. But no. Do not open the cool room. Trust me."

"Rotten food?" Chloe asked.

"Yes, but it's also where we put West and Smithy's bodies."

"Ew, why would you do that?" Kat's face screwed up.

"Where is Zed?" Rachel spoke over the top of Kat's disgust.

"We want to bury him, so we put him outside," Jesse explained. "But we weren't digging holes in the frozen ground for those other two assholes."

Rachel blew out a breath. It was late, probably nearing midnight. She wanted to reach a decision so they could move forward. Make plans.

"I saw a box of potato chips under the counter in the kitchen. Want me to get them?" Cassie asked.

"What flavor?" Kat replied, perking up.

"Barbecue."

"Hell yes!"

Rachel turned to Stephen as Cassie disappeared into the kitchen. "So, what's your vote?"

"Cassie and I are both a cross against Terrence. Cass is against Jefferies too. But I'd like to ask him some questions before I decide if that's okay?"

Rachel hated to admit it, but giving Jefferies a chance to explain himself before deciding on his fate was probably the right thing to do.

"Fair enough. Jesse, you want to vote now, or wait until we speak with Jefferies?"

"I don't think either of them deserves to live. And you were right before. We don't know exactly how the antifreeze is going to work and we need to. I've only ever prescribed drugs to help, not to kill."

Rachel had forgotten that Jesse was a pharmacist, and the realization that someone else had some kind of medical knowledge relieved some of her burden. "You know I'm a vet, right?" she asked.

"Yeah, I was there when you stitched up Jake's bullet wound when I first came to Sanford. I figure between the two of us, we should be able to get the job done. Because if we mess up when we try this in Sanford, we might not get another chance."

"Okay then, let's bring Jefferies out." Rachel walked towards the closed broom closet with Jesse behind her.

Their prisoners were sitting up inside, bound and gagged, both appearing asleep. "Wake up, asshole." Rachel kicked at Jefferies' boot and his head jolted upright. He immediately tried to speak through his gag.

"Save it for the jury," she muttered, stepping back so Jesse could help Jefferies to his feet and guide him over to the others.

Rachel slammed the door on Terrance's blinking eyes.

Jesse had dumped Jefferies into a chair, placed in front of the booth where everyone could see him.

Rachel had been pushing down what a chauvinistic pig John Jefferies had been to her mother over the years they'd both been on the Sanford town council, but seeing him now made her mouth twist.

She hadn't wanted her dislike of the man to bias her decision, but she remembered vividly the time Jefferies had asked her mother to collect his dry cleaning. And the time he'd dismissed her idea to apply for a grant to beautify their main street, and then went and won the grant—and the glory—himself.

None of that was grounds for a death sentence, but since the outbreak of Sy-V, he'd been Townsend's right-hand man—helping to establish the totalitarian regime that now gripped their hometown.

They were only accusing him of one atrocity... who knew how many others he had committed?

"You want to hear this?" Rachel called out to Jake and Buddy at their respective ends of the diner. They both shook their heads.

Jesse untied the bandana gagging Jefferies, who winced as the fabric pulled over the bloody mess Jake had made of his face.

"I saved you from those men. Doesn't that mean anything?" he implored, glancing between each of them. "I could have stayed out of it. I didn't need to step in and shoot them. I saved you!"

"Do you know who I am?" Chloe asked him, calm. Collected.

"Sure, you're Chloe Brent. Married Ash Maxwell."

"I'm Iris Brent's granddaughter. Remember her?"

Jefferies' face blanched.

"Townsend told me to. I..." He hung his head. "I was following orders."

"Your defense is that Townsend *told you to*?" Chloe swept her arms across the table, knocking the potato chips to the floor. "No. No, I don't accept that. You don't get to sit there and tell us you were *following orders*." Tears were streaming down her cheeks.

"What if..." Jefferies faltered. "What if I could tell you where her... body is?"

"How does that help?" Chloe screamed, jumping from the booth and pushing his bound body from the chair and onto the floor. "How does that change *anything*?"

Chloe's agony ripped through Rachel's pretense of composure and she gasped, throwing a hand over her mouth to stifle a sob. How much more could they bear? When would this emotional torment end?

Mackenzie got to her feet, wrapping her arms around Chloe and dragging her over to Jake, where they huddled together.

"You admit you murdered Iris Brent?" Rachel asked, the words dry and cottony in her mouth. When Jefferies said nothing further, she turned to Stephen. "You want to ask him anything else?"

Stephen wordlessly shook his head. It felt like there was a consensus in the room. Rachel looked at Jesse, who lifted his chin.

"I'll take him back to the cupboard and then you want to check out the gas station to see if it has what we need?" he said.

"Take a gun," Jake called.

It looked like they were really doing this.

RACHEL STOOD over the pile of firearms on the floor, and a wash of fatigue swamped her. She had no idea what she was looking at. It was a motley collection of rifles, shotguns and handguns, and none of them looked remotely accessible.

She took an inadvertent step back.

"Here, take this." Jesse pushed one into her hands. "You know how to use a gun?"

"Uh, no. Why would you assume that?"

"Okay. Fair point. I'll carry the gun. You hold the flashlight."

Together, they exited the diner, the feeble light from the flashlight picking up softly falling snow. It was bitterly cold, the frigid air assaulting Rachel's respiratory system, causing her to gasp and cough.

"Damn, I hate the snow," Jesse grumbled.

It was only a couple of hundred feet to the gas station, where they found the automatic doors busted open and snow and trash piled up at the entrance. Inside, the shelves were ransacked and knocked over. A slushie machine lay on its side surrounded by pink ice.

"Automotive supplies over here." Jesse waved her over, and they surveyed the merchandise stand.

"Guess it doesn't matter which brand we use?" Rachel asked.

"This is so fucking surreal." Jesse picked up a container of antifreeze and shook it.

"They're not going to willingly drink it, and we can't inject them." Rachel chewed on her bottom lip. This was fucking insane. How was this her life now? "I guess we put it in their water?"

"I believe it tastes sweet, so it would probably be better in soda. Let's get back to the diner so I can read this container and we can work out dosage rates."

It was quiet when they returned, the late hour and hectic day taking its toll.

"So, how does this work?" Mackenzie asked, handing Rachel a bottle of soda.

"Jesse thinks this is the best way for them to consume it. How quickly their bodies metabolize the chemical will depend on how much we give them, but they should show signs of grogginess and slurred speech. Then it's a waiting game for us, to see how long it takes for their organs to shut down."

"And what happens when that starts?"

Rachel looked at Jesse.

"Convulsions," he replied. "Coma and then death by shock."

"That sounds... intense." Mackenzie curled her lip. He

was only verbalizing what she'd suspected, but hearing it out loud was uncomfortable. Would her friends think she was a monster for instigating this, when they saw what the poison did?

Why had no one else thought of a better way to take back Sanford?

"Hold this." Jesse passed the gun to Rachel and took the container of antifreeze, sitting on a stool at the counter.

The weapon was weighty in her hand, and she grasped it awkwardly.

"Like this." Mackenzie took it from her and showed her how to grip it, making sure she saw where the safety was and how to use it.

"Since when did you become proficient at handling deadly weapons?" Rachel asked, taking the gun back and attempting to balance it in her grip like Mackenzie had.

"I told you, Apocalyptic Upskilling. I'm a pretty decent shot, too. But I'm rubbish at picking locks."

Rachel couldn't help herself. She burst out laughing. It was either that, or scream.

JAMES HAD SPENT the last *fuck-knew* how many hours trudging through the snow in near-pitch darkness, the cold steadily seeping into his soul and stealing his will to live.

After their truck had plowed into Caroline's stationary van, fucking the engine beyond immediate repair, they'd had no choice but to walk.

He felt for Caroline. He did, but she had cried almost the whole trek back to the roadhouse, and he was *so fucking tired* of using Quinn as a crutch.

And the dog. The *damn* dog. Dex walked at his heels,

continually threatening to cause James to stumble. He'd been impressed the mutt had tracked them from Sanford, and grateful the animal had kept Caroline safe when she'd driven the van into a ditch with enough force to deploy the airbag and give her a decent whack to the head.

She'd been confused and stumbling when they'd found her, and he suspected it was only Dex's presence that had kept her from losing it.

But now, with the roadhouse just steps away, the dog's eagerness combined with a string connected to tin cans pulled tight across his path finally brought James to his knees.

He wanted to cry.

"Stop right there!" Jake appeared, rifle held low and threatening. "Shit! I nearly shot you!" he exclaimed, recognizing them.

Stumbling inside, James was again thrown off balance by Dex, who barreled past him straight to Mackenzie, barking like mad.

Mackenzie spun around, dropping to her knees and opening her arms to the advancing dog. Surprised, Rachel also swung around, raising a shotgun as she did so.

The clarity with which James saw Rachel's finger slide off the safety was terrifying. Pulling on Quinn's arm, he dropped to the floor, yelling at Jim and Caroline to do the same.

The sharp crack of the shotgun discharging was shockingly loud.

He saw Rachel yelp and drop the weapon; the horror etched on her face causing his heart to clench as time slowed.

Seconds passed.

"Is everyone okay?" Jim asked, getting to his feet and helping Caroline stand.

"What the fuck was that?" James fumed, accepting Quinn's help to stand. "Davenport, why the hell are you carrying a loaded weapon?"

He wanted to strangle her.

He wanted to throw her over his shoulder and take her some place private and search every inch of her to ensure she was whole and safe.

"I'm sorry! I'm so, so sorry." She gasped. "I don't know what happened. It just..."

"It's my fault," said Mackenzie, bending to pick up the weapon. "I shouldn't have given it back to her when I knew she didn't know how to use it properly."

"Damn right you shouldn't have!" Jake stormed over, sweeping Mackenzie into his arms. "You could have been killed."

"I'm so sorry." Rachel's bottom lip was trembling.

"Why are you all still awake at this godforsaken hour of the night?" Jim asked, allowing Maggie and Kat to take Caroline from his grasp, enfolding her in a hug.

"You're freezing," Maggie exclaimed. "What happened out there?"

"Long story," James muttered. "We need to get out of our wet clothes. Did anything happen while we were away?"

"No contact from Terrence's people." Jake tucked Mackenzie under his arm. "But we're keeping guard on the doors."

Mackenzie wriggled from Jake's grip and crouched down to hug Dex. "I didn't know if he would remember me." She buried her face in his fur.

"We need to sleep," Maggie said. "Buddy and Jake, you want a break?"

They both declined, returning to their posts at the two exit doors.

"Between me, Buddy and Jake, we should have enough spare clothes to get you guys changed." Jesse dumped a couple of backpacks in front of James and Quinn.

"Yeah, thanks..." But James was distracted, watching as Chloe led Rachel like a child over to a mattress on the floor. She appeared small and brittle, and his heart ached to hold her. But she closed those haunted eyes, not looking in his direction.

DAY 24

James was roused from a deep sleep by the shuffle of feet and low voices. He guessed it was morning, although the newspaper-covered windows gave no indication of time. Kat and Maggie had done a good job on them.

His whole body was stiff. Sore. He'd once run the Boston Marathon, and had felt nowhere near this ravaged the morning after.

He rolled over, groaning. If he didn't need to take a piss, he'd go right on back to sleep. But with his bladder reminding him he was, in fact, still alive, he got to his feet, mumbling a greeting to Maggie as he made his way to the restrooms.

Running water and flushing toilets lightened his mood somewhat, and he went to search out Rachel, only to find her mattress empty. There was a group congregated around the biggest booth.

"We're agreed we'll tie them up out here so we can monitor them?" Rachel was saying, her long hair a tangled mess and her eyes bloodshot.

"Monitor who?" He came to stand beside her.

"We voted," she replied flatly, without looking at him.

"Voted on what?" James tried to keep his voice level, but was she really talking about what he thought she was talking about?

She didn't need to answer, because Jake and Jesse walked over with Terrence and Jefferies.

"This vigilante justice is bullshit!" James growled, surprised when Rachel grabbed his arm and pulled him away and into the kitchen.

"You can't do this," he said.

"Would you keep your voice down? We need them to drink the soda, and they won't do that if they know what's in it!" she hissed.

"Rachel..."

"We voted. This isn't just me, so back the fuck off."

"We're going to poison them like they're lab rats?"

"Terrence has raped and killed multiple times since Sy-V broke out, and Jefferies admitted last night to killing Grams. So yeah, we're doing this."

James grimaced. "I understand they're not innocent. But doesn't this make us just as bad as them?"

"I can live with that." Rachel crossed her arms, glaring at him. "You don't have to agree, you get to have your own opinion. But majority rules."

"I don't want to become this person," he said, sitting down heavily in a chair.

"What person?" She was losing patience with him, her voice sharp.

"I get the world has ended. But I just want to live a quiet life, away from people and drama." He sighed. "And I want you there too."

"So, you're just going to walk away?"

"I didn't say that."

"Well, you're welcome to bury your head in the sand, but right now, we have a situation to deal with. If you'll excuse me, I'm done talking."

Watching the sway of her hips as she stalked away, something in him cracked.

This woman was going to break his heart.

HE STAYED in the kitchen for another half an hour, making himself breakfast and then tackling the pile of dirty dishes that were stacked in the sink.

"Don't bother with those." It was Chloe who came up behind him.

"Washing the dishes?" He turned, flicking the dish towel over his shoulder.

"It's a diner. They have a ton of dishes. We're not going to be here long enough to use them all."

James looked at Chloe properly for the first time in a long while. They'd all lost weight, but she seemed gaunt— her cheeks hollow.

"How're you doing, Chlo?"

Once upon a time, they'd spent a lot of time together— he as Rachel's boyfriend and she as Rachel's best friend. Chloe had been bright, bubbly and quick to smile. She and Ash were joined at the hip and the four of them had spent countless hours at the river, swimming and lying in the dappled shade, coming home as the sun went down with sandy feet and kiss chapped lips.

"You know Mackenzie is only doing this for me, right?" She picked up a plate and put it back down. "If Jefferies had killed someone else's grandmother, she wouldn't care. She'd get on with her life. So if you want to be mad at someone, be mad at me."

"I'm not mad," he said, realizing it was true. "I'm frustrated. Remember how easy it used to be when we were kids? Rach and I never had to try to fit together. There was never friction or misunderstandings. And now that I'm back..." He sighed. "I just don't know if we fit together anymore."

"Maybe you don't," Chloe said bluntly. "Or maybe you just need to work at it. Since when was life meant to be easy?"

"Was it like that for you and Ash?" he asked. "Did your relationship change over time?"

Her face shut down and James leaned back against the sink. He'd over-stepped an invisible boundary. "Sorry."

She shrugged. "I just came in for snacks."

"How's it going out there?"

"See for yourself."

James didn't know what he was expecting when he came back into the diner, but he wasn't surprised to see Terrence and Jefferies on the floor, one sitting in a pool of vomit and the other retching. They appeared inebriated, belligerently demanding to know what was wrong with them, tripping over their words and leaning haphazardly against each other.

"Rachel said ethanol was the antidote?" James asked Jesse, who was sitting on a counter stool staring into a mug of coffee.

"Yeah."

"Where do we get that from?"

"The whiskey distillery."

James paused, digesting that.

"So, you're not testing it on these two?"

"Nope."

"You're good with that?"

Jesse looked up then, drilling James with an intense stare.

"Bro, you need to get onboard with this. We're going to need everyone if we're going to take back Sanford. You need to decide if you're in, or out."

CHAPTER NINE

"Now that we know it's going to take roughly twelve hours for the antifreeze to kill, we have a timeframe to set our plan to," Rachel said, taking the time to look everyone in her group in the eye.

They'd moved to the other end of the diner, to avoid the bodies.

The last twelve hours had been excruciating for them all. Monitoring two men die was insanely fucked up. No matter how evil those men may have been.

James' words from earlier, asking if their doing this made them as bad as Terrence and Jefferies, echoed in her head. She shook it, wanting to dislodge the memory and concentrate on what needed to be done.

"Girlie, it's been a tough day. Why don't we eat something and get some rest? Make our plans in the morning?" asked Maggie.

"She's right, you look like shit, Rach. Did you even sleep last night?" piped up Kat.

Rachel wanted to disagree, but her eyes were gritty, and

her shoulders ached with tension. She was tired. So damn tired.

And the more she'd thought about it, the more she didn't want Cassie and Stephen to go into Sanford alone. She just didn't have the brainpower right now to come up with a better option.

"Go have a shower. Hot water will do you a world of good," Maggie instructed. "We've been using room one, because whoever's on lookout can cover that door, too. I put a bunch of clean towels on the bed in there."

Rachel stood on wobbly legs, finally acknowledging the extent of her exhaustion. She was a wreck, and no good to anyone in this state. The weight of James' gaze had plagued her all day, and she was happy to leave the diner, and him, behind.

Cassie and Stephen were sharing lookout at the rear exit, and Rachel gently tugged on the girl's long braid as she passed her.

"Going okay, honey?"

"Better than you," Cassie replied. "You need to rest."

"I will. Just grabbing a shower."

"We've got your back." Stephen dipped his chin at her.

It had stopped snowing at some point during the day, and someone had shoveled a walkway to the motel room. Wearily, Rachel let herself in and was overcome with the intense urge to sink down onto the bed.

She'd just rest, and have a shower in a minute...

"DAVENPORT, HEY. WAKE UP."

Someone was shaking her shoulder and when she slapped at it, mumbling a protest, James' rough chuckle seeped into her consciousness.

That snapped her into alertness.

"What're you doing here?" she demanded, instantly on the defensive.

"You've been gone for a while. I just wanted to check you were okay."

She rolled onto her back, staring at the ceiling. She felt like death warmed up.

"I haven't had a shower yet," she muttered.

"I can tell. You look like shit."

"So everyone keeps telling me."

It was the fucking apocalypse. It wasn't like anyone else was getting blow outs or painting their nails. Turning her head, she sniffed surreptitiously under her arm. Okay, maybe she really did need a shower.

"Give me ten minutes and I'll be back in. Does anyone need me?"

"No, Davenport, no one needs you. Well, we *need* you, of course. But you're not the only captain on this ship. We're holding the fort without you."

"You're mixing your analogies. Are we on a ship, or at a fort?"

James shook his head, his small smile forced.

"Just get in the shower." He cocked his head. "Unless you're waiting for some help?"

Rachel took a moment to consider his offer. A big, firm hand rubbing shower gel down her back, over her ass, between her legs... They'd only ever had one shower together, on a snowy night their senior year when her mother had been out of town and he'd stayed over.

She'd been blissed out from an afternoon beneath the blankets with him, and when they'd ventured into the shower—the hot steam, combined with his relentless tongue against her clit, had actually made her black out.

James had carried her, dripping, from the bathroom, terrified there was something seriously wrong, and equally terrified they would get caught together.

She pushed the memory away.

They were not in the right place to be getting that intimate. She knew she shouldn't be mad that they were on different pages—he had a right to his own opinion. But she was mad. Mad that he wouldn't get off his high-horse and acknowledge the world was different now.

The rules were different.

"I'm fine." She got off the bed, wincing as something twinged in her back.

"Suit yourself." James shrugged and turned to leave.

And why did that sting? That he didn't push it, didn't try to break down her barriers again? It's not like she wanted him to.

"And, James? What happened before between us? It's not going to happen again."

He paused and then continued out the door without saying a word.

"Fuck!" Rachel swore, slapping at the bathroom door and then slamming it closed.

Why did he make her act like a bitch all the time?

She stripped off her clothes, grateful that between Mackenzie, Caroline and Maggie they had enough spare clothes to make a clean outfit. It was incredible how well they had prepared and stocked the roadhouse, making it into an excellent base for numerous people.

If Sanford weren't an option, this could have made a great alternative. They could set up raised garden beds and chicken coops in the parking lot...

She stopped herself. Sanford was their home, and they

would get it back. There was no need to consider alter-
natives.

Viewing herself critically in the mirror, she scowled.
Her lean frame had never boasted curves, but after weeks of
not enough food and plenty of manual labor, she was
thinner than she'd ever been. She was a haggard, cold-
hearted bitch, and it was better she'd said that to James now,
before he realized exactly what she was.

Getting dumped by him once was enough, thank you
very much.

The hot water of the shower was a miraculous balm on
her tired muscles, until she started thinking about the generator producing the hot water, and then how much diesel
generators consumed, and then how Sanford was going to
source enough to get through this winter... the snow had only
just started—they had some hard months ahead of them.

Sighing, she turned off the water and stood, shivering
and dripping. She'd left the towel in the other room.

Swearing, she stomped out of the bathroom, giving a
startled yelp when she saw Kat reclining on the bed.

"Jesus! You scared the crap out of me."

"Here." Kat tossed her a towel. "When was the last time
you waxed? I feel I need to stage an intervention about the
state of your va-jay-jay."

"Like you've had time for personal maintenance?"
Rachel huffed, wrapping herself in the towel. "It's the
fucking apocalypse."

"Remember when I tried to convince you to get laser
hair removal with me? Bet you wished you'd done that
now." Kat's expression was smug.

"So, you have a tidy lady bush?" Rachel looked at her,
eyes narrowed.

"No, Mackenzie and Chloe have tidy lady bushes, because they listened to me. I have no lady bush; I am smooth and bare."

"Too much information, Kat."

"No, seriously. You need to sort that shit out. I can't believe you slept with James in the state you're in. First thing in the morning, I'm finding you a razor."

"I hate you, you know that?"

"I love you, too. Come on, let's get some sleep. Today has been all kinds of fucked up, and I need it to be over."

DAY 25

Rachel slept deeply, awakening the following morning to Kat spooning her and the smell of coffee coming from the kitchen. This roadhouse really was a miraculous sanctuary filled with all the good things.

Quinn's enormous boots filled her vison, and she looked up from her mattress on the floor to find him looming over them, Dex by his side.

"It's PT time."

"No, it's FO time," answered Kat, sliding an arm around Rachel's waist. "My girl and I are having some cuddle time."

"FO?" Quinn widened his stance and put his hands on his hips.

"Fuck off."

"Harsh," Rachel said.

"He calls it personal training. I call it pure torture. Go away, Quinn."

"We're doing gun safety this morning, and it's mandatory. Ten minutes, girls."

"Is it just me, or is he grumpier than usual?" Rachel mused.

"Mmm."

Rachel rolled over to face Kat, who was otherwise distracted.

"Are you perving on Quinn's ass?" She raised an eyebrow.

"There's no harm in looking."

"Weren't you and Suzanna a thing just before all this?"

"We'd called it off, and I haven't seen her since, so I don't think she was in Sanford when Sy-V hit. Or, you know, she was one of the ones at the hospital..."

"Sorry, Kat."

"It's okay. We've all lost someone. Multiple someones. And we weren't serious."

"So, Quinn?"

Uncharacteristically, Kat appeared lost for words.

"Uh, guys?" Buddy called out, the note of hysteria in his tone causing both Rachel and Kat to sit up. "Something is happening with this walkie talkie."

He was holding up the two-way radio that Terrence had brought, and it was flashing with a small green light as a staticky voice cut in and out over the line.

Rachel's stomach dropped.

That more of Gemma's gang were out there was now a terrifying reality.

In seconds, there were all gathered around Buddy, who was holding the radio at arm's length. "What do I do?" he panicked.

"Shut up so we can listen," instructed Jim.

The indistinct voice came again, and Rachel strained to understand what it was saying.

"Did he say 'FEMA'?" Maggie asked.

There was nothing else for long moments, and Rachel's heart remained lodged in her throat. Who was on the other

133

end of the radio? Could FEMA be active somewhere close?

Caroline brought out a pot of coffee, pouring it into mugs for the silent group.

Rachel was excruciatingly aware of James, noticing he didn't appear to be favoring his good ankle, which meant his bad one must be healing. She watched him stir creamer into his coffee, and then looked away quickly when he raised his head.

"West, this is Dale. Over." The male voice came over the radio loud and clear.

"Holy shit," Rachel breathed.

"What do we do?" Buddy asked, dropping the radio as though it were hot.

Jim scooped it up and, putting a hand over his mouth to disguise his voice, answered.

Jim: Dale, this is West.

Rachel held her breath. Would Dale believe him?

Dale: Where are you? Over.

Jim: Secure location. Don't go back to the Plaza. Over.

Dale: Already saw it. What happened? Over.

Jim: Long story. Are you still in Dutton? Over.

Dale: Yeah. Over.

Jim: Find somewhere to bunker down. I'll check next steps with Gemma and get back to you. Over.

Dale: Tell her we got supplies, hit up a FEMA camp. Got ourselves a military tactical vehicle, too. Over.

Jim paused, and Rachel's eyes widened. She wasn't sure

exactly what a military tactical vehicle was, but it sounded good. The kind of good that could be used against Townsend.

Jim: Give me a couple of hours. Over and out.

Jim placed the two-way with unnecessary gentleness onto the counter, a slight tremor in his hand. "This could change things." He looked around the group. "We could use them to get into Sanford, especially if we have a military tactical vehicle."

"And how are we going to do that?" James asked. "He might have been dumb enough to think you were West over the radio, but that's not going to play face-to-face."

"We don't go face-to-face!" Rachel blurted, adrenalin running high and hot. "This is perfect. We tell them Gemma's taken over Sanford and wants them to leave the supplies and tactical vehicle here, at the roadhouse. Say she's making it a secondary base. And we get them motorcycles to ride into Sanford and they can be a distraction and—"

"And we get these motorcycles from where?" James interrupted.

Rachel glared at him. What was his *problem*? Why was he still here, if he had no intention of helping them?

"I don't know! A motorcycle garage, off the street. Wherever! We use their arrival as a distraction to get our people inside, and they can start the poisoning process, and then the rest of us can follow up in the tank, or whatever this tactical vehicle is." She stopped, short of breath.

"We could workshop that," Jake agreed. "It's a solid idea."

"It could work," said Jesse. "My neighbor in Dutton rode a hog. Bet it's still in his garage."

"Or, we could just not respond to those psychopaths and they disappear into the distance, never to be heard from again." James slid out of the booth so he could stand with his arms crossed across his chest. "This is insane. We already have to contend with one asshole dictator. Why would we bring more crazies into the mix?"

"Because those crazies could be useful," Rachel shot back.

"You going to experiment on them, too?"

All the oxygen left the room and Rachel was momentarily dizzy.

"*What* did you say?"

———

THAT MAY NOT HAVE BEEN the smartest thing James had ever said.

But he stood by it.

Rachel was spiraling out of control, and someone needed to call her on it. The risk attached to bringing in these unknown variables to an already half-cocked plan was off-the-charts stupid.

He already had major reservations about attempting to reclaim Sanford. He understood that Caroline and Jim were invested because their children were still there, and he respected that. Wanted to help, even.

But why was everyone so fixated on endangering their lives to take back a town, when they could re-settle—safely —elsewhere?

"Explain to me why it's not a better option to just ask for Jim and Caroline's kids, and then go somewhere else? Without killing anyone, without—"

"You mean without killing anyone *else*, right?" Rachel's

face blazed with righteous fury. "Because I'm such a monster for wanting to save my people from tyranny, right?"

"Rachel, look at what you're willing to do to *save people*. You're willing to *kill others* for it." James' fists clenched. He didn't know how to make her understand. She was so goddamn stubborn, she needed saving from herself.

"You're right, I am!" she shouted, ignoring Dex's whine and Mackenzie, who had placed a hand on her heaving shoulder. "Because I *care*. Because these people need help, and I'm not going to walk away from them. I'm not like you!"

That hit low, hollowing out his insides. But didn't he deserve it? He had left her, once. And he'd been contemplating doing it again just yesterday.

Why was loving this woman so damn hard?

"You're talking about *mass murder*." He fought to keep his voice calm, even as blood thudded in his ears.

The rest of the group had stepped back, witnessing their battle without comment, but James rounded on them.

"It's not just her, we're all complicit in this. Tell me I'm not the only one uncomfortable with what's happening here? Killing Terrence and Jefferies was one thing, but going into a town and poisoning fifty men? Some of whom may just be following orders so they can feed their families? That's not right, and you know it."

"We'll have the ethanol," Jesse countered quietly. "Not everyone has to die."

"Right, and that's so foolproof. Who decides who lives and dies? Why are we the ones to make that decision?"

"Because we're the ones left," Rachel said flatly.

Deflated, James slumped into the booth seat, bracing his elbows on the table and dropping his head into his hands.

Because we're the ones left.

"I don't like it either," Jim admitted quietly, "but I need my kids back."

James raised his head wearily. "I get it, I do. But you haven't even tried going to Sanford and asking for them. For all we know, they'd hand them over."

"And for all we know, they could shoot us on sight," Jim responded.

James nodded. His arguing was pointless.

The decision was made.

But just like those guards in Sanford had a choice to subjugate their fellow townspeople in order to feed their own families, he had a choice, too.

And he didn't choose this.

"I'll leave. Take one of the vehicles from the parking lot. If it's okay with you, I'll fill my backpack with food?" He kept his voice steady and didn't look at Rachel.

"Where will you go?" asked Quinn.

"My brother is in Oklahoma City. I'll head there."

"What about your ankle?" That was Kat, and James was touched by her concern. She didn't even refer to him as 'fuckboy'.

"It's fine, almost back to normal."

"You don't have to do this." Mackenzie glanced between him and Rachel, like she wanted to push them together and tell them to kiss and make up.

If only it were that simple.

"I do."

Still, Rachel didn't say a word. She'd taken a seat at the booth, facing away from him.

"Do you know if any of the vehicles left in the lot have their keys?" He hoped Jake and the others had canvassed them when they'd first set up base here.

"There's a pickup at the back with snow chains, and I

know it had keys behind the visor," said Jake. "Not sure how much gas is in the tank, though."

"Thanks." It was settled then.

It took less than ten minutes for James to gather his belongings and accept food supplies from Maggie. Quinn walked him out to the parking lot. Everyone else said their goodbyes from the door.

Rachel was nowhere to be seen.

"You sure about this?" Quinn tugged his ball cap low on his forehead. "I get you don't want to be involved, but you don't need to leave. You could wait here at the roadhouse until after..." he trailed off.

"There was only ever one thing for me here, and she... It's time for me to go. Check on my family."

"I get that. Here, take this." He placed a handgun into James' hand. "It's only got a quarter box of ammo, but it's better than nothing."

"Thanks." The weight of the weapon was reassuring in his grip. "I appreciate it."

"You can always come back." Quinn surprised him by pulling him into a one-armed man-hug. "I'll watch out for her for you."

An unexpected lump came to James' throat. He hadn't realized he'd made a friend here until it was time to leave.

The wind was too bitter for prolonged farewells, and so James simply tipped his chin at Quinn and got up into the pickup, which Stephen and Buddy had generously de-iced for him.

The frigid interior created clouds with his breath and as he started the engine, he glanced back towards the others at the entrance of the diner, one last time.

He knew before he even looked, she wouldn't be there.

And so, he drove away. Leaving his heart behind.

CHAPTER TEN

DAY 26

"Rach, enough. You need to pull yourself together."

It had been twenty-four hours since James had walked out, and apparently Chloe's patience was at an end.

"Go away." Rachel pulled the pillow over her head, curling up as small as she could on the mattress on the floor of the diner. She had been buried under the blankets for the last twenty-three hours and fifty-nine minutes, and had no intention of coming out any time soon.

"It was bound to happen. You didn't really think he was going to stay, did you?"

Yes.

A small, fragile part of her had had the audacity to hope. To believe.

She choked back a hot, hiccuppy sob. "No."

"Oh, honey," Chloe soothed, her voice gentling.

The mattress dipped, and then Chloe was crawling under the covers with her. Rachel shifted to share the dark space, sniffling back her tears and accepting her friend's embrace.

"I hate that I care so much," she admitted. "He just felt inevitable, you know?"

"Yeah, I do."

They lay quietly, Chloe's soft breaths comforting Rachel's flayed heart.

"I feel empty. Just, done. There's been *so much* that has happened, and I can't do it anymore. I don't want to," she whispered. "Maybe James was right, to want to get away and start fresh. To leave all this behind."

"You don't mean that."

"I do. What we've done, what we're going to do... it's all so *hard*. I wish..." She paused. "I don't even know what I wish. That none of this had ever happened. That life was normal again. Our lives are *never* going to be the same, and I don't know if I can cope with that."

"Of course, you can. You're Rachel Davenport. You're the smartest, most capable person I know. And, honey? We don't have a choice."

Rachel groaned, hating that Chloe was right. No amount of crying was going to change the way things were. Change who she was.

"Caroline's fried up some chicken wings. You hungry?" Chloe cajoled.

"Isn't it morning? Why're we having wings for breakfast?"

"Kat felt like eating them, and it's the apocalypse, so, you know, we figured why the hell not?"

That made Rachel snort.

Throwing back the covers, she blinked against the overhead light, suddenly nervous to know what she'd missed in the time she'd been hiding. Time seemed to move faster now—so much could happen in the space of a day.

Had they buried Zed? Had they made contact with the remnants of Gemma's gang?

She looked at Chloe. "Has there been more contact with Dale?"

"It's all in motion." Chloe nodded. "Come on, let's catch you up."

IF RACHEL HAD REALIZED that everything being "all in motion" meant she'd be manhandling a half-frozen corpse, she would have stayed under the covers.

"I got the idea from that movie, *Weekend at Bernie's*," Jim said, sliding West's legs into the front passenger seat of an SUV.

Rachel, propping the dead man up so she could fasten the seat belt, just looked at Jim blankly.

"You're showing your age, Jimbo," Caroline said, puffing slightly from having helped them carry West from the cool room to the parking lot outside the diner.

"This is hands down the most fucked up thing I have ever done," Rachel muttered. "Kat, where are the sunglasses?"

"The finishing touches." Kat leaned across Rachel to slide the dark frames over West's slack features. "Give a man a new jacket with no bullet hole or blood, and he's a new person!"

"I find it disturbing that you're enjoying this." Rachel eyed her friend.

"I'm making the best of a shitty situation," Kat shrugged. "Now hurry and get out. I need to get myself comfortable down on the floor so I can play puppeteer with our friend."

Quinn, lying across the back seat of the SUV, lifted his

chin at Rachel's worried expression. "I'm covering her. It'll be fine."

There was so much about this plan that terrified Rachel, but leaving Kat vulnerable to the two incoming gang members was currently topping the list.

Dale: West, we're five minutes out. Over.

Pulling on Terrance's ball cap, Jim got into the driver's seat and motioned for Rachel and Caroline to go back inside.

They didn't move, straining to hear the radio conversation from inside the SUV.

Jim: I'm in the blue SUV. Gemma wants those FEMA supplies ASAP, so you need to move fast. Leave the tactical vehicle and change into the red truck. I'll head out when I see you pull up. Over.

Dale: I still don't see why we have to leave the tactical. Over.

Jim: I told you, we're getting some resistance at Sanford. Gemma doesn't want the townspeople to know she has it until she needs it. Over.

Dale: Seems to me like she needs it now, then. Over.

Jim: Are you questioning Gemma? Over.

Rachel held her breath until Dale's voice came over the radio again. All of this could go wrong so easily.

Dale: Tucker and I get the credit for the tactical. Over.

Jim: We already agreed to that. Over and out.

"What are you two doing? Get inside!" Jim yelled through the partially closed window.

Running, Rachel and Caroline headed for the diner, acutely aware of time ticking down until their plan fell into motion.

Stephen opened the door at their approach, closing and locking it after them, and then they crowded at a window where they'd removed the newspaper covering.

"You're sure they can't see in here?" Rachel asked Cassie for the third time.

"I'm sure. The sun's glare from the angle they're going to be makes it impossible to see inside," Cassie reassured her.

Rachel couldn't tear her eyes from the blue SUV. They'd parked it strategically, so Jim in the driver's seat was on the opposite side to where Dale and Tucker would pull in. With the sun bouncing off the snow, it was practical for West to be wearing sunglasses, and by communicating over the radio, they negated the need to lower vehicle windows or get too close.

Time slowed.

"Can you see Jesse and Jake?" Maggie asked. "I don't see them."

"That's the point." Mackenzie chewed on her bottom lip. "They're hidden out there as backup."

Rachel's heart was in her throat.

They were counting on Dale and Tucker obeying "Gemma's" instructions to unload the FEMA supplies and re-load them into the red SUV, without asking questions. The idea was, if they thought West could arrive in Sanford before them and take credit for the tactical, it would make them hurry.

"It's killing me that we can't hear the radio," Rachel said.

"Here they come!" said Mackenzie.

Rachel wasn't sure what she was expecting a military tactical vehicle to look like, but this thing would have looked at home in a war zone. It was huge.

It was strangely squat-looking for its size, brutish and blunt with its enormous tires wrapped in snow chains. It was scary as hell.

Before the tactical could come to a stop, the blue SUV pulled away. West's arm rose in a casual wave, and Rachel's stomach rolled, thinking of Kat manipulating the dead man's limbs.

A man jumped down from the tactical, yelling into the radio handset he was clutching. "You could have waited to help us unload!"

Rachel recognized his voice as Dale.

She couldn't hear the response over the radio, but Dale slammed his hand onto the hood of the red SUV. "Come on, let's get this shit transferred," he instructed Tucker.

Together, the two men hauled crate after crate from the tactical—all stenciled with the word FEMA. They crammed them into the SUV with little care, cursing the whole time.

Rachel was strung tight with tension. Even knowing Jake and Jesse were out there with their rifles ready, she felt exposed.

Why was it taking so long?

Finally, they slammed the back of the SUV and Dale rounded to the driver's door.

"I need to take a piss." Tucker turned towards the roadhouse.

Rachel froze, her breath catching and her eyes refusing to blink as Tucker took a step towards the diner.

"What are you, a bitch? Do it in the snow and let's get going. West is already ahead of us," Dale shouted.

Cassie grimaced beside Rachel as Tucker unzipped his pants and took out his penis, using it to create a yellow pattern in the snow.

"Gross." Chloe screwed up her nose.

Once Tucker had pulled away in the red SUV and was out of sight, Rachel's chest eased, allowing her to take her first full breath in what felt like forever.

There was no time for relief.

"You ready?" she asked Mackenzie.

"Yup. Let's go."

The two of them raced outside to join Jake and Jesse, each emerging from different vantage points in the parking lot.

"Man, I cannot *wait* to drive this baby," Jake crowed, running his hands reverently over the body of the tactical.

"You *can* drive it, right?" Mackenzie asked.

"Babe, you wound me," he replied. "Let's do this. The back road we're taking should get us there before them, but we can't take any chances."

It required a stretch and a jump for Rachel to pull herself into the back of the tactical vehicle, and once inside, the utilitarian military aesthetic made her think she jumped right into a video game.

"Check it out," Jake breathed. "This is a marvel of modern engineering. The transmission is six-speed automatic. We've got independent suspension and a maximum speed of seventy miles per hour. This beast is *beautiful*."

"How about you put your hard-on away and drive the beast?" Jesse suggested.

Rachel exchanged an amused glance with Mackenzie and was immediately chagrinned. There was nothing funny about their situation.

The tactical growled to life, the snow chains gripping as they rolled out. Anticipation—threaded with fear—rose in Rachel as the snow-covered terrain passed by in a blur. Jake was right, even without the back road shortcut they would have arrived at Sanford before Dale and Tucker, because the tactical handled the road conditions so much better than a normal vehicle.

As they drove, Rachel concentrated on taking long, slow breaths. The plan was in motion and she had to relinquish control. What would happen, would happen.

She just hoped they weren't all driving to their death.

THEY PULLED into the barren parking lot behind Sanford's pizza shop ahead of schedule and encountering no one. As predicted, Townsend had continued to concentrate his guards around the old Benson warehouse, the distillery and The Strumpet.

Kat, Quinn and Jim emerged from behind a dumpster as they disembarked the tactical.

"We've cut a hole through the chain-link fence at the back of The Strumpet," Quinn said, "and there's cover for us to wait until Dale and Tucker provide our distraction."

"No one in the streets between here and there?" Rachel asked. If they'd been spotted, the whole plan could backfire.

"Not a soul," Jim replied. "We think they're still waiting for an attack from Gemma."

Together, they jogged the few blocks to the bar, using overgrown vegetation to advance to their hiding spot.

"They're doing a shit job of guarding the back of this

place," Kat puffed. "They should have spotted us half a dozen times by now."

"Jogging a couple of blocks shouldn't have you out of breath, Kat. We need to work on your cardio," Quinn commented, eyeing her thoughtfully.

"Fuck off, Quinn." Kat stuck her tongue out at him.

"Shut up, both of you," Jim snapped.

Hunkering down, they waited.

And waited.

"What's taking them so long?" Rachel finally hissed, stretching out a cramp in her calf. "I wish we had two walkie-talkies so we could have someone watching the front to see what's happening."

"If we don't hear what's happening, then it's not a big enough distraction. We don't move until we hear something," Jake warned.

Rachel refrained from snapping at him. She knew the goddamn plan. But this waiting was torturous. Was it only this morning she'd been thinking that time moved quicker now?

It was a single gunshot that alerted them to action at the front of the warehouse, followed by running footsteps thudding along the back of the bar and disappearing around the side of the building. This was what they were waiting for.

"Remember, *follow me*," Quinn stressed. "I know where the explosives are rigged. Step where I step."

Without a word, they all scrambled out, sprinting in single file to a back door that led to the bar's kitchen. The freezing oxygen rushing in and out of Rachel's lungs was stinging her throat, and she prayed to a god she didn't believe in that they wouldn't trip a hidden explosive.

Quinn, reaching the door first, wrenched it open and

rushed inside without checking what they were running in to.

Entering last, Rachel slammed the door behind her and spun, coming face-to-face with several wide-eyed women, their hands raised at the gun Quinn had leveled on them.

"Don't yell," he warned. "We're not here to hurt you."

"Get that gun out of my face, Quinn Brent, or I'm going to scream bloody murder." A woman stepped forward.

Fuck. Vivienne *bloody* Oxley.

———

SEVERAL HOURS INTO HIS JOURNEY, James had realized he'd been naïve to think it would only take a day or two to reach his brother. The roads and highways were virtually impassable without the snow trucks that usually kept them clear at this time of year.

He'd snatched an hour or two of sleep the night before, pulling over onto the side of the road but not leaving the pickup. He'd refueled at a deserted gas station, but continued on. While the pickup was handling the built-up snow well, it was slow going, and he'd turned down the interior heating to conserve gas. The cold was serving the double purpose of keeping him alert and keeping him focused on his physical discomfort rather than each bruised palpitation of his heart.

The empty landscape surrounding him was taking its toll—everything was eerily still. A while back he'd come across another set of tire tracks, but they'd turned off onto a back road and he'd seen no evidence of human life since. There was the odd abandoned vehicle on the road, which were easy enough to maneuver around, and nothing else to break up the tedious trip.

Nothing to distract him from every mile he put between him and Rachel. His jaw ached from clenching it against a suspicious prickling behind his eyes, and he was continually swallowing to dislodge the rock of remorse wedged in his throat.

But fuck that. He'd done what he had to do.

Seeing a sign for the town of Bexingham ahead, he decided not to bypass it; the sun was already low in the sky and he needed to find shelter; he couldn't spend another night in the pickup.

Knowing how Dutton had fallen to the rebel motorcycle gang, James held a certain trepidation about entering an unknown urban area—who knew how Bexingham had fared after the fall of civilization?

He shook his head. He didn't want to be around other people now, anyway. He'd find an abandoned house and rest until it was light enough to move on in the morning.

He slowed to a crawl as he entered the built-up area, the suburban roads showing signs of both vehicle and foot travel. Driving further into the residential streets, he found it claustrophobic to be surrounded by buildings again. The back of his neck itched, imagining eyes watching him from the darkened structures.

An alley cat darted across his path and he reached across to the handgun lying on the front passenger seat, shifting it to his lap for easier access.

He'd barely placed his hand back on the steering wheel when a man stepped out from behind an SUV, a rifle slung across his back. Pumping the brake pedal, James held his breath as his pickup slid forwards on the iced surface.

The man hadn't raised his weapon, but that didn't assuage the wariness that gripped James by the balls. One—

apparently unthreatening—stranger didn't mean there weren't several more on rooftops, rifles trained on him.

The pickup finally ceased its forward momentum and James slowly raised his hands to wave at the man through the windshield. The stranger was Black and middle-aged, but in the encroaching darkness and bundled against the weather, James couldn't make out many details. Until the man smiled, his bright white teeth a beacon of friendliness.

James slid the handgun into a side pocket of his jacket, concealed but easy to reach, and wound his window down as the stranger approached.

"Hi there. Where are you headed?" the man asked.

"On my way to Oklahoma City."

"Long way to go."

James nodded, searching the man's face for any hint of malice.

"We're good people. You've got nothing to fear. I'm Asaad. Are you looking for somewhere to stay the night?"

James shifted uncomfortably. He was too raw to be around people, especially new people.

"I was hoping to find an empty house," he finally said.

"You're welcome to stay on our street. We have a couple of empty homes. Our neighborhood has banded together and we're doing okay, but I wouldn't advise straying too far from these parts. It's a lawless world out there now."

As Asaad spoke, two women stepped out from an apartment block to their left, carrying cooking utensils. Watching them, James realized they were cooking over an open fire on the street, probably because there was no electricity inside.

"No streetlights," he commented to Asaad. "Your electricity is out?"

"Water too. One of our neighbors worked for the city,

151

thinks he knows a way to get it back on. Hasn't happened yet, though."

"You don't know me. You're taking a risk letting a stranger stay in your community."

"Yep, and I'll respectfully ask you to leave your weapons with me until you're on your way again."

James narrowed his eyes. "Then I'm the one taking the risk."

"We both are," Asaad countered. "But I believe in trusting my fellow man. Now more than ever, we have to look for the good and help where we can."

In his gut, James felt Asaad was genuine. It was also reassuring to see the women calmly preparing food, and several children emerging from a house on the corner, laughing.

"You're not worried about catching Sy-V from me?" he asked.

"Didn't you hear? The CDC said whoever is left is immune."

"Okay, I'll take you up on your offer. Thank you."

Assad smiled that toothy grin again, and patted the side of James' pickup with satisfaction. "Let's get you settled, and then we can share stories. It's always good to get news about what's happening outside Bexingham."

James hid a grimace. So much for a quiet evening in solace, licking his wounds.

"JOIN ME FOR A DRINK?" Asaad had showed James into an uninhabited house, telling him to make himself at home. Now he stood at the open front door, on his way out. "I've got some exceptional red wine, which goes down better with company."

As much as James wanted to lock himself away from the world to wallow, he owed Asaad for his hospitality, and he was curious about this neighborhood.

Nodding, he dumped his backpack and followed the other man across the street and into a quaint, cottage-style house with an enormous wrap-around porch. "Have you lived here long?"

"Maria and I inherited the house from my grandmother and moved in when we got married. Thirty-five years ago." Asaad smiled.

Inside, it was cozy and warm, lit by candles.

Leading the way into the kitchen, Asaad waved at the wood-burning fireplace, which was crackling merrily. "Never been so happy to have a fire to chop wood for."

"Is Maria...?" James bit his tongue. If she wasn't present, chances were she hadn't survived Sy-V.

"She's checking in next door. We've got a lot of kids on this street and not many adults, and a couple of them have come down sick. And we just took in a new teen yesterday, Blane. She's making sure he's settled."

"Come down sick?"

"We're not sure what it is, but I'm worried it's dysentery from not boiling the water they're getting from the river. If they get worse, I'll need to find antibiotics tomorrow." Asaad pulled a bottle from the wine rack. "Can you grab some glasses from that cupboard to your left?"

James complied and then took a seat at the kitchen table with his host.

"You treat all strangers this way?" he asked.

"Not what you expected?" Asaad answered, uncorking the bottle and generously pouring.

"Not really, no. From what I've seen, most people are

too wary to reach out. That, or dodging Sy-V flipped their asshole switch."

"Where've you come from?" Asaad exuded an affability that relaxed James, encouraging him to open up. Over a glass of red that was, in fact, exceptional, he told Asaad about Sanford, and the events that led him to leave, seeking his brother.

When he finished, Asaad topped up his wine, eyeing him thoughtfully.

"Seems to me you're a good man. And apparently there aren't too many of them left," he commented. "We could use someone like you here, in the neighborhood. You could make your home here, that fresh start you were talking about."

James was saved from declining Asaad's offer by Maria —a thin, wiry woman of mixed-race descent, her long, graying hair in a knot on the top of her head. She had Blane, the newly arrived teenager, with her.

When introductions had been made, and Asaad had poured Maria a glass of wine, they sat in companionable silence. James, exhausted from his journey, was drowsy from the alcohol and the hypnotic flames of the fire.

"Are you hungry?" Maria eventually asked, getting to her feet. "Blane, will you help me chop some vegetables?"

"What about those military MREs you have in storage?" the teenager asked.

"You have military ready-to-eat meals?" James asked.

"They're for emergencies," Maria explained. "It's going to be a long winter. In the meantime, we're eating the fresh food we've been able to stockpile."

"How much do you think you've stockpiled?" Blane asked.

James studied the kid. He sure was interested in the food situation.

"He's been hungry," Asaad volunteered quietly. "He's a good kid who's had to rough it for the last couple of weeks."

Blane, obviously having heard their conversation, stopped chopping a carrot and spoke up. "I'm grateful you've taken me in."

"Where have you been?" James asked, a niggle of doubt about the kid's genuineness surfacing. There was something about his earnest expression, like he was trying too hard.

"My parents and sister all died when... well, you know. There were two guys in our apartment block and they brought in others, but they aren't... nice. I went to my uncle and aunt's house, but they weren't there. I stayed for a while, but there wasn't much food."

"I found him on the streets when I went out yesterday, half frozen," Asaad said.

Okay, so maybe that was why he was trying so hard.

James yawned.

"As good as that smells, I'm beat. I'm going to call it a night," he said. "Thanks again for your hospitality."

"Thanks for the company," Asaad responded, handing James back his handgun. "And think about what I said. We need people like you if we're going to survive and rebuild. It's a long way to Oklahoma City, especially in these conditions. And you could go all that way and not find your brother. You could stay."

The idea was tempting. The journey to Oklahoma was going to be lonely and grueling, and he appreciated what Asaad and Maria were doing here. He had seen little of the neighborhood, but it was the kind of community he could see himself happy in.

His gut twisted. As happy as he could be without Rachel.

"I tell you what, if I get to Oklahoma City and he's not there, or didn't survive, then I'll come back. Deal?"

"Deal."

CHAPTER ELEVEN

Vivienne Oxley looked like hell.

Her acrylic nails were chipped and torn, she had yellowing bruises across her face and her normally immaculate hair was a greasy mess.

"Don't look at me like that," she snapped at Rachel.

"Like what?"

It was like they were back at high school all over again.

"I don't need your pity." Vivienne stalked forward. "I meant what I said, Quinn. Put that gun down or I'll alert everyone to the fact you're here."

Quinn lowered the weapon, and Rachel narrowed her eyes. They didn't know who of these women could be trusted. Jean Fiskette and Tabitha Teale had both lost their husbands to Sy-V and Gemma's motorcycle gang, respectively.

"What are you doing here?" asked Jean, her hands flapping. "You've got to get out. If Mrs. White catches you here—"

"—it won't be good," finished Tabitha.

"Someone's coming!" Vivienne hissed. "Get into the storeroom."

There was no way all seven of them were going to fit into the kitchen's storeroom, so Rachel and Mackenzie dived beneath a bench, out of sight from the doorway. If whoever it was came into the kitchen properly, they'd be seen straight away.

"Fuck. Fuck-fuck-fuckity-fuck," Mackenzie muttered.

Jean and Tabitha came up behind them, leaning over their crouched forms to stand casually against the bench top.

"Something's happening at the front gate!" A man rushed into the kitchen, but Rachel couldn't identify his voice.

"Is it the gang?" asked Vivienne.

"I think so, but there's only one vehicle. We should take this opportunity to escape."

Rachel and Mackenzie shared a look.

"You know anything about this?" Vivienne's feet came into view. "Oh, for God's sake, get up. It's only Charlie."

Of course. Rachel should have recognized Charlie Nixen's slightly nasal voice; he had been her mother's assistant at Town Hall for almost a decade. Charlie was a stickler for the rules and, at thirty-three, still lived at home with his mother.

Rachel and Mackenzie got to their feet as the others emerged from the storeroom.

"What the hell?" Charlie screech-whispered. "What are you doing here?"

"That's what we'd like to know." Vivienne propped her hands on her hips. "Charlie, lock the door. The last thing we need right now is Mrs. White coming in."

"She'll be mad if she finds the door locked." Jean fretted, clutching the stained apron she was wearing.

Vivienne shot her a withering look. "Mrs. White being pissed is the least of our concerns right now."

"Do you know where my kids are?" Jim asked, as a round of semi-automatic gunfire could be heard from outside. Everyone paused.

Jean began sobbing in the silence.

"My kids, where are they?" Jim repeated.

"Again, low priority," Vivienne snapped. "What the hell is happening out there?"

"Calm down," Rachel said, stuffing down a grin at the way those words had the color rising in Vivienne's cheeks. "We have time to tell you everything. What's happening at the front gate was a distraction to get us in here. We have a plan to help everyone, but we need to know you're willing to help us."

"And I need my kids," Jim said, clenching his fists.

Rachel got it. It had been weeks since Jim had seen his children and he was so close, but still so far.

"Can we trust you?" asked Jake.

"We can't trust Vivienne." Kat pointed at the woman. "She taunted us about being trafficked to the motorcycle gang."

Rachel had forgotten about Vivienne's goad when they'd been locked in the room at The Strumpet.

"Oh, for God's sake, you're such a drama queen." Vivienne rolled her eyes. "I was *warning* you. I had people watching me. It wasn't like I could come right out and tell you to bloody well hurry up with your escape plans."

"What's your plan now?" Charlie had his back against the locked kitchen door, but his gaze was steady as he assessed each of them.

"We can get rid of Townsend," Maggie promised.

"Really?" Vivienne's tone was doubtful.

"Just bring me my kids, and we can explain everything," Jim said. "Archer is two and Stephanie is fifteen."

"I know who your kids are, Jim. Who do you think has been looking after them?" Vivienne said scornfully. "Fine, I'll get them. But you better have a fucking good plan to get us out of this."

"WHY ARE you bringing us to the kitchen?" Stephanie's petulant teenage voice preceded her as she entered the kitchen, Archer perched on her hip.

"I'm trying to do something nice, kid. Would you quit with the questions?" Vivienne said from behind, pushing them both forward so she could close and lock the door behind them.

"I'm not rostered to help with dinner," Stephanie protested, swinging around to face Vivienne.

"Steph!" Jim ran towards his daughter, tears streaming down his face.

"Dad?" Stephanie spun again, gripping tight to her baby brother.

The shock on the girl's face was quickly replaced by utter joy and Rachel got a lump in her throat as Jim embraced his children, engulfing them in his arms.

Archer let out a squeal of indignation at being squeezed so tightly and Jim laughed, loud and gruff, squeezing tighter.

This was why they were doing what they were doing.

This was why James was wrong.

Family—community—was everything. Especially now.

"You better start talking," Charlie said. "People are

going to be arriving for the dinner prep shift, and you can't be in here then."

"How many are loyal to Townsend?" Rachel stepped forward.

"Not many. It's been... bad. Only the guards and their families want to be here. The rest of us want out," said Charlie.

"Why haven't you left then?" asked Kat.

"Uh, the guards? With guns?" Charlie squinted at her, as though she were stupid.

"I thought they were to protect Sanford and keep people out, not keep them in," said Mackenzie, sliding under Jake's arm to nestle against his side.

Rachel had a moment of missing James, like an amputee misses a phantom limb. He should be there, but he wasn't.

"If they let us leave, they'd have no one to cook the food and wash the clothes and look after the kids," answered Tabitha.

"Or keep their beds warm at night," Vivienne added bitterly.

Acid twisted Rachel's stomach.

Things were worse than she'd feared.

"Do Townsend's men still have the monopoly on coffee and whiskey?" she asked.

"Is the sky blue?" Tabitha's lips pursed.

Rachel nodded. "Good. That's what we were hoping."

Tabitha looked confused. "Why?"

"We're going to poison them."

Rachel waited for exclamations of disgust. To be told they couldn't do something so despicable.

No one said a word.

"Are they still using those enormous coffee pots from Town Hall?" asked Quinn. "Because that's our starting point. Someone sneaks in tonight and gets the poison into them, ready for the morning."

"What are you going to use? Will it kill them straight away?" Vivienne asked.

"Antifreeze. To begin with, they'll think it's food poisoning. It takes twelve hours to kill them."

"And who's going to get the blow back on that?" Vivienne exclaimed. "We can't have men sick for twelve hours. We'll get the blame and be dead before they are."

"As soon as we see enough of them are incapacitated, we move in. We offer them the antidote if they agree to stand down."

"No way is Townsend going to stand down," Charlie scoffed.

"And no way does he get the antidote," added Vivienne, her mouth twisting viciously.

"Agreed," said Rachel.

Vivienne met her gaze and then looked away.

Sympathy welled in Rachel. She could only imagine what life had been like for these women since Townsend had bunkered down. No matter the cost, this had to end.

"I can put the antifreeze in the coffee pots," Charlie volunteered. "I'm on the cleaning roster tonight and will have access to the tea room they use in the warehouse."

"Here," Quinn thrust a backpack at Charlie. "Divide it evenly between the three pots. Use it all. And for fuck's sake, don't get caught."

Watching Charlie take the backpack, Rachel had a flash of dread. They were entrusting the execution of this plan to one person. Charlie Nixen. Did he have the balls to pull it off?

"Tabitha and Jean, we can hide them in the side room on the first floor, where all the extra furniture is," Vivienne instructed. "Charlie, go out first and act as a decoy so they can get up the staircase."

"We're staying with you!" Stephanie clutched at Jim's sleeve. "Don't leave us."

"Of course, you are. I'm never leaving you and your brother again," Jim replied, glancing at Vivienne as though expecting her to disagree.

"Have you got Archer's pacifier?" Vivienne asked Stephanie. "It's on you to keep him quiet."

Stephanie nodded. "He'll be good, I promise."

Vivienne hugged the teen and kissed the top of the toddler's head. "Go on then. Be safe."

Rachel's mouth fell open.

The world really had changed.

IT WASN'T until Tabitha and Jean had stowed them away and left that Rachel realized Maggie was not with them. "When was the last time anyone saw Maggie?"

"Just before Vivienne came back with my kids," said Jim. "We had a disagreement about her going to find Townsend."

Rachel raised an eyebrow. He looked at her blankly.

"Ah, fuck." The light switch finally went off in Jim's head. "She's gone off to find Townsend."

"Dad!"

"What?"

"Don't say the f-word in front of Archer!" Stephanie scowled. "What would Mom say?"

Jim smiled so hard it must have hurt his face.

Rachel turned away, biting down on her anger that Maggie had gone off alone. She could jeopardize not just the plan, but all their lives.

"Should we be worried Maggie might compromise us?" Jake rubbed at his facial hair.

"I don't know about you all, but I'm more worried about that Charlie guy. How confident are we in him being able to follow through with the antifreeze?" asked Jesse.

Rachel realized that, until now, Jesse had been fairly quiet. She was reminded that Sanford wasn't his town; he was risking everything to help them. Risking everything for a chance at a safe place to start again.

"We have to have faith that Maggie knows what she's doing, and Charlie can do it," Rachel said. "We can't do anything but wait now, anyway."

Kat flopped onto an armchair, sneezing when dust motes flew into the air. "I *hate* waiting," she whined. "We go from one extreme to the other, and it's not good for my chakras."

"Your chakras?" Mackenzie laughed, pushing Kat over so she could squeeze in beside her.

"The energy points in my body are not dealing with all this adrenalin," Kat said. "You know there are, like, twenty different chairs in this one tiny room. Why are you trying to sit on my lap?"

"Because I love you, Kitty Kat," Mackenzie said, blowing in Kat's ear.

"Aren't you two meant to be adults?" Stephanie eyed them disdainfully.

"I think we just got dissed by a teenager," said Mackenzie.

"No one says 'dissed' anymore." Stephanie took Archer from Jim, settling him into a bed of cushions she'd made on the floor. "Now keep it down so I can get him to sleep."

Jesse came to sit beside Rachel, who was leaning against

a wall with her elbows resting on her knees. All of a sudden, she was exhausted.

"Charlie seemed... more beta than alpha," he said.

Rachel smirked. "Charlie is gamma. But I shouldn't be surprised that he's survived here. He's always flown under the radar. He was my mother's assistant for years, and she doesn't tolerate fools. He gets shit done. I think we're good."

"Your mom? She's still alive?"

"I don't know. I'd like to hope so. She and the other women from the council were away on a retreat. It was only a couple of hours away, so you'd think if they'd survived... Anyway. None of them have come back."

"I'm sorry."

Rachel shrugged off his condolence. She didn't need it. Everyone had lost someone, and she couldn't think about her own losses right now.

Quinn joined them, lowering his big frame with surprising grace.

"How tall *are* you?" Jesse asked.

"Six foot five." Quinn stretched out his long legs and cracked his neck. Rachel was reassured by his presence. He had her back.

"And you're cousins with Jake and Chloe?"

"Our fathers are brothers."

They watched Jake sit on the floor between Mackenzie's legs, resting his head against her knee and swatting away Kat's hand when she tried to ruffle his hair.

"Do you think they killed Dale and Tucker at the gate?" Rachel asked.

"I think from the gunfire we heard, we can assume so," Quinn replied.

"I bet they took all those FEMA supplies straight to the warehouse." Rachel ground her teeth. "Did you see how

thin everyone looks? And what about those bruises on Vivienne's face?"

"Their time is up, Rach. We just have to wait," said
Quinn.

And so, they waited.

————

DAY 27

James was woken the next morning by Blane knocking
on the front door.

Cursing that he'd over-slept, he let the boy in and immediately set to work packing up the sleeping bag he'd rolled
out on the couch.

"You didn't use one of the beds?" Blane asked.

James looked up. "It felt weird to sleep in someone else's
bed," he admitted.

"I get that." Blane walked around the room, inspecting
the contents. "Maria wants me to move into this house.
That lady and all those kids next door who are sick? It's
dysentery. They have bloody diarrhea and—"

James held up a hand. "Okay, I get it. Dysentery."

"Crazy, right? It's like we're living in third world
country."

There was another knock on the door, and Maria let
herself in.

"Hope you don't mind me sending Blane over. Now
that the sickness has progressed from stomach cramps, it's
highly contagious. I didn't want him in that house."

"No problems. I'm just about to head off." James hefted

his pack onto his back, pleased he could bear his full weight on his bad ankle with no pain.

"Oh." Maria's face fell. "I know Asaad was hoping you'd have breakfast with us. He's going to ask if you'll go out with him to find medicine."

"You don't have medical supplies?" Blane asked.

"We have some, but not the kind of antibiotics we need to treat this," Maria answered. "Did you want to go out with Asaad, too?"

Blane quickly set down the photo frame he was holding and shook his head, taking a step back. "No. No, I'll stay. If that's okay? I just... I'm not ready to go back out there yet."

"Sure, of course. You can help Alison at number twenty-six. She's setting up hydroponic vegetable gardens in her greenhouse." Maria smiled sadly. "I didn't mean to push you; you don't have to go anywhere any time soon."

James rubbed a hand across the bristles on his face. He wanted to be on his way. The sooner he reached Oklahoma City, the sooner he'd know the fate of his brother and nephew.

But he couldn't leave these people if they needed help.

"Alison has chickens, and we're cooking up eggs," Maria said, gesturing across the road. "Sure you can't at least stay for breakfast?"

James grinned. "You've twisted my arm."

"Blane, you're okay to unpack and settle in?" Maria asked.

"Yep. Thanks for breakfast. And for, well, everything."

Maria hugged the boy and then escorted James across the road to where Asaad was frying eggs on a skillet over the open fire.

"You're still here!" he called, straightening up and slapping James on the back. "We weren't sure if you would have left already."

James didn't know what to say to that. He'd prefer to have been on his way, but these people had been nothing but kind to him. If he could help them, then he would.

"Maria mentioned you needed my help to get some medicine?"

"I do, if you'd be so kind as to oblige. Lucy from fifty-seven just came by, and they've got several more who've come down with dysentery. She's just gone to get her rifle, and then she's going to head into the town centre with me. We sure would appreciate your company."

A hot flush swept James' chest. He was a fool. He'd left his handgun beneath the cushion on the couch where he'd slept. "If you need my help, then you've got it. I just left something across the road. I'll be back in a minute."

"Sure, sure. I'll plate you up some eggs. You like ketchup?"

"Who doesn't like ketchup?" he faux-laughed, heading back out the hallway to the front door.

How could he have been so stupid? The idea of having Rachel with him, and his forgetting the gun, leaving them unprotected and in danger, made his skin prickle with shamed heat.

He was grateful for the slap of cold air in his face as he crossed the street; he needed to get his head in the game. Jogging up the front steps to the house he'd stayed at, he swung open the door, Blane's startled reaction making him cringe with guilt.

"Sorry, I didn't mean to scare you."

"It's okay, I'm still a bit jumpy, I guess."

"That's understandable. What've you got there? A walkie talkie?"

The boy held an object loosely at his side.

"Yeah. It's broken. I used to play with it with my little brother. Now, it reminds me of him. It's stupid, I know." He shrugged, putting the radio handset into his duffle bag.

"Not stupid at all. It's good to remember the people we've lost." James' mind flashed to Rachel as yet another crack fractured his heart.

"I'll put this away in the bedroom," Blane said, picking up his duffle and heading down the hallway.

"I'm just grabbing something I forgot," James yelled after him. "I'll catch you later."

The weight of the handgun in his grip was reassuring as James returned to Asaad and Maria's home, his appetite returning now that he had his weapon on him.

"This is Lucy." Asaad waved at a petite brunette who looked to be in her twenties. "She used to be a librarian, but now she's our crack shot sniper."

"I don't know about crack shot, but I've definitely developed a useful skill." Lucy eyed him speculatively. "And you're James, our newest recruit."

James looked at Asaad. "Recruit?"

"I'm still working on getting him to stay," Asaad told Lucy. "But as you know, I'm a very persuasive man. Here, I made you both breakfast burritos to go. We're going on foot, so it's best we get going sooner rather than later."

Before they set out, Maria handed them each a wide-headed broom, laughing at James' puzzled expression. "Drag them behind you to cover your footprints in the snow," she explained.

"So where are we headed, exactly?" James asked as they started off, boots crunching through the snow.

"There's a mom-and-pop store on the corner of East and Tamworth Streets, and they operated a small pharmaceutical dispensary. I'm hoping it's been overlooked in the looting," Asaad replied.

"Has there been much looting?" James asked. "Did FEMA make it here to Bexingham?"

"We've heard rumors they set up at the Army Base on the other side of the town, but we haven't confirmed that," Lucy said through a mouthful of egg.

"Why not?" That's the first place James would have gone.

"There are a couple of gangs fighting it out for control of the streets, which makes it dangerous to move around unless it's absolutely essential," she said.

James guessed that an outbreak of dysentery made it essential.

They walked another couple of blocks, skirting snow-covered mounds that James realized were piles of dead bodies. He shuddered.

The residential area gave way to commercial buildings, and the mounds grew fewer. It was cold, and the bright sun offered no warmth.

"These gangs, exactly how fucked up are they?" Even as he asked, James wasn't sure he wanted to know. Why did it seem like Sy-V had upset the ratio of asshole to normal human beings, with the assholes coming out on top?

"They are *all kinds* of fucked up." Lucy stopped chewing and looked around, eyes alert. "Do you hear that? Vehicles. A lot of them."

Asaad cocked his head. "Sounds like they're headed this way."

In unison, the three of them halted.

"This way." Asaad took off, darting between parked cars and into an office building—its front windows smashed wide and yawning.

Crouched inside beneath the window, panting, they waited. Several moments later, a truck fitted with a snow-plough lumbered past, pushing snow and debris to the side. The enormous plough had the head of a jackal spray painted onto it, and an assortment of trucks followed, all emblazoned with the same graphic.

"They call themselves The Jackals," Asaad said.

"How are there so many of them?" Lucy whispered from behind her rifle, which she had balanced through the broken window. "Have they always been living amongst us, and it took an apocalypse for them to flip their switch?"

"The CDC said those with a natural immunity to Sy-V appeared to mostly be in clusters, some kind of environmental factor that's protected us," said Asaad. "My guess is a lot of those clusters were in prisons. Which means most of the survivors were already criminals."

James was equally captivated and repulsed by the people driving the trucks and riding in the cargo beds. Men and women alike, they looked like extras from the *Mad Max* films; sporting war paint and wild hair and facial tattoos.

They appeared primed and ready—maliciously purposeful.

"Where are they going?" James asked.

"Can you hear that?" said Asaad. "They're yelling between the trucks."

Between the revving and rumbling of the engines, they could make out Jackals calling to each other.

"Are they taking bets?" James asked, confused.

"What are they..." Asaad fell back on his haunches, his eyes wide with terror.

"Did they say..." Lucy whispered.

"Maplewood Drive. They're heading to our neighborhood." Asaad clutched a hand urgently to his chest and then dropped to the ground.

James just watched, shocked. Jesus Christ, he was having a heart attack.

"It's a panic attack." Lucy dropped to Asaad's side. "Close your eyes, and breathe deep. In and out. It'll pass. That's it, in and out."

Her hands were shaking, and her face was ashen.

"We have to get back!" James urged. "We need to warn them."

Lucy shot him a look. "That's it, Asaad. Keep breathing. It's just a panic attack. You're going to be fine."

"We have... to go." Asaad struggled to his feet. "Maria. The kids."

How many Jackals had just passed them? Ten trucks? Twelve? Even if they sprinted, they wouldn't make it back to the neighborhood before the Jackals. Before they wreaked a horrific kind of havoc there would be no recovering from.

"Go, go!" Asaad shouted, stumbling out onto the street.

James grabbed at his shoulder, pulling him down behind a parked SUV. "We can't follow them directly. They could see us. We need to take a parallel street."

"Come on, this way!" Lucy shouted, her rifle slung across her back as she darted down a side street. Together, James and Asaad followed, their heavy footsteps sinking into the snow-covered ground, making their panicked movements slow and sluggish.

Concentrating on putting one foot in front of the other, James ran—pumping his arms and praying his ankle could handle this exertion. He was sweating beneath his layers of clothes, the freezing air sharp in his lungs and making his eyes water.

One block. Two.

How many more?

Lucy slowed, holding a hand to her side.

"Stitch." She gasped. "Don't wait for me."

Asaad had fully recovered from his crippling anxiety, powering ahead like a man possessed. James put his head down and pushed forward with his thighs, making each step count as he kept pace.

Three blocks. Four.

Gunfire erupted in the distance. Continuous and deliberate.

"No!" Asaad fell to his knees, his chest heaving.

"Come on." James grabbed his arm, pulling him to his feet as Lucy caught them up. She took Asaad's other arm and together they half ran and half dragged him between them.

The closer they got, the louder the gunfire echoed.

And then they heard the screams.

CHAPTER TWELVE

There were a lot of things Rachel was never taking for granted again.

Since this whole shit-show had begun, she'd had very few nights sleep in an actual bed, and her stiff joints and aching body reminded her of that this morning.

Nine bodies packed into one small room had ensured they didn't get too comfortable, but at least a working generator had kept the heating on throughout The Strumpet.

Archer was grumpy, which had Stephanie, Jim and Mackenzie fussing to keep him quiet.

Rachel was thrilled for Jim that he had his kids back, but less thrilled she had to endure the toddler's incessant whining. They were all irritable and on-edge, not knowing what was happening in the warehouse.

Tabitha had slipped in not long ago, bringing them food and confirming that Charlie had got the antifreeze into the coffee pots undetected. He'd even put a little in each of the thermoses the guards took with them out on duty, figuring it would be handy to have them sick and off the fence as soon as possible.

The knowledge brought no relief, just ratcheted the tension higher.

All this sitting around gave Rachel far too much time to think. She was obsessively going over every interaction she'd had with James since he'd come back—second-guessing every word she'd spoken.

Had she been too hardline? Had she dismissed his opinions too easily, afraid he was judging her? She was well aware her stubbornness wasn't an attractive trait. Had she driven him away, or was he always going to leave?

Had she been right to pursue this course of action?

Right now, she could be in a little farmhouse, curled up with him in front of a crackling fireplace, far away from danger and drama. There would be chickens and cows and goats in a barn, and a little stream out the back.

How far was too far, when it came to securing your freedom?

When the door opened and Vivienne burst in, she jolted out of her daydream.

"It's working!" Vivienne cried. "They're getting sick. Coming down with stomach cramps and vomiting."

"And you've cleared out the kitchen?" Rachel jumped to her feet. "There's no one there if they come looking for someone to blame?"

"It's clear," Vivienne said, scooping up Archer, who promptly flung his chubby arms around her neck.

"How long do we wait before we go down there?" Jake asked, looking around.

"It's chaos at the moment, and no one can find Townsend," Vivienne replied.

Rachel's mind flashed straight to Maggie. It was no coincidence she'd disappeared, and now Townsend was nowhere to be found.

"We have to find him," Mackenzie said. "This doesn't work unless we cut the head off the snake."

"I can go to his rooms, see if he's there," Vivienne said.

"There's no way you'll get close," Rachel argued. "He'll have guards everywhere."

"Sick guards." Vivienne smiled viciously. "And anyway, they're used to seeing me there."

Rachel winced, and Vivienne crossed her arms defiantly, like she was daring anyone to pity her.

"I'm going with you." Rachel stepped forward.

"What?" Mackenzie cried.

"No. No way." Kat grabbed hold of Rachel's hand.

"It'll be fine." Rachel shook her hair out of her ponytail. "I'll cover my face with my hair and keep my head down."

"Take my handgun," said Jim, passing her the weapon.

"No! It's too dangerous for her to be seen." Kat tugged on Rachel's hand. "Please Rachel, no."

"I'm not letting Vivienne go by herself." Rachel gently pried Kat's hand loose. "Jake, can you give Vivienne your gun?"

Mackenzie was white-knuckling Jake's sleeve, but he handed his weapon to Vivienne, who nodded her thanks and tucked it into the waistband of her jeans.

"You don't have to come. I can do this myself." Something that looked a lot like vulnerability flashed across Vivienne's face.

For the first time in a long time, Rachel's internal conflict settled. Yes, she'd taken a hard line on Townsend. But that didn't mean she was losing her humanity. It meant she was protecting it.

"I'm coming," she stated firmly.

. . .

"WHERE IS EVERYONE?" Rachel was walking a step behind Vivienne as they navigated the corridors and stairways of The Strumpet.

"We told them to stay in their rooms. They don't know exactly what's happening, but they know enough to stay out of the way."

They were almost at the front entrance when Vivienne pushed her back into a dark alcove around the corner. "It's Mrs. White."

Vivienne shielded Rachel with her body as Mrs. White walked in, talking with someone whose voice Rachel didn't recognize. Oblivious, the pair stopped just feet away, Mrs. White impatiently giving instructions to take clean water and Tylenol to the warehouse, before expressing her displeasure about the kitchen not being manned.

Rachel and Vivienne burrowed further into the alcove, and Rachel let out a heavy breath when they heard footsteps moving away.

"We should probably wait until they head back out," Vivienne whispered.

Disturbed dust tickled at Rachel's nostrils, and she shot Vivienne a panicked look. "I'm going to..."

Vivienne's hand slapped over Rachel's mouth, muffling the sneeze that exploded in a puff against her palm. Taking her hand away, Vivienne's thumb rubbed across Rachel's bottom lip.

There was something about the action, something intimate and intentional.

Vivienne blinked slowly, her eyes heavy lidded and a softness to her features. "Just in case we die today, I've loved you since the seventh grade."

Rachel's head pounded. "You hate me," she protested.

"I hate that I love you," Vivienne said simply.

"Oh."

"You don't have to say anything, but I wanted you to know."

They stared at each other, breathing the same air in the closed space, Vivienne's yearning palpable. Confusion and guilt warred for dominance within Rachel, along with the knowledge that, deep down, maybe she'd known? Because there was a distinct lack of surprise at the revelation.

Vivienne sighed and took a small step back. "Where is James? I thought you were back together?"

"He left."

"Like last time."

Rachel blanched.

"Sorry," Vivienne said. "That was harsh."

Rachel shrugged. "But true."

"For what it's worth, I didn't hate you two together. If it couldn't be me, then I was glad you had him."

The front door opened, and Mrs. White exited the building, pulling them from the moment.

"You ready?" Vivienne squared her shoulders.

"Where are we going exactly?"

"Townsend has set himself up in the distillery, taking over the boardroom. He had men bring all the furniture from his house, including a king-size four-poster bed." Vivienne's top lip curled. "Just stay behind me and I'll do the talking."

Rachel nodded, hoping her apprehension wasn't visible.

She'd come with Vivienne to prove to herself she wasn't a monster. She had empathy—she *cared*. Even if James would never see that. "Hey," Rachel reached out to touch Vivienne's shoulder. "We're not dying today."

. . .

THE GUARD at the door to the distillery looked decidedly green, but it didn't stop him leering at Vivienne as they approached.

"Come see me when Townsend's finished with you, Vivi."

Rachel's stomach turned.

Vivienne ignored the man and walked right past. Keeping her hair over the side of her face closest to the guard, Rachel followed, tightly gripping the handgun concealed in her jacket pocket.

The distillery's front foyer featured a high atrium ceiling, showcasing the snow-heavy clouds outside, and one entire wall was covered with stacked oak barrels. The long tasting bar had, according to Vivienne, been re-purposed as a general check-in station where guards clocked-in and picked up a weapon, and returned it when they clocked-off.

Rachel was relieved to know many of the men wouldn't be armed. It was only those on duty who would be carrying.

There were several men congregated on bar stools, one of whom leant over to vomit on the floor as Vivienne and Rachel passed.

No one paid the women any attention.

"It's quieter than usual," Vivienne whispered.

"Maybe they're sick enough to have gone to their beds?"

Vivienne shrugged, leading the way down a long, glassed-in corridor where visitors to the distillery could see into the factory and watch the whiskey being made.

When they got to the end, Vivienne turned right and stopped at a set of enormous double doors. She turned to face Rachel, her mouth set in a tight line. "There's usually a guard stationed here. Even if he's not here, Townsend always has someone protecting his rooms."

"Is it locked?"

Vivienne tried the handle and nodded.

"So, we knock?" Rachel expected Vivienne to shoot a withering glare her way. Instead, she gave two sharp raps on the door.

Rachel fingered the safety on the handgun in her pocket, wishing Quinn had given her more than two minutes' instruction on how to shoot the damn thing.

Nothing happened.

There was no sound from the other side of the door.

"It's Vivienne." She knocked again.

He was in there. Rachel knew it. He'd probably realized his people were getting sick and, thinking it was contagious, barricaded himself inside.

Footsteps ran up the corridor behind them, causing Rachel's heart to jump into her throat. She whipped the handgun out and turned towards the sound, only to release a shaky breath when the steps turned in the other direction and kept going.

Vivienne raised her hand to knock again, but Rachel held up a finger.

"Hang on, I have an idea." She was acting on a hunch, which could very well get them killed, but they'd come this far.

"Maggie?" She tapped on the door. "Maggie, are you there? It's Rachel."

Either she was right, and Maggie had infiltrated Townsend's rooms and was holding him hostage, or Townsend would be curious enough to open the doors.

Seconds ticked by.

Rachel was just turning away when she heard a muffled tread beyond the door.

"Rachel?" a soft voice said from the other side.

"Maggie! Oh, thank God."

Vivienne gave her the side-eye. "That could have ended very differently."

The door swung open and Maggie hustled them inside, looking over their shoulders. "No one else is with you?"

"Just us. Is Townsend here?" Vivienne replied.

Rachel turned in a circle, taking in the utter unreality of a boardroom having been converted into living quarters, complete with draping curtains and enough furniture to fill Pottery Barn.

"Insane, right?" Maggie said, her voice at a normal level. "It's okay, there's no one else here," she reassured, noticing their panicked expressions. "Well, except for him." Maggie gestured contemptuously to the four-poster bed.

Townsend was sitting on the floor at the foot of the bed, bound and gagged. His barrel chest heaved and his eyes widened at the sight of Rachel and Vivienne.

"You forgot to mention him." Rachel raised an eyebrow at the slumped form of a man beside the door. "Is he dead?"

"One less for us to deal with," Maggie replied.

"You've been busy."

"Which is lucky, because Townsend wouldn't have had the antifreeze. He has his own fancy coffee machine in here."

Vivienne walked over to Townsend and, without a word, kicked him viciously in the gut. "Anyone want a cappuccino?" She continued on to the kitchenette.

Townsend yelped through his gag and tried to slump forward, but was held back by his ties to the bedframe. His naturally ruddy face darkened to a deep red as he attempted to yell through the material stuffed in his mouth.

"Lots of creamer and two sugars," Maggie called out, settling nonchalantly into an armchair.

"Maggie, what are you doing? This wasn't part of the plan." Rachel hugged her arms across her chest.

"The plan was to take out Townsend," Maggie replied.

Rachel sighed, eyeing their captive. "What now?"

"I was waiting until I knew the antifreeze had worked. You know, I walked right in here, easy as could be. Acted like a nice, submissive little woman, and no one asked a damn question. That one," she tipped her head at the dead guard, "didn't even see the knife I slit his throat with."

"You what?" Rachel's mouth dropped open, noticing the dead body was surrounded by a pool of congealed blood.

"Black with one sugar." Vivienne handed her a mug.

Rachel took it with trembling hands. "You know how I like my coffee?"

Vivienne ignored her. "I like the idea of that, up close and personal," she said, handing Maggie another mug. "Where's the knife?"

"In the sink. I washed it up." Maggie took a deep sip of her coffee. "This is heaven."

"Hang on!" Rachel cried. "I like plans; I like making plans, I like following plans. We are totally off script here and I don't like it."

"You've gotta go with the flow, Rachel." Vivienne returned from the kitchenette with a gleaming silver hunting knife and kneeling beside Townsend's prone form. "What was it you said to me, the first time you raped me?" she asked Townsend conversationally. "That's right. It was 'scream as loud as you want, no one's coming to save you'. I wonder how loud you're going to scream when I gut you like the pig you are?"

The air thinned of oxygen and Rachel gasped, stepping forward.

Maggie stopped her with a hand on her arm. "No, girlie. This isn't your fight."

Townsend's bound boots thumped on the ground in agitation as he leant away from Vivienne's crouching menace, unintelligible sounds getting caught in his gag.

There was no way Rachel could witness what was about to happen. As the first wet stab punctured Townsend's body, he screamed.

Rachel turned into Maggie, who wrapped her arms around her.

"This is between Vivienne and him," Maggie murmured into Rachel's hair. "We've got no business getting between her and her vengeance."

Rachel clung to the older woman. She wished she could close her ears, and not hear the brutality Vivienne was inflicting. The guttural moaning of Townsend was incessant, and the metallic scent of his blood permeated the air.

Rachel flinched as a drop of it flicked onto Maggie's shoulder.

And then Townsend was silent, and the only sound was Vivienne's panting breaths. Rachel turned and held out a hand to Vivienne. "It's time to go," she said, resolutely ignoring the bloody mess on the floor and instead holding Vivienne's gaze. "Come on."

Vivienne stood as the door to the boardroom flung open, semi-automatic gunfire erupting. And Vivienne fell back. Dead.

———

JAMES AND LUCY had to restrain Asaad from running headlong onto Maplewood Drive. He struggled with them in the snow as they dragged him down behind a neighboring fence.

The gunfire had ceased, but so had the screaming.

James knew that didn't bode well for the small community.

"Lucy, can I use the sight on your rifle?" he asked, working to widen an existing gap in the slatted wooden fencing.

She thrust it at him and then fell to the ground with Asaad. "I can't look," she said. "I just can't."

It only took James a moment to adjust the sight. As everything came into hyper-sharp focus, he wished the street beyond them had remained a blur.

The snow-plough had rammed through the vehicle barricade at the top of the street—the road now swarming with Jackals jovially loading up the trucks with pillaged goods. James couldn't see a single person who looked to be from the neighborhood.

Not one.

"Tell me. Can you see them? Anyone? Maria?" Asaad asked, his voice breaking.

James swallowed, pulling back from the rifle and shaking his head.

"It's just the Jackals. I can't see anyone else."

"What do we do?" Asaad crumpled in on himself, looking to James for direction.

"I don't think there's anything we *can* do," James replied. "Not until they've gone."

"They can't get away with this!" Lucy stuffed a fist in her mouth, tears tracking down her face. "We have to do something."

It would be suicide to show themselves. They were outmanned and outgunned.

His heart in his throat, he turned back to the rifle. The least he could do was to bear witness to the ruin being wrought. Was this it? Was this what humanity had been reduced to?

Knowing how vulnerable the women and children of Maplewood Drive were, fearing their slaughter, James realized Rachel had been right all along. If good people didn't do what had to be done, this was what the future held.

A light snow began to fall.

Suddenly, a familiar blonde head crossed James' vision. Blane.

"Oh shit," he breathed, wanting to close his eyes against what was coming, but unable to. Someone should be with the boy in his last moments, even if the kid would never know it.

An enormous Jackal carrying an axe approached Blane and James cringed, seeing the kid's death playing out in his mind's eye. But instead of being bludgeoned to death, the Jackal gave Blane a thump on the back, and kept walking.

James shook his head in confusion, losing his focus and impatiently readjusting the rifle's sight. It made no sense.

Until it did. Until it made perfect sense.

The boy was pointing directions and received another congratulatory slap to the back, helping to stuff chickens into crates and hoisting them onto a truck.

Blane had betrayed them. He was a Jackal—a fucking spy—and had infiltrated the community in order to exploit them.

"Blane never had a brother," he muttered, thinking back to the walkie talkie.

"No, he had a sister," Asaad said from the ground.

James had the burning need to squeeze the trigger right now, with Blane's head in his sights. His teeth ground together. By doing so, he would be signing his own death warrant, and Asaad and Lucy's, too.

The Jackals climbed back onto the trucks, and the first engine roared to life. In minutes, only the oily smell of exhaust remained.

James couldn't move. If he stayed still, he wouldn't have to confront the devastation before him. He wouldn't have to tell Asaad he'd allowed a wolf into their midst.

He started when Lucy touched the back of his jacket.

"Come on," she said.

Asaad was running, stumbling, in front of them.

James had the strongest urge to turn and run away.

But he was done with running.

THE JACKALS HAD BEEN RUTHLESS. Men, women and children were gunned down, blood soaking into the floors of homes, macabre splatters coating walls hung with framed family photos.

Asaad ran from his home, yelling Maria's name into the street.

"She's not there! She's not in there!" he screamed at James. "Where is she?"

"Asaad, stop! Stop!" Lucy pleaded with him, having come from the house next door. "She'd gone to help the kids. They... She's at the back door. They almost made it out. I'm so sorry."

Asaad fell to his knees, wailing his grief to the sky.

Impotent rage flooded James.

He was helpless in the face of humanity's desecration.

· · ·

JAMES WAS STARVING; not a single food item had been left behind and Asaad wouldn't leave the neighborhood until every body had been covered in a sheet. The man was operating on auto-pilot, and Lucy had to help him pack the personal possessions he wanted to bring.

Sitting alone in Asaad and Maria's now-freezing kitchen, James debated where exactly the three of them were going to go. He couldn't drag them with him to Oklahoma City; it would be a tedious journey with no guarantee at the other end.

They could attempt to cross Bexingham to reach the army base with the supposed FEMA setup, but after the trauma of today, none of them would cope with facing roaming gangs.

Which left Sanford.

And Rachel. He got it now. He'd allowed his own history with Sanford to blind him to Rachel's investment in her home, in her people. He hadn't wanted to see that community was what was going to bring them through this. To survive.

He was shamed at the judgement he'd harbored against her.

He'd let her down. Again.

Asaad was too shellshocked to have an opinion on their next move, and Lucy was happy for James to take the lead. He hadn't told them Blane was responsible for the downfall of Maplewood Drive, and he doubted he ever would. It wasn't knowledge that would ease their grief.

It was obscene that it was only midday. How could so much have changed in such a short amount of time?

When Asaad finally shuffled into the kitchen, James knew what they had to do.

They were going to Sanford.

. . .

THEY DROVE THROUGH THE NIGHT, slowly and silently. When James was too exhausted to keep his eyes open the next morning, Lucy took over the driving.

Seeing a farmhouse down a tree-lined driveway, he gestured for Lucy to take a detour. They needed food desperately, and would need gas shortly, too.

With no footsteps or tire marks marring the snow-covered driveway, James hoped the house would be abandoned. He didn't have faith they would be warmly greeted if the occupants were still alive.

Sitting out front in the idling truck, they watched for movement within.

"You think there's anyone in there?" Lucy eventually asked.

"Only one way to find out," said James. "But the snow's blown right up to the front door and no one's cleared it, so chances are it's empty."

His legs were wobbly when he got down from the truck, the combination of low blood sugar and exhaustion. He had to push and pull Assad out of the truck; the man was catatonic and hadn't spoken or moved since they'd gotten into the vehicle.

Leading with her rifle, Lucy called out a greeting as she approached the house. At the lack of response, she climbed the porch steps and knocked on the door.

Stepping back, she looked at James and shrugged.

"Cover me." He moved forward to try the handle. It was unlocked and opened easily, but the *putrid stench of decomposition* had him quickly falling back.

"Take Asaad to the truck," he said to Lucy. "I'll see what food I can find and bring it out."

Lucy nodded gratefully. "I'll check the barn for gas."

Pulling his scarf up and over his nose and mouth, James re-entered the house, bile rising in his throat when he walked into the living room to find it crowded with rotting corpses. Far too many for one family. Neighbors must have gathered here when they fell ill.

Although the cold had delayed the putrefaction process, it was horrendous.

Walking quickly through the grisly room, he found the kitchen. Grabbing a shopping bag from a hook on the wall, he began filling it with anything edible he came across, his grumbling stomach demanding he stuff a handful of dry crackers into his mouth, regardless of the scent of death hanging heavy in the air.

When he made his way back to the truck, Lucy had just finished re-fueling from a jerrycan, and they sat in the truck inhaling the random assortment of food James had foraged. Asaad refused to eat, his eyes blank and empty.

They set off again, in slightly higher spirits now their bellies were full.

Lucy and Asaad asked no questions about their destination, and the nearer they got to Sanford, the more anxious James became about what they would find when they arrived.

How would Rachel react to him returning?

Each mile closer honed an almost unbearable ache to see her. How had he thought he could live without her? If the events in Bexingham had taught him anything, it was how precious the ones you loved were. And how fragile.

He kept recalling the second he'd had Blane in the sights of the rifle, and how intense the urge had been to pull the trigger. That one moment abolished any concept of right and wrong. Black and white.

189

They were living in shades of grey and, while Rachel was impossibly stubborn, he'd been firmly rooted in solid colors and unwilling to contemplate the various shades she was wading through.

He'd left her.

Regret calcified inside of him, making it difficult to swallow. To breathe.

He gripped the steering wheel and pushed harder on the gas.

CHAPTER THIRTEEN

DAY 28

It took twelve hours for order to be restored in Sanford.

Twelve hours of negotiating and deliberating, as the ethanol anti-dote was distributed to just six of Townsend's men. Several who were deemed worthy had died from the antifreeze before that conclusion was made.

Along with Townsend, his guard and the man Maggie had shot dead after murdering Vivienne, there were thirty-three casualties.

Most of the residents had made themselves scarce, fearful of being involved in the overthrow of their dictator.

Many of the guards hadn't had surviving family; if they did, chances are they wouldn't have followed Townsend's orders so easily. It was the guards who had family that Rachel hadn't factored into their planning... it was those family members who were now being held at gunpoint, crying bloody murder.

Rachel was exhausted. Emotionally and physically.

She needed time to unravel the mess of feelings she had over Vivienne, and her death.

"I hate to leave you, but I need to get Caroline," Jim said, casting his eye around the distillery foyer, where they were also monitoring the six recovering guards.

"Of course. Jake has the keys to the tactical," Rachel replied, keeping an eye on Mrs. White. The elderly woman had helped to implement Townsend's draconian domestic rules, and her son was one of the guards who'd succumbed to the poison.

Rachel had not an ounce of pity for her.

"Untie me right now," Mrs. White demanded. "What you're doing is highly illegal."

Mackenzie burst out laughing.

"Sorry, sorry." She buried her head in the front of Jake's jacket to muffle herself. She pulled back. "Sorry. I know this isn't funny. But *come on*. You don't think trafficking me as a sex slave was just a little illegal?"

"Jake Brent, what are you doing with a girl like that?" Mrs. White huffed. "Her father is white trash, and she's no better."

"Can we gag her?" Jake asked, tipping his chin at Mrs. White.

Mackenzie just laughed harder.

Rachel wondered if the adrenalin dump from the last few days wasn't affecting her.

"Mac, help Maggie and Jesse distribute food from the warehouse to the people," Rachel instructed. "Jake and I are good here."

"Fine. Where's Kat?"

"I actually don't know." Rachel looked around. "Quinn has got a crew disarming the explosives that were rigged around the perimeter, but I have no idea what Kat's doing."

"I'll go find her." Mackenzie pulled on the lapels of Jake's jacket, and he obliged by dropping his head. Rachel had to look away from the raw and heated kiss that followed.

"You're a vile hussy!" Mrs. White shouted after Mackenzie as she walked away, giggling.

"If you don't shut your mouth now, I *will* gag you," Jake growled, standing over Mrs. White, glowering.

He walked over to the long bar and took a seat on a stool, and Rachel followed. Her shoulders ached from the tension she'd been carrying. They may have overthrown Townsend, but their re-building job was only just beginning.

"What are we going to do with them?" She gestured to the nine mothers and wives whose sons and husbands they had just killed. "And we're going to have to deal with all the bodies, too." She sighed.

"I've been thinking about that," Jake said. "We could get some excavation machinery from that hire place out on Sandhills Road. There's an empty field beside the town cemetery and we could dig new plots."

Rachel nodded. That could work.

"I'll have a whiskey, straight up," Kat called, walking into the distillery and heading straight for the bar.

"Where have you been?" Rachel asked.

"I got you a present, look!" She brandished a disposable razor with glee.

"Kat, seriously?"

"I told you we needed to do something about your personal grooming."

Rachel turned away from Jake and raised an eyebrow at Kat. "James left, remember? I don't think it's going to be an issue," she muttered.

"Mmm."

"What's that 'mmm' for?"

Kat tipped her head to the side. "I think he'll be back."

Rachel quickly stamped down her flare of hope. He wasn't coming back, and it was because she'd been too stubborn to accept his truth. She'd driven him away, claiming he was judging her. But she'd been just as guilty.

"I think you're delusional," Rachel replied. "Why don't you make yourself useful and start bringing everyone here to the distillery? We need to hold a meeting."

Rachel figured Jim should have returned by the time they got everyone together. They needed to catalogue who was still here and what they needed, and then decide how they were going to manage their community as they moved into the middle of winter.

She pushed down the ache of longing that resurfaced at the mention of James. He had no place in what had to be done. He was gone.

IT TOOK another two hours before everyone was gathered in the distillery's foyer. Most of the residents looked haggard but relieved. Chloe was working her magic, walking among everyone, listening and reassuring, and Dex was stuck to Mackenzie's heels.

Caroline was smothering her kids with weeks of pent-up love; Jesse had set up an impromptu medical clinic, and Cassie and Stephen had reunited with their friends Lucas, Jimmy and Sami.

Rachel watched it all with a glad heart, able to stop doubting herself and her decisions, because this was the proof they'd done the right thing.

Nothing great ever came without great sacrifice, and she would happily live with the blood on her hands if this was the outcome. She nodded at Jim as he stood before the bar and, nodding back, he called the meeting to order.

"I want to start by saying that everyone in this room has a voice, and every decision made today will be voted on by a show of hands. Anyone over the age of fifteen can vote."

Cassie stood beside Rachel and nudged her gently. She knew it was Rachel who'd pushed to give the teenagers a say. "Thank you," she whispered.

Rachel put her arm around Cassie, pulling her closer. "You're welcome."

"You didn't take a vote before you killed our sons and husbands!" Mrs. White shouted.

"No, we didn't. and I'm not apologizing for that." Jim stood firm. "The voting starts now."

"Well, that's convenient," hissed one of the widows.

The crowd shuffled uneasily.

This was what Rachel feared. Would they face resentment for the liberation? Would the residents of Sanford accept the extreme measures it took to secure their freedom?

Could Sanford live with the actions taken in its name?

"I propose our first vote concerns what happens with the families of the guards who were killed," Jake called out.

"Go on." Jim nodded.

"We understand you're not happy with how things went down," Jake started, moving to the front of the room.

Mrs. White snarled something unintelligible.

"If you want to leave, we'll provide you with supplies. But if you choose to stay, then you have to get onboard with how things are going to be now."

"Sounds fair," agreed Jim. "Does anyone have anything to add?"

"You're going to throw us out?" Mrs. White glared

daggers at everyone around her. "This is my home. I was born and raised in Sanford, and I know each and every one of you. Are you going to let this happen?"

"Look around, Mrs. White. Look at what *you* let happen to these people you know." Mackenzie waved at the gathering.

"We're not throwing you out. We're giving you a choice," Rachel added. Although privately she wished Mrs. White had poured herself a big mug of coffee yesterday morning.

It was people like her who had allowed Townsend's rule to thrive.

"Raise your hand if you agree with Jake's suggestion," Jim said.

There was muttering from the nine women being voted on, but bar them, every single person raised their hand.

"Motion passed. What's next?" said Jim.

"I want my rifle back," called out Tony Mitchell. "Are you going to let us carry weapons for protection?"

Rachel wasn't surprised this was one of the first requests. And honestly? She got it.

"What if everyone over the age of fifteen is allowed to carry, but there are old-world consequences? If you shoot someone, you face a jury of your peers and are punished accordingly," she suggested.

"Sounds fair," Tony agreed.

The room voted, and it passed.

They were another step closer to unifying their town.

In this manner, they decided as a community to continue living at The Strumpet and the distillery. Keeping everyone—and their limited resources—in the one fortified location made sense. At least until they got through the winter months.

However, living spaces would be re-allocated via ballot and each family would be given twenty-four hours with a truck to bring across possessions from their homes.

"Everyone will need to contribute," said Jim. "There are lists up on the bar with jobs: childcare, cooking, washing, scavenging, gardening, burying the dead." He paused. "Those who choose to help with that task will receive extra rations. When this meeting is finished, I'd ask you to come on up and write your name under what you'd like to do."

Most people nodded, but Rachel noticed they were looking tired. Edgy. "Cass, can you grab some of the others and bring in the ready-to-eat meals that were in the FEMA crates?" Having a full belly solved a multitude of problems.

"What about guards? You didn't mention that job," someone called out.

"That's because it's a job I think we should all share." Jim looked around the room. "Quinn has offered to give lessons in weaponry and also run physical fitness training. Our safety is everyone's responsibility. Let's vote on it."

It wasn't unanimous, but enough people voted that it passed.

With impeccable timing, Cassie reappeared and, together with Stephen, Stephanie and Lucas, began handing out the military food supplies.

"Come on, people, sit on the floor. Let's have a picnic!" Kat encouraged, taking an MRE and settling herself onto the ground.

Rachel watched, bemused, as everyone followed her lead.

"Last, we need to decide on our policy for newcomers," Jim continued. "Townsend wanted to isolate us to consolidate his power. He didn't share with you the radio transmission from New York, which confirmed the CDC had released a statement saying those who were still alive have a natural immunity. There is no longer a threat of contracting Sy-V."

The mellow vibe of the room erupted as the townspeople digested this information. Rachel had forgotten the relief she'd felt when first hearing this news and realized they should have started the meeting with this knowledge.

"Okay, okay. I know this is a shock," Jim called over the buzzing. "But it's good news and means we're not at risk of getting sick from outsiders. Are we going to help others if they come to us?"

This little sanctuary had been hard won, and Rachel was apprehensive about the burden even more people would have on their already limited resources.

She stepped forward and cleared her throat. "I want to help people, and I'm open to trading with others. But our food won't stretch all winter. I say we don't take any newcomers until we've set up scavenging teams and established some sort of indoor hydroponic gardening system to grow food."

The buzzing of conversation intensified.

Rachel's mouth was dry, and she swallowed. Were they going to think she was heartless? She'd instigated the poisoning and now this... She wanted to help people, *she did*. But they couldn't help anyone if they depleted themselves.

"Anyone have anything to add before we vote?" Jim asked.

Everyone quieted.

"Okay then. Raise your hands if you think we should consider outsiders only after we have put ourselves in a better position in relation to food supplies."

Again, the vote was just enough to pass.

"Is there anything else that needs to be said?" Jim held up his hands.

"Are you the boss now?" Tony asked.

"No, I'm not. I think we should create a board of towns-folk who will govern, and set up an election process to appoint a leader. I don't know that right now is the time for that. Does everyone agree to postpone management to a different meeting in a couple of days?"

This time the vote was unanimous, and a tiny seed of hope unfurled in Rachel.

———

DAY 29

Regret had a flavor, and it was very similar to how James imagined the bottom of an ashtray would taste. If he'd thought he was nervous when he'd returned to Sanford weeks ago, it was nothing on the trepidation he felt now.

Before, he could only imagine what Rachel's reception to him would be. He had hope. Rejection from the Rachel he grew up with would have hurt, but rejection now—when he knew the woman she'd become—would be annihilation.

As he drove past the 'Welcome to Sanford' sign, fear hollowed out his insides. He didn't think the guitar he'd brought with him to beg Rachel's forgiveness was going to cut it now. Not after he'd left a second time.

But it couldn't hurt.

"I just need to make a quick stop," he said to Lucy, navigating the streets that would take him to the Airbnb he'd stayed in when he'd first arrived.

"Where is everyone?" Lucy eyed the empty streets.

"They've set up base on the other side of town. Give me two minutes to grab something." Parking the truck, he headed inside, thankful he remembered the code to retrieve the key from the lockbox.

Everything was as he'd left it. Looking around, he contemplated taking all his things, but the apocalypse had a way of removing value from possessions. He'd always been hopeless at keeping track of physical photographs and had instead stored them digitally on his phone—which was still in his back pocket. And who cared about the Italian leather loafers or the designer sneakers?

The guitar, though. That was something he needed.

Slinging the strap of the case over his shoulder, he walked back outside, leaving everything from his old life behind.

"SANDFORD HAS A DISTILLERY?" Lucy perked up. "They're sitting on a gold mine. Medicinally, recreationally... imagine the leverage they have in negotiating trade."

"It's also made them a target," James replied grimly. He slowed the truck as they drove within sight of the barricade of vehicles surrounding the base Townsend had made.

The fact a sniper hadn't already blown out their windshield reassured James that Townsend was no longer in power. That, and he'd stopped at the roadhouse when they'd driven by and found it empty.

The idea that Rachel wouldn't be here... he swallowed against a suddenly dry throat.

Movement ahead caught his eye. Someone was standing on the back of the local fire truck, which was planted sideways in the middle of the road. Whoever it was had an AK-47 assault rifle on their back but didn't raise it, instead speaking into a walkie talkie.

As they got closer, James recognized Tabitha Turner.

She held up a hand, requesting he stop, and he pulled up speaking distance from the truck. Winding down the window, he waved at her.

"Tabitha, hey. It's James O'Connor."

"Who else do you have in there with you?" She wasn't overly friendly, but she hadn't shot them yet, either.

"Two friends."

"Hang on." She turned and got down from the fire truck, walking towards him. "Where have you come from?"

"Bexingham. Are Rachel and the others here?" James' heart ceased all movement, only beating again when Tabitha nodded.

"She's on her way out here."

Now his heart beat double-time. "You can't let us in?"

"Nope."

Lucy shifted anxiously in the passenger seat. "What's going on?" she whispered to James.

"It's okay. It's fine." He opened the driver's door and made to get down, but Tabitha shook her head. "Okay, I get it. No problems." He settled himself back into the seat.

What the fuck had happened here for Tabitha to be acting like this?

"Who is *that*?" Lucy breathed, looking through the windshield.

And there went that irregularly beating heart again.

Rachel was striding towards them, looking fierce as hell in bad-ass cargoes and aviator sunglasses, long hair whipping in the wind. She was flanked by Quinn and Jim—all three heavily armed.

James hoped someone had given Rachel a lesson in using the handgun she was carrying.

"What are you doing here, O'Connor?" she asked.

The chill in her tone cut straight through him, and he hated he couldn't see her eyes behind the mirrored lenses.

"I've brought people. Friends. They need someone to go," he answered.

"James, you're putting us in a situation here," Jim said.

"Not intentionally. What's the problem?" James was confused. And tired. And trying really hard not to get pissed about the way this was going down.

"It's not personal," Quinn reassured. "We voted, and we're not letting in newcomers until we're in a better position ourselves."

"You voted? Townsend's definitely gone then."

"We did what we had to do, and now we're re-building," Jim said.

Quinn turned to Rachel and Jim. "Can we talk about this? It's not like James is a newcomer."

"Who have you got with you?" Rachel asked.

"Lucy and Asaad. I met them in Bexingham. They were good to me and then... things went sideways. I thought Sanford could be a safe place for them." Frustration had his knuckles whitening on the steering wheel. "Am I wrong? *Is* Sanford a safe place? I thought that was the whole reason you did what you did."

"James..." Lucy warned.

He bit his tongue, wishing he could take back those last words.

"We stayed, and we fought, and we made this place safe." Rachel's voice was low. "We're the ones with blood on our hands, so that people like you can be safe."

"People like me?" That cut. Deep. "So you can't take us in?" A tension headache threatened at his temples.

"Son, we're starting over here, and we've promised the people we'll vote on things," said Jim. "We can't turn around less than twenty-four hours later and say we've changed the rules."

"We can't turn them away, either," Quinn argued.

It was an impossible impasse that James couldn't see a way through.

"James, you go. I'll take Asaad somewhere else." Lucy smiled sadly. "You were one of them. They'll take you in without us."

The smart thing would be to accept Lucy's offer. But it wasn't the right thing.

"No. I'm not going in if you're not." With a sigh, he put the idling truck into gear.

"Wait!" Rachel called, taking a step forward. "We could compromise. We said no to newcomers because our food won't last much longer, even with Dale's FEMA supplies. But what if you brought food with you?"

"What does she mean?" Lucy asked James. "What do you mean?" she shouted over him to Rachel.

"We don't have any food," James said.

"But you could get some," Rachel pointed out.

James looked to Lucy, and then back to Asaad, who didn't appear to be registering any of this. "We could..."

"Go to Quinn's house. I'll meet you there with some food for now. From my own rations," she tossed over her shoulder to the others. She turned back to James. "We'll work it out, okay?"

Relief bloomed in James' chest cavity, allowing him to take his first deep breath in what felt like forever.

"Okay."

"SHOULD I BE NERVOUS ABOUT THIS?" Lucy asked, settling into an armchair in Quinn's living room.

"What's with you and this Rachel chick?"

"What do you mean?" James was pacing before the window that overlooked the street outside.

"There's obviously a story." Lucy curled her legs beneath her. "So, out with it."

"We have... history." He ran a hand through his hair. "Look, I don't want you to worry. I'm going to make this right."

He *had* to make this right.

There was a knock at the front door. James and Lucy looked at each other.

"Are you going to get that?" Lucy said.

James started toward the door, willing his thundering pulse to settle into something close to normal. When he opened the door to Rachel, his heart hurt so bad he had to push the heel of his palm into his chest.

She was the most divinely beautiful, fierce creature he had ever met. He wanted to pull her into his arms and never let her go. He wanted to talk and explain and listen and understand.

He wanted forever with this woman.

"James."

"Come in." He stepped back awkwardly, allowing her to pass. "But keep your jacket on. It's cold in here."

"I'm sorry we didn't let you in—"

"I'm not complaining. Thank you for thinking of a compromise," he assured her.

"Hi, I'm Lucy." Lucy stood and shook Rachel's hand. "We appreciate you doing this for us."

Rachel gave a small smile, handing her a bag of MREs and then looked to Asaad, who'd been sitting in an armchair staring at the wall since they'd arrived.

"This is Asaad." James cleared his throat. "There was...

he lost his wife. He and Lucy lost their community in Bexingham."

"I'm so sorry." Rachel's eyes softened.

Taking a seat on one end of the couch, James waited for Rachel to sit as well.

"What's the plan?" he said. "I can drive to some nearby towns and see what supplies I can find."

"Jake told me there was a commercial bakery in Dutton they were going to hit before they blew up the Prestige Plaza, but they ran out of time. We could get enough food staples to last a long time," Rachel explained.

"We?" He didn't want to hope, but his stupid heart wasn't listening to his head.

"I mean, if you want me. To help," she quickly clarified.

"I want you." His voice was thick, hoarse.

Rachel's cheeks pinked, and she looked away. "Well, should we get going?"

"Now?" Lucy sat up straight. "I don't think Asaad is up to doing this right away, and I don't want to leave him by himself."

"You're right, he's not doing so great," James agreed. "But we probably only need two people..." He rubbed at his beard. "And I'd really like your help, Rachel."

"Okay, let's do this." Rachel stood. "Cassie gave me the keys to the mini-van, and Quinn put snow tires on it. We should be back by nightfall."

James was a fumbling teenager all over again, grabbing his stuff and farewelling Lucy. He *could not* fuck this up a third time. He was playing with the forever-kind of stakes, and he had to believe Rachel being here was a positive sign.

At least she hadn't kneed him in the balls. Yet.

CHAPTER FOURTEEN

They hadn't been inside the mini-van for more than a minute before their breath began fogging over the windows. It was insanely cold, and James began furiously rubbing his palms together.

"An apocalypse in winter fucking sucks," he grumbled.

"It'll heat up in a moment." Rachel turned the ignition. "And at least it's slowing down the decomposition of the dead."

"The silver lining at the end of the world." James mentally berated himself. He didn't want to be joking with her; he needed her to know he'd come back for her, but he didn't know where to start. "How are the kids?"

Rachel paused in reversing down the driveway to look at him, eyebrow raised.

"Cassie and Stephen," he clarified.

"They're fine."

"I'm sorry. It's like we're married and talking about the kids so we don't have to confront the issues in our relationship." He cringed. How did he explain the mind shift he'd experienced when the Jackals had decimated Bexingham?

"James..."

"Rach..."

"Sorry. You go." Rachel blew a strand of hair off her face, competently handling the vehicle in the icy conditions.

"You are frighteningly capable." He couldn't take his eyes off her.

She hummed in agreement.

"I want to say that I get it, that nothing is black and white in this new world. And I'm sorry for not trying to understand the greys. I'm sorry for making you feel bad about your choices."

"That's all you're sorry for?"

Was that the hint of a smile?

"Baby doll, there are not enough words to describe the many, many things I am sorry for. I should have listened to you. I should have trusted your judgement."

"And..."

"I should *never* have left. No matter how bad things were, I should have stayed so we could work through it." He paused. "Rach, it's kind of hard to grovel when you're concentrating on the road. Do you think you could pull over for a minute?"

"I thought you said I was frighteningly capable?" But she was already shifting down gears to bring the mini-van to a stop. They were on the outskirts of Sanford, with not a soul for miles.

Hi pulse sped up. This was either very, very good. Or very, very bad. Either way, he had her attention. Hope surged in his chest.

It took a moment for her to take her hands from the steering wheel and turn to him, her eyes glossy with unshed tears. "First of all, I..."

His balls shriveled.

If Rachel said "first of all", it meant she had prepared research, data and charts, and would destroy him.

"I'm sorry, too."

It took a moment for her words to reach him. He'd been expecting a verbal dressing down that would take several therapist visits to recover from—and chances were low at finding a therapist these days.

"You... you're sorry?"

"I was furious at you, and I let that drive you away. I should have tried to listen, too. I'm not saying you were right," she quickly added, "but I didn't give you a chance to explain."

That hope in his chest grew wings and soared.

He grinned. "You're not saying I was wrong, either."

"Let's agree to disagree." Her mouth tipped at the corners, the beginnings of a smile curving her lips.

"You are such a beautiful, fragile woman," he murmured, reaching out a finger to run it down the tip of her nose.

"Fragile?" She pulled back, smile slipping.

"Not like a flower," he hurried to reassure her, mentally kicking himself. "You're fragile in the way a bomb is fragile. Powerful and potent and explosive."

She narrowed her eyes, thinking. "Okay, I can accept that."

"Rachel, I want you. I want all of you... all your emotions and thoughts and feelings and moods. I want forever with you. Can you give me another chance?"

He picked up her hand, threading their fingers together. This was it. If she forgave him now, she was signing away the rest of her life to him. Because there was no way he was ever letting her go again.

"Tell me the truth. Did you come back for me? Or

because you needed to take Lucy and Asaad somewhere?" she asked, her gaze steady.

He swallowed.

"Bexingham turned bad really quickly. And all of a sudden I just *knew* that coming back to you was the only way forward for me. It was like there was a string, tugging at my insides and leading me back." He paused, searching her eyes for understanding. "Bexingham changed how I see the world. What happened there... it made me appreciate the messy complexities of right and wrong. I'm not saying I wouldn't have come back if that hadn't happened, but it may have taken me longer to get outside my own head. I *can* tell you I missed you with every fiber of my being from the second I drove away from that roadhouse."

"I missed you too," she said softly. "And I forgive you. Do you forgive me?"

The fact Rachel Davenport was asking his forgiveness *slayed* him.

Before she could blink, he'd hauled her from her seat to straddle his lap, his mouth devouring hers with a raw intensity that stole their breath. It was unrestrained and messy, teeth clashing and tongues aggressive.

Reaching, he gripped the curve of her ass, encouraging her to spread wider for his insatiable lust as he groaned into her neck. He wanted to sink his teeth into her soft skin. He wanted to mark her. To claim her.

"I can't live without you," he growled, threading his fingers through her hair and tugging her head back, exposing more of her neck for his lascivious kisses.

"You don't have to," she panted, digging her hands under his layers of clothing until her nails could scratch into his skin.

His dick jerked in response. Eager and hard.

"Was this easier when we were kids?" He fumbled with the zipper of her jacket. Shifting, he tried to stretch out his legs. "I don't remember it being this difficult."

"We were never crazy enough to do this in winter." She laughed. "It's hard to do anything wearing this many layers."

"I can fix that," he muttered, finally stripping her jacket from her shoulders and using it to pin her arms behind her back. Impatiently, he shoved at her upper clothing, baring her lace-covered tits and praising her when she arched them into his eager hands. Cupping them, he thumbed her bra aside and dipped his head, latching onto a peaked nipple and feasting.

Her whimpering breathlessness urged him on, sucking and licking as he kneaded each plump breast, alternating his attention between them. She was panting his name, rhythmically clenching her thighs around his hips and grinding her pussy down onto his cock.

"Baby doll, you've got to quit with that or I'm going to blow my load like a teenager," he warned, releasing her breasts and taking a firm hold around her waist to hold her aloft.

In answer, she shucked her jacket to free her arms and went for the zipper of his jeans, her top front teeth leaving little indents in her lush bottom lip.

With a smirk, he obliged, lifting his hips to pull down his jeans and briefs as Rachel shifted to the side to wriggle out of hers. They were a tangle of limbs, intent and urgent. Taking possession of her hips, James guided her pussy down onto his dick, the tight warmth drawing a guttural growl from him. He surged upward, holding her steady as he bottomed out.

Stars exploded behind his eyes.

She gasped, tugging at his hair and widening her thighs impossibly further, seating him deeper inside her until he swore there was no beginning, and no end. Just now. Just this.

And then she clenched her inner walls, and there was no holding back. He fucked up into her, thrusting long and hard with each stroke, building momentum until he was heaving with exertion and she was screaming obscenities.

"Touch your clit, baby doll," he panted. "I need you to come."

Her hand immediately dove between their straining bodies, the fluttering of her pussy walls heralding her orgasm. She shuddered and cried out, biting into his shoulder.

Letting go of the last of his control, James drove upwards one final time, his own orgasm wrenching from him in flashes of pure bliss.

Breathless, they held each other, slick with their combined release. Content.

Until Rachel shivered, and James felt the goosebumps on her skin as the cold impinged upon their languor. Sitting her up, he kissed her, a drugging, soft melding of their lips.

Releasing her, he lifted her off of him, picking up her discarded jacket as she settled into the driver's seat and righted her clothing.

Searching the glove compartment, he found tissues and passed a handful to her before cleaning himself up. He looked up to find her watching him.

"No condom," he said.

"I have an IUD."

Hmm. Interesting she hadn't mentioned that earlier.

As though reading his mind, she smiled. "There was no way you were leaving semen inside me, before."

"Fair call."

When they were both fully clothed, he leaned forward to rub the condensation from the windshield and Rachel rubbed her forearm against the driver's window.

She clicked on her seat belt. "You ready?"

"Let's get this done, so I can get you home and into a bed," he replied, placing his hand onto her thigh as she began driving.

"Would you rather... find true love today, or win the lottery next year?" she asked.

"Win the lottery next year," he replied promptly.

She raised an eyebrow. "Wrong answer, O'Connor."

"If I win the lottery next year, it means the world is back to some kind of normal." He smirked at her. "And I found true love when I was seventeen."

BY SOME MIRACLE, or the fact that people who knew about it were either dead or gone, the bakery was untouched, although James was still feeling the reverberation from having to smash open the iced-over door lock. He shook out his shoulders and rolled his neck, looking around the near-dark interior.

"Did you break the lock?" Rachel twisted at a lock of her hair. "I'd feel better if we knew no one could get in easily. I swear I heard a car engine out there."

"You probably did, Dutton's not empty. But if no one's found this place yet, I think we're safe."

James was on a high and refused to allow Rachel's jumpiness to affect him. They'd be in and out of here in no time, and back to Sanford. Together.

"Can you believe this place?" Rachel breathed, turning in a circle to take in the space. He followed her eyes, and knew why her apprehension now sounded more like excitement. The bakery had floor to ceiling industrial shelves filled with pallets of flours, leaveners, sugars and salt. It was a much needed bounty for the town and would ensure Lucy and Asaad's safety.

The sudden thought of Asaad and all he'd lost wrenched at James' insides. If he lost Rachel... He shook his head, determined to stay in the moment.

"We should have brought a truck. We won't get even a quarter of this into the mini-van," he said. "I owe Jake a solid for this intel."

"You can bake him a cake." Rachel grinned, patting an enormous bag of vanilla cake mix.

"Maybe I will," he said, pinching her on the ass. "I'll even bake you one if you're a good girl."

"Oh, you have *no idea* how good I can be," she teased, biting into her lower lip provocatively.

He groaned. "Stop being a minx. We have a job to do."

"I need to find a toilet first," she told him. "They're such an underrated commodity in the apocalypse."

"You might get one flush out of the water in the cistern."

"Wish me luck."

When she returned, they found two hand trolleys and began the laborious task of moving the sacks and bags and boxes, loading them into the mini-van they'd parked in the delivery bay.

Despite the cold, James was sweating by the time they'd filled every square inch of the vehicle with easily enough dry ingredients to get their community through the rest of winter.

"Here," Rachel handed him a bottle of water from her backpack, which he chugged gratefully. Wiping the back of his hand across his mouth, he caught her watching him.

"What's on your mind, Davenport?"

"I found a tub of frosting..." She raised that sexy eyebrow of hers.

He propped a hip against a bench, crossing his arms over his chest. He liked where she was going with this and crooked his finger to draw her closer.

A loud guffaw from behind them made the hairs on the back of his neck prick and he spun around.

"I don't mind me a bit of frosting." An enormous, tattooed man stepped forward, holding an axe loosely at his side. "What about you, Blane? You like frosting?"

James pivoted to where a familiar blonde teenager had flanked them, shotgun trained on Rachel.

"Nah, too sweet." The teenager shrugged. "Brax, what do you think about bringing her back with us after we kill him?" The gun barrel waved to James.

"What's going on, Blane?" James struggled to keep his voice even. Why the *fuck* had he left his rifle on the flour bins in the next room? Hot anger at his own stupidity warred with ice-cold determination.

He was not dying, and they were *not* taking his woman.

"Hands up, little lady." Brax smirked. "I see that handgun in your jacket."

"You can have everything here. You can even take the mini-van." The desperation in Rachel's plea caused James' resolve to harden. He'd never thought he'd want to kill another human, let alone a kid. But these two were already dead, they just didn't know it yet.

———

FEAR MADE RACHEL HOT. Too hot. She couldn't drag in enough oxygen and gulped in a lungful of air. She had to get it together. She hadn't survived Townsend to then end up with these two.

Her fingers itched to grab for the handgun in her pocket, but she'd have a bullet between her eyes before she could blink.

The boy, Blane, was just a *kid*. What was he doing?

She'd have no problem shooting the brute, Brax. But Blane... Cassie's sweet face flashed before her. How had this kid gotten into this situation? Just a month ago, he'd have been sitting in a classroom learning algebra.

She inched closer to James, who was cooly assessing the situation.

"I said, hands up." Brax moved fast for his bulk, using the handle of his axe to tip Rachel's chin up. His breath was sour, and he had a teardrop tattooed beneath his eye.

Rachel couldn't meet his gaze. She wanted to cry. Just when she thought thing were better, they were back fighting for their lives. Is this what living is now? A constant fight to the death for survival?

James shifted, so that he stood at her back. They both raised their arms.

"Why are you here?" James' tone was calm, measured. "What do you want?"

"I like tying up loose ends." Brax grinned, showing tobacco-stained teeth as he stepped back to stand beside Blane.

"We followed you." Blane explained. "We can't risk you and Asaad coming back for revenge."

"Revenge for what?" Rachel looked between the two.

"It was them, at Bexingham," said James.

Dread slithered through Rachel. So, this wasn't random. They weren't opportunists, looking for supplies.

They had hunted them.

"That's a long way to come." James pressed closer to Rachel.

"You talked about the whiskey distillery, we wanted to check it out." Blane spoke casually, as though he weren't holding her at gunpoint. As though he weren't threatening her town.

He was unnerving.

"Enough talking. Blane, you want the woman?" Brax ran his tongue over his teeth. "Let's get this done and go get us some whiskey."

"Shoot Brax," James hissed in her ear.

Before she could register what he was doing, he'd leapt from behind and launched himself at the teenager. They toppled to the floor and somehow her shaking hands were holding the handgun and her finger was pressing the trigger.

Two shots went off simultaneously.

Brax's big body crashed to the floor, a red hole blooming across his jaw. She dropped the gun, mouth gaping at the lifeless body.

James and Blane's struggling snapped her from her shock and she spun to find them on the ground, both grappling for control of Blane's weapon.

Was James shot? She'd heard the shotgun discharge at the same moment she'd shot Brax.

Adrenalin forced her to her knees, hands frantically searching for the gun she'd dropped. Where the fuck was it? The side of her sweeping hand knocked into the weapon, which slid further under the bench.

Someone grunted in pain.

Fuck, fuck, *fuck*.

Finally, her fingers grasped the gun and she rose, planting her feet wide and raising the weapon.

James was sitting astride Blane, his forearm and elbow

pressing into the teenager's throat. They were both still, apart from heaving chests.

They were fine, no one else had been killed. The vice of anxiety on her chest loosened.

"Rach, get the shotgun for me, please." James didn't look up, his concentration trained on the boy beneath him.

"Where is it?" Rachel hated that her voice wavered. She needed to be strong.

"It was kicked behind those boxes."

Her legs felt like jelly, but they carried her forward until she located the weapon. "I've got it. Are you hurt?"

"No." James leant harder against Blane, whose face was turning red. "Don't move a fucking muscle," he growled. Getting to his feet, he took the shotgun from Rachel's trembling hands.

"Are you okay?" she whispered. Her ears hurt and her teeth chattered.

"Are you?" He gathered her against his side, brushing a quick kiss against her temple.

"James—" Blane lifted a hand in supplication, seeming to have shrunk into himself.

"I said don't move a muscle!"

The venom in his voice made Rachel recoil. They were safe, the danger was over. Brax was dead, and they could take Blane back to Sanford. The kid clearly needed help.

James' arm dropped from around her as he raised the shotgun to his shoulder, pumping it loaded.

"James! What are you doing?"

"He attacked us. He was going to kill me and take you," James replied grimly, bringing his cheek to the side of the shotgun.

"He's just a kid!"

"You don't know what he's capable of."

"James, no." She stepped in front of him, she couldn't let him do this. He'd never forgive himself. She had no idea what had happened at Bexingham, but she knew together they could sort this out.

"We don't have to do this." She put her hand out, lowering the gun towards the ground. She felt him resisting her. "He's just a boy and he's unarmed."

She'd already been responsible for so much death. No matter what else she had to live with, she could not kill a child. And she would not let the man she loved do it either.

A hand, strong and tight, snaked around her ankle, pulling her off balance. She fell into Blane with a shriek. A sharp sting bit into her neck and everything inside her went cold.

"Move a single fucking inch and this knife is going to finish you off before your pussy of a boyfriend can—"

A boom shook the room. Blane fell away. The cold bite of the knife pressing into her skin disappeared.

Rachel rolled away from Blane, the room swimming around her. Suddenly, James dropped to his knees beside her. His mouth opened, but his words drowned beneath the ringing filling her ears.

"... baby. Rach! Are you okay? Did the pellets get you? Are you hurt?"

As his words finally filtered through the ringing, she hurled herself into James' chest.

"He can't hurt you now." James was cradling her face in his hands, his thumbs wiping at the tears that would not stop.

"That was..." She couldn't choke out more words.

"It was the smart thing, and the right thing." His arms wrapped tight around her, lifting her off her feet to bring them face-to-face. "I won't ever let anyone hurt you," he promised, pressing a kiss to her forehead.

RACHEL HAD SOBBED herself empty in James' arms, and then he'd taken them to the staff tearoom. Finding a slightly lumpy sofa, she curled up against him and slept.

Waking sometime later, she was disoriented; her arm was tingling painfully with pins and needles and the skin at the base of her throat stung. The memory of pulling the trigger, of Brax falling back dead, made her start.

"It's okay, Davenport. I've got you," James murmured, running his hands through her hair. "We're safe, I promise."

She realized her head was resting in his lap, and raised a hand to her throat, wincing at the long, shallow cut.

"I cleaned the blood away. It shouldn't even scar."

"You killed him."

"I had to. Someone very smart taught me that sometimes, you have to do the hard thing in order to be safe." He brought her hand to his mouth, kissing the inside of her wrist.

Shame overwhelmed her. It was her fault that Blane had almost got the upper hand. She had jeopardized them both, because she couldn't do what needed to be done.

"I couldn't. I couldn't..."

"Shh. You don't always have to be the one making the tough decisions." His breath was a warm balm against her skin. "I'm here. We're in this together."

"James..."

"I've got you, baby doll."

They lay quietly together then, his big hands soothing as they rubbed up and down her arms. It was such a relief to hand over responsibility. No, not hand over. To share. To know that he had her back. That they were a team.

She could sense his surprise when she raised her head to catch his lips in a heated kiss. But she needed him. Right now.

She needed to know they were alive and together and forget everything that had just happened.

His facial hair, untrimmed for weeks now, was soft as he nuzzled between her breasts, muttering and worshipful. Digging her fingers into his hair, she held tight, silently begging for more. More of everything. Just, more.

Growling, his warm mouth latched onto her tightly furled nipple and she wanted to scream with the exquisite torture. Every suck and lick caused a corresponding throb between her thighs until she was lightheaded with lust.

When he pulled back, she mewled in protest, pouting.

"What's wrong, baby doll?"

"You *know* what's wrong."

"I do. Your jeans are still on."

Pulling her up, he moved them to a table, depositing her on top of it and standing between her spread thighs. He flicked down the zip of her jeans, lifting her butt with one hand so he could undress her with the other. The cold air was brutal against her naked skin and she whined.

"I'm going to make it all better," he shushed her. Hooking his hands beneath her knees, he dragged her forward so her ass was at the edge of the table. When he pushed on the back of her thighs and settled her ankles over his shoulders, she went faint with anticipation.

"Hands above your head, baby doll," he instructed, and she obeyed instantly. Anything to get his mouth on her aching core faster.

The dark edge to his chuckle made her insides flutter.

"Good girl. You want me to lick your pretty pussy?"

The filthy words ignited every single one of Rachel's deepest desires. Her answering moan was desperate. Needy.

The first wet swipe of his tongue between her folds had her writhing against his touch, pushing into his waiting mouth. His adoration and complete lack of inhibition had her mind blanking to anything other than the sensations he was inflicting.

Her thighs clenched tight around his head as he circled her sensitive nub relentlessly with his tongue, pushing first one finger, and then two, into her pussy.

She bucked against him, driving his fingers deep enough to touch on that magic spot, instantly igniting an orgasm that shattered her into a million tiny fragments.

Trembling and boneless, her arms fell to her side. She watched in a blissful daze as James released her legs and tenderly re-dressed her before gathering her into his arms. Lifting her, he carried her back to the sofa.

With her cradled against his chest, he lowered himself and drew her close, running his lips over her chin, her cheeks, her forehead.

She burrowed into his chest, luxuriating in the strength of his hold. They had endured so much since the outbreak of Sy-V, and this bubble of contentment was a salve on her ravaged soul.

It was inconceivable less than a month had passed since James had arrived back in Sanford—so much had changed in that time. Not the least of which were her feelings.

She cleared her throat, blushing at the knowledge it was hoarse from screaming his name. "You know, I don't think I've told you that I love you."

"You know, I don't think you have," he whispered into

221

her neck. She could feel his lips curving into a smile against her skin.

Pulling his head level with hers, she traced a finger over the planes of his face, so changed and yet so familiar.

"James O'Connor, I'm in love with you."

"You said a couple of weeks ago that we didn't get a second chance. But you were wrong, Rachel Davenport. And this is our happily ever after."

EPILOGUE

"Okay, I'm ready. Bring on this grand gesture you've planned to apologize with." Rachel settled back against the bedhead in their room at The Strumpet. "But it better be good, O'Connor."

James was leaning against the closed door, all tousled and bearded and scrumptious.

"I know we've got running water again, but I wouldn't hate it if you kept the facial hair," she commented, running her eyes over him appreciatively.

"Woman, stop looking at me like that," he growled. "Or I'll bury my face between your thighs and you can forget about the grand gesture."

"That's not an incentive." She not-so-subtly arched her back. "We've got a lot of years to make up for."

"I think we've made a good start," he smirked, referring to the last twenty-four hours they'd spent locked away in their room, fucking themselves senseless. "Close your eyes, and no peeking, or you'll get spanked."

"Again, not an incentive." But she followed his order,

feeling the mattress dip when he sat on the edge, curiosity warring with the need to obey.

"Okay, open."

Her eyes popped open to find him holding a beat-up looking guitar.

"This is your grand gesture?"

"Baby doll, I learned the guitar for you."

His fingers lightly strummed the instrument, the vibrations from the chords hitting her deep inside. When he started playing the tune, she melted.

He began singing Van Morrison's *Brown Eyed Girl* in his deep, gravelly voice, eyes holding her hostage the entire song. It was her favorite, and he'd sung it to her endlessly that one rainy summer, limbs entwined and hearts tender.

The last note faded, and she smiled tremulously, a tear slipping down her cheek. Her heart had always belonged to him, and she was thankful she'd finally acknowledged it.

"Even when I wasn't with you, you were with me, my brown eyed girl." He placed his hand over his heart. "It was so hard to find my own way, but I came back to you."

Sobbing, she launched herself into his lap, covering his face with loud, messy kisses. With a laugh, he tossed her onto her back and covered her body with his own, pressing them into the mattress with his delicious weight.

Turning onto his side, he tucked her head against his chest, humming as he ran his hands through her unruly hair, gently teasing out the knots. Breathing in sync, they listened to the sounds of their new community, re-building itself around them.

Maggie had taken Asaad and Lucy under her wing, and in just a few days the two of them were making Sanford their home. Lucy had teamed up with Quinn to start weapons training for all residents, and Chloe was helping Asaad talk through his trauma.

Mackenzie had instigated a hydroponic garden in the distillery, and Jim had plans to get the distillery producing again so they could trade with other communities.

The ham radio that Townsend had restricted access to was now manned day and night, although mostly their communications had been with small family groups; they hadn't heard of any communities of significant size.

With enough food to last them through the winter, the residents of Sanford were settling into a semblance of calm. There were still dead to bury, and people to mourn, and not everyone was satisfied with the way things had ended.

There were grumbles and disagreements, which were bound to happen with one hundred and twenty people living in such close proximity.

But the dread of imminent danger had passed. They could breathe easy, and look to what comes after.

THE END

STAY IN TOUCH!

Want to keep up-to-date on what's happening in Jacqueline's world? Sign up to her email newsletter! You'll receive behind-the-scenes photos, romance memes, book reviews and other awesome stuff. (Jacqueline is well aware "awesome stuff" is a broad term).

Sign up! https://bit.ly/2W1y31C

Or, you can jump over to her Facebook group - Love at The End of The World for giveaways, memes and more!

ABOUT

Jacqueline picked up her first Mills & Boon novel when she was fourteen, and fell head over heels in love with the romance of a happily-ever-after. *Sweet Valley High* just couldn't compete after she got hooked on dashing heroes and plucky heroines.

She has a Bachelor Degree in Print Journalism but, having always been tempted to embellish the facts of a story, decided she was more suited to writing works of fiction. She writes in between wrangling two daughters and her very own tall, handsome husband. *wink wink*

For more on Jacqueline, you can find her at:
www.jacquelinehayley.com
Instagram @jacquelinehayleyromance
Facebook /jacquelinehayleyromance

ALSO BY JACQUELINE HAYLEY

THE AFTER SERIES

Prequel (novella)

The Beginning of the End

Book 1

After Today

Book 2

After Yesterday

———

Coming soon...

Book 3

After Tomorrow

Book 4

After The End

JACQUELINE HAYLEY

PANDEMIC

THE BEGINNING
of the end

PREQUEL TO THE AFTER SERIES

THE BEGINNING OF THE END

It's the beginning of the end...

Seventeen-year old Cassie is home alone planning her first ever house party, unaware the deadly Sy-V virus has begun to ravage humanity. But when most of her classmates fail to show for the party, she can't contact her parents, and her best friend becomes sick, in the blink of an eye her entire world changes.

Stephen has lived next door to Cassie forever, only as the virus tears their friends and family apart, the boy-next-door suddenly becomes a hero burning brightly in the devastating dark of their new world. But no way could she fall in love. Not at this moment. With this boy. Right?

This novella is a prequel to The After Series, which begins with *After Today*.

READ ON TO SEE HOW IT ALL BEGAN...

THE BEGINNING OF
THE END

CHAPTER ONE

The rolling thunder stirred a primitive fear in Cassie Blackley, which had nothing to do with the impending storm and everything to do with the knowledge there were some things—*many* things—outside her control.

Why did an outbreak of the flu have her so unsettled?

Sighing, she began the laborious process of moving the lawn chairs she'd set up around the backyard onto the covered deck. The reduced party space meant there would be unavoidable over-flow into the house, but so many of her classmates were off sick at the moment. Maybe it wouldn't be an issue.

After spending weeks counting down the days until her parents left town on a business trip and she could hold this party, she was now wishing they weren't so far away. What if she got sick? Who would look after her?

Her cell chimed with a message just as the first fat drops of rain fell.

Hallie: Can't find the string lights in the Christmas decorations. Soz.

Cassie: Okay. I'll check my basement again.

Hallie: Still want me to come over and get ready together?

Cassie: Yep.

Hallie: Is JEREMY still coming?

Cassie: Why did you write his name in capitals?

Hallie: Because it's JEREMY.

Cassie: You're such a child.

Hallie: You love me.

Cassie rolled her eyes at her best friend's response, a smile tugging at her lips.

Thoughts of Jeremy Tait were enough to distract her from the havoc weather and sickness were playing on her carefully orchestrated plans.

Her classes yesterday had been subdued and the cafeteria eerily quiet with so many students away sick, but Jeremy had caught her at her locker and confirmed he was coming. *And he'd reached out and pushed a stray lock of hair behind her ear.* She was still feeling the tingly aftershocks from it.

Fizzing with giddy excitement, she pushed down her worries. It was the start of the weekend. She had no homework, a pilfered bottle of vodka, the hot tub was warming up and Jeremy Tait was coming to her party.

"Hey, Cass! Open the gate," her neighbor, Stephen Worthington, called from across the fence.

Dashing into the rain and hauling open their shared gate, she faced a keg of beer.

"Cass, move! This is heavier than it looks," he grumbled.

"Sorry!" She stepped back to let him pass, looking back into his yard.

"Your parents are still away, right?"

The last thing she needed was her parents finding out about this evening's plans. Her other neighbor, Stacy, was pretty young and cool—she wouldn't care. Although her dog, Dex, might bark if they got too rowdy.

Stephen dropped the keg onto the deck and rolled his shoulders, his wet t-shirt plastered to his well-defined chest. Cassie wondered absently if he'd been working out recently. Since when did Stephen have muscles?

"They're not, actually."

"What?" Cassie snapped back to reality. "They came back early?"

Shit-shit-shit.

"They cut their trip short because they came down with this flu that's going around. Don't worry, they're feeling like death warmed up. They won't be leaving their bedroom for long enough to know what's happening over here."

Stephen and his family had lived next door for as long as Cassie could remember and, being the same age, she and Stephen had grown up together. In their small town of Sanford, that basically guaranteed they would be best friends. Hallie completed their trio nicely.

"Are they okay?"

"They'll be fine. It's just the flu. When is Hallie getting here?"

Recently, Cassie had been wondering if maybe Stephen was developing feelings for the pocket-sized Hallie, and the thought caused a sticky niggle of jealousy. Not over Stephen, *obviously*, but out of concern for the dynamics of their friendship.

"Soon. Are you staying to set up?"

"Unless you've learnt to tap a keg?" He raised an eyebrow at her.

"Ha ha."

"Actually, I kind of wanted to talk to you about something."

Cassie tensed when he couldn't meet her eyes, his hand sweeping through his over-long hair in a telltale sign of awkwardness.

They were *never* awkward.

She was sure this was about Hallie, and she was sure she didn't want to have this conversation. She was not prepared to become the third wheel.

"Uh, sure."

Shit-shit-shit.

"You want to sit down?" He didn't wait for her to answer, taking advantage of a lull in the rain and walking to the old swing set in the corner of the yard. His long legs folded comically when he sat on the swing seat. Cassie couldn't remember the last time they'd used the swings.

She perched on the other seat, her feet trailing in the wet grass and her mind racing. Did Hallie know he felt this way? Had they already been together, and he was only now telling her? A flash of betrayal sparked in her belly.

"What is it?" she asked, sharper than intended.

After all, maybe it had nothing to do with Hallie?

"Cass, we've been friends for like, ever..."

He exhaled heavily, reaching a hand to her knee and leaning forward so he could look her in the face.

Now he wanted to make eye contact, and she'd never been more uncomfortable in her life. His face was shining with sincerity and she swallowed, her throat dry.

"Hey, guys!" Hallie broke the moment, emerging from the house onto the back deck. "Uh, what are you doing?"

Her gaze bounced between them, and the swing rocked wildly when Cassie jumped to her feet.

"You know it's raining, right? And we're seventeen, kind of old for swing sets." Hallie planted her hands on her hips. "Are you guys drunk? Did you start drinking without me?"

"No! No," Cassie squeaked, hurrying onto the deck and throwing her arms around her friend. "But there's no time like the present, right?"

She pulled away, looking down at Hallie in apprehension.

"You're burning up. Do you have a fever?"

"It's nothing." Hallie brushed her away. "Where are the snacks? Did you buy Doritos?"

"No offence, Hal, but you look like shit," Stephen commented, coming to stand beside them.

"Thanks, asshole." Hallie punched him playfully on the shoulder. "It's just the flu. Give me some alcohol and it'll nuke my germs."

Cassie narrowed her eyes, taking in the pallor of Hallie's skin and the sheen of perspiration on her forehead.

"Now who's the asshole?" Stephen said, only half joking. "You're probably contagious and are gonna make us all sick."

"I'm not missing this party." Hallie spun on her heel and headed indoors. "And I feel fine, I just have a mild version of it."

They settled on barstools around the island bench in the kitchen, Cassie pouring them each a generous shot of vodka into red solo cups while Hallie hooked her cell up to the Bluetooth speakers, filling the room with her Billie Eilish playlist.

Stephen's cell rang, and he laughed. "It's Mom. She has a parental sixth sense for when I'm about to do something I shouldn't." Taking a swig of his drink, he answered.

His conversation was brief, and when he lowered his cell, Cassie's fingers tightened around her cup at his furrowed brow. A trapdoor of uncertainty creaked open inside her.

"What is it?"

"Mom's taking Dad to the hospital, she said he's getting worse."

"Isn't she sick too? Should we drive him?" Cassie asked, already standing.

"She said for me to stay here, so I don't catch it, too. She was coughing pretty badly..." he trailed off, looking out the window at his own home.

"Hospital is the best place for him," Hallie said. "She's right, stay here. But are you going to go home to change? You're soaking wet."

Stephen stared at them blankly, before pulling the back of his t-shirt over his head and removing it, shaking his shaggy wet hair as he did so.

"Oh. Wow, well..." Hallie's eyes were wide and unblinking.

Cassie hastily raised her drink to cover her surprise and spluttered as the vodka burned her throat, her attention riveted on the broad expanse of Stephen's muscled chest and the light smattering of hair that trailed enticingly between the hard v framing his hips.

Oblivious, Stephen walked into the adjoining laundry. "I'm gonna throw this in the dryer," he tossed over his shoulder.

"That was... unexpected," Hallie whispered. "And hot. *Really* hot."

"Hal! He's our best friend. Stop ogling him."

"You were ogling too," she accused. "And come on, can you blame us? When did he fill out like *that*?"

Cassie blew out a breath and acknowledged the quickening of her pulse. Wow was right.

CHAPTER TWO

Cassie was vaping with feigned nonchalance, excruciatingly aware of Jeremy's knee bumping hers as they sat on the top step of the deck, watching the rain sheet down across the backyard as the party pumped behind them.

She glanced at him from beneath lowered lashes, adoring the fullness of his bottom lip and the cocky smirk he always wore. He had a confidence, a *sureness,* that Cassie found mesmerising, even as it made her question why he'd be interested in her.

"Want to hit up the hot tub?" he asked, the column of his throat tantalising as he swallowed the last of his drink.

"Uh, yeah. I mean, yes." She stood quickly and cursed herself for coming across as too eager, looking away from him to survey the party.

If you looked at it objectively, it should be bombing. Less than a quarter of the senior class had showed, so there were none of the usual cliques that defined them. But everyone was mingling and chatting, hyped up on the uncertainty the flu pandemic had wrought.

Lucas Hernández rarely attended parties, but he was

currently smashing Stephen at beer pong and regaling everyone with news from downtown. He and Jimmy Fowler worked at the Dairy Queen and it had closed, as had many of the local businesses. Too many people off sick to open them.

"Mayor Townsend has stationed councilmen at the front doors to the supermarket, to stop people panic buying," Jimmy said, "And I heard that Marie Jenkins is so sick, her parents took her to the hospital."

"Didn't you hear?" asked Sami Thomas, their class president. "Marie died this morning."

Everyone stilled. The rain was loud on the deck roof and someone muted the music.

"What?" Cassie breathed. Marie was *dead*?

She shook her head in denial.

Shocked faces mirrored back at her, and two girls started sobbing. If they believed it was real, maybe it was? Maybe Marie really was gone.

A hollow pit bloomed inside Cassie. She wanted her parents. She wanted Hallie. Where *was* Hallie?

"Was it the flu?" someone asked.

"That's what I heard," Sami replied. "The hospital is full of sick people."

"But the flu doesn't *kill* you," Jimmy argued.

A buzz of frenzied conversation swirled like a disturbed hive of bees, and Cassie hugged her midsection with trembling arms. All of a sudden, she wanted the party to be over.

"Intense, huh?" Jeremy slung an arm around her shoulders, angling them towards the hot tub. "What temp have you got the water at?"

"Jeremy, I don't really..." Cassie ducked out from beneath his arm, confused by his lack of concern. How did that news not affect him?

243

"Come on," he cajoled. "It'll relax you."

Was she really turning down the opportunity to get in a hot tub with Jeremy Tait? She'd been crushing on him their whole junior year and now he was stripping down to his board shorts *right in front of her*, holding out a hand for her to join him as he stepped into the steaming water.

"Oh yeah, this is the bomb!" he called, sinking down. "Come on, Cass."

She knew if she backed out now, she would lose her chance with him. If she wanted this to happen, and *god* she wanted this to happen, she needed to push down this stupid, inconvenient reluctance.

Swallowing, she pulled her dress over her head to reveal her new black bikini, studiously ignoring her flipping stomach and hoping she looked at least a little more casual than she felt.

Slipping into the water, she let the heat envelop her, her skin tingling at the abrupt change of temperature. Jeremy grinned, motioning her closer. "Told you this is what we needed. Get our minds off this whole flu thing."

His breath puffed over her, yeasty with the scent of beer and thrilling her. Instinctively, she clenched her thighs together.

If she could just forget the flu and overlook the childish niggling need for her parents, this was perfect. Romantic with the twinkling of the string lights overhead and the billowing steam. And hadn't she been dreaming of this forever?

For Jeremy to notice her, to *want* her.

She wondered if he could see her heart palpitating right through her skin. Did he know how inexperienced she was? She'd only been on a few dates, and apart from that one time she and Stephen...

Nope, not thinking about that right now.

She needed to pull herself together.

She bit her lip, encouraged when his eyes tracked the movement.

Tucking herself under his arm, she settled on the ledge seat beside him. Immediately, his hand began tracing patterns on the skin of her shoulder before dipping lower and stroking the side of her breast. It was terrifyingly electric and had gooseflesh breaking out despite the heat of the water.

It was suddenly difficult to drag enough oxygen into her lungs and, oh god, could he see her nipples puckering beneath her bikini top? Did she even care?

A reckless rush of longing had her turning into him, raising her chin and parting her lips. She had barely closed her eyes before his mouth was on hers, his tongue stroking in a request for entry. On a sigh, she opened, submitting herself to the pressure of his rhythmic, practiced thrusts.

"Cass!" Stephen's shout was enough to drag her from euphoria.

She blinked her eyes open, finding him standing beside the hot tub with an inscrutable expression on his face.

A flash of... *guilt*? pricked her, but she shoved it away. Who cared if Stephen saw her making out with Jeremy? It was none of his business.

"What?" she snapped.

"Yeah, man. What's your problem?" Jeremy drawled, his hand flexing possessively on Cassie's hip.

"Sorry to... interrupt. But I need you," Stephen muttered, which was when Cassie saw his barely leashed panic.

"What's wrong?" She was already clambering from the tub, wrapping herself in the towel Stephen offered.

"Cassie..." Jeremy implored, but she didn't glance his way.

"It's Hallie. She's sick. Really sick," Stephen said, his tone low and ravaged.

"I'll call her parents."

"I already tried, cell coverage must be down because I couldn't get through."

"Okay, we'll drive her home."

"I think she needs the hospital."

Shit-shit-shit.

CHAPTER THREE

"Hold up, you're leaving your own party?" Jeremy was incredulous, not making any attempt to leave the hot tub. "Come on, Cassie. This will all blow over. Everything is fine."

Cassie glanced at him and then continued trying to reach her parents on her cell. Neither of them were picking up, causing her flutter of anxiety to flood into tsunami proportions.

"We need to leave, Cass. Now," Stephen called. He'd already carried Hallie to his jeep as Cassie was shutting down the party.

"Are you going to the hospital?" asked Lucas, flanked by Jimmy and, surprisingly, Sami.

"Yeah. She's really sick," Stephen said. "She's started bleeding from her nose, and her temperature is, like, super high."

"We'll follow you. My Mom was taking my Abuela to the hospital earlier this afternoon," Lucas said.

"And maybe we can find out more about what's going on," Sami added, clutching tight to Jimmy's hand. Cassie flicked a look between them, but there was no time for that kind of curiosity.

She started for the door and then hesitated, looking back at Jeremy. He was getting out of the tub, but refused to catch her eye. What was his problem? Couldn't he see this was an emergency?

Shaking her head, she followed the others through the house and out to the cars, not bothering to lock up behind her. The sight of Hallie's pale and listless form had her heart clenching.

She'd been so wrapped up in Jeremy she hadn't even thought about her best friend. Guilt had bile rising in her throat and she scrambled into her seat beside Hallie, laying her unconscious friend's head in her lap and stroking her sweaty forehead.

"It's okay. You're okay," she soothed.

Stephen was frantic and his driving erratic, causing Cassie's fear to rachet into something bordering on terror. Sami's words from earlier bounced on repeat through her head.

"Didn't you hear? Marie died this morning."

They had slowed to a crawl and then stopped all together.

"Fuck. Fuck!" Stephen roared, banging his fist against the steering wheel. "This must be the first time in fucking history Sanford has had a traffic jam."

Cassie lent forward to better see through the windscreen. A stream of red tail lights trailed all the way down the block, taking up both lanes of the water-slick street.

"Are they all…"

"Heading to the hospital? Looks like it," Stephen said.

For the first time, Cassie turned to check the others

were behind them. Jimmy was driving a family-sized mini-van and waved at her when she caught his eye.

"We're going too slow!" she called, swinging back to face Stephen. "Hallie doesn't have time to wait in this kind of traffic."

And she wasn't the only one with that thought. The doors to the vehicle in front of them opened and Mrs Smithson from the drug store emerged, helping her son to his feet. He was also bleeding from the nose.

They started the two-block walk to the hospital, without even glancing at them. Cassie's elation at seeing an adult was short-lived. Everyone was too caught up in their own drama to ask how anyone else was.

She and Stephen both jumped, startled, when Lucas knocked on the driver's side window.

"We're going to have to walk," he said when Stephen lowered it.

"Let's just reverse and take another road," Cassie argued.

"Can't. We're already blocked in by other vehicles." Lucas waved over his shoulder.

A car horn blared ahead of them, soon joined by several others. More people began getting out of their vehicles and walking towards the hospital.

"Guys!" Jimmy skidded to a stop beside Lucas, waving his cell. "The internet is blowing up. They're calling it the Sy-V virus and it's *bad*. So bad that the army just bombed O'Hare International because of rioting!"

"What?" Stephen shook his head.

"That's just crazy," Cassie chimed in, leaning between the front seats to better see Jimmy. "Our military wouldn't bomb Chicago's airport because of a flu outbreak."

"It's not the flu." Sami had come to stand with Jimmy. "Sy-V has flu-like symptoms, but it's... deadly."

"What are you? A doctor? Hallie has the flu, and just needs a fluid IV or something," Cassie insisted. "Who's going to help me carry her?" She opened her door with force, feeling a kick of satisfaction when Sami jumped out of the way.

"It's *really* contagious, Cassie." Sami's expression was stricken.

"What, and you think you haven't already been exposed?" Cassie couldn't help the vicious twist to her mouth. It would be just like Little Miss Class President to think she was too good to catch the flu.

"We're not saying to leave Hallie," Jimmy placated. "We know she needs to get to the hospital, and we need to get answers. But we also need to be smart. If Sy-V is as contagious as the media is reporting, then we should take precautions."

"Cover our faces," agreed Stephen, unbuckling his seat belt and getting out of the jeep. It was night, and it was October. The rain had stopped, but it was cold. Too cold to be using their jackets as makeshift masks.

"Hold on, Mom was on laundry duty for my little brother's soccer team. I think their shirts are in the back of the van," Jimmy called, already running to check. He returned with an armful of navy and yellow tops, throwing one to each of them.

Cassie leaned against the jeep, the shirt hanging limply from her hand. The reality of their predicament rudely shoved through the emotional barriers she'd hastily erected, leaving a debilitating fear to crash over her. She wasn't sure if her legs would continue to hold her up. If her lungs had the capacity to keep her breathing.

She wanted her Mom. She wanted Hallie. She felt bad about being a bitch to Sami, and why was she even worrying about something like that right now?

A tear tracked down her cheek and she hiccoughed a sob, stuffing her fist into her mouth to stem the rising tide of hopelessness. How had this happened so quickly?

"Hey, hey. It's going to be okay." Stephen stepped in front of her, his hands cupping her face as he thumbed away her tears. Bending, he pressed his forehead against hers.

"Hallie needs us to be strong right now," he murmured. "I know this is scary as hell, but we have each other. I've got you, Cass."

She breathed deep, swallowing her fears and blinking up at him.

"Okay."

"Here, let me help you tie the shirt as a mask," he offered, tugging her closer by the belt loops of her jeans and then lifting her hair from her neck so she could tie beneath it.

The silky material restricted her breathing, but that was the point, right?

A rattling distracted her.

"I found this," Sami said. "I thought a shopping cart would be easier than carrying Hallie all the way."

"Thanks." Cassie offered a grim smile and they watched the boys extract Hallie from the jeep, her body limp and unresponsive, and place her carefully in the cart.

Cassie looked around at the five of them, and then turned towards the hospital, holding tight to the side of the cart as Stephen pushed forward.

The weight of despair permeated the air, but, apart from the earlier blasting of car horns, it was weirdly quiet. Just desperate people making their way towards salvation.

CHAPTER FOUR

It took an interminable amount of time to walk the two blocks to the hospital, only to find vehicles spilling from the carpark, parked haphazardly all along the street. There was a growing throng at the door to emergency with people jostling for a position, muted muttering punctuated by the occasional shout.

"Why are they crowding out the front?" Cassie asked, immediately feeling Hallie's forehead when Stephen stopped pushing the shopping cart. She was burning up, hotter than it should be possible for a human to be.

In the darkness outside, the crammed capacity of the ER was horribly visible—seats were full and patients were lying on the floor and lining the walls. They looked grey under the harsh fluorescent lighting, and many were racked with fits of coughing, blood streaming from their noses.

As they approached the back of the crowd, a small nurse wearing a surgical mask opened the door, backed by a security guard.

"One at a time, and only the sick. We're at capacity and

don't have the space for family. You'll have to wait outside," she called out.

There was grumbling as the group complied, handing their sick loved ones off and backing away. Sami, Jimmy, and Lucas stood back as Stephen rolled Hallie forward.

"Please look after her," Cassie implored, as another nurse received them at the door.

"How long has she been in a coma?" the nurse asked.

"Coma? She's not in a coma!" A flutter of panic choked Cassie. "She's got a fever, but she's going to be okay, right?"

"We'll do our best." The nurse looked worn and frayed at the edges, her own body shaking with a suppressed cough. "It's good you've got your face covered. Stay safe, okay?"

And Hallie was whisked away.

"Wait! I didn't even tell you her name!" Cassie called, taking a step to follow.

"Sorry, Miss. You can't enter," the security guard said, his voice not unkind.

Mr Bilpin, a local farmer who supplied barley to Sanford's whiskey distillery, pushed her to the side. Stephen steadied her on her feet and tugged her away.

"What do you mean I can't come in?" Mr Bilpin's voice echoed back at them. "She's just a baby, she's only four!"

Cassie looked over her shoulder and saw Mr Bilpin shouldering the unarmed security guard. When the guard stood firm, Mr Bilpin pulled a shotgun from his belt and brandished it wildly.

"Oh shit," Stephen breathed, tightening his hold on Cassie as they watched the scene unfold. The door swung shut, a nurse fumbling with the lock as Mr Bilpin and others pushed against it.

"My little girl! You've got to let us in!"

Crazed with desperation, Mr Bilpin fired into the night sky.

"Let us in!"

The remaining crowd began banging their fists against the door, watching helplessly as staff inside pulled furniture and equipment to barricade themselves.

"This is fucked up," Lucas muttered as they joined the others, staring back at the commotion. When another gunshot rang out, cracking but not breaking the glass door, they turned as one and sprinted back the way they'd come.

Their burst of adrenalin didn't last long. It was two in the morning and they were exhausted. Sami dropped back first, Jimmy slowing to match her, and then they were standing in a circle, panting.

"What now?" Cassie asked, her throat tight with unshed tears. "It's too far to walk home, and our cars are parked in."

"My parents are going to be freaking out," Sami said.

"Have you tried calling them?" Jimmy rubbed tenderly between her shoulder blades.

"They're not answering." She looked up. "But I work after school at the vet clinic, and it's only a block away. I have a key. We could sleep in the staff room and work out what to do in the morning?"

They reached consensus without a word, and began trudging behind Sami, Cassie's chest blooming with comfort when Stephen slipped his hand into hers.

THE SOUND of the back door to the vet clinic opening had Cassie forcing her eyes open, the morning sun streaming brightly into the staff room. The night before they had repurposed clean towels and blankets meant for the animal cages as bedding, and Cassie had been asleep before she could lament the uncomfortable floor or the barking of a dog they had disturbed.

Sitting groggily, she realised Stephen had been curled around her back, and she instantly missed his body warmth.

Footsteps had her alert in seconds and she looked around, seeing Sami was also aware they had company.

"Who is it?" Cassie whispered.

Sami shrugged, getting to her feet.

"It shouldn't take me long to check the animals..." The female voice was getting closer, and Cassie recognized there were two sets of footsteps. The voice trailed off as she entered the staff room, and Cassie saw it was Rachel Davenport, one of the veterinarians, and Chloe Brent-Maxwell, their guidance councillor at school.

"Sami! What are you doing here?" Rachel asked, looking at them in surprise.

"Rachel. Miss Brent-Maxwell. Hi," Sami stammered. "Our cars got stuck in the traffic jam to the hospital, so we thought it would be okay to stay here." Cheeks stained pink, she glanced between the two women. "I mean, it was okay, right?"

"Yeah, sure," Rachel assured her. "Do you need a lift home? Do your parents know where you are?"

By this time, the boys had woken in varying degrees of alertness.

"Mr Bilpin was shooting a gun at the hospital doors, trying to get in," Stephen said. "It was fucked–" he paused. "Sorry. It was messed up."

"Don't apologise," Miss Maxwell said. "It *is* fucked up out there."

Their normally calm teacher appeared rattled, which scared Cassie. A lot.

"Guess we won't be having that meeting about college applications," Cassie said, hoping they would contradict her. She wanted the adults to tell her everything would be back to normal by tomorrow.

"I don't think so, Cassie. I had an email from the department, and schools are closed until further notice."

"Give me ten minutes to sort out the animals, and we'll drop you home," Rachel interrupted. "Mayor Townsend wants everyone at the Town Hall at ten o'clock for a meeting."

That centred Cassie. In the absence of her parents, she needed to know that someone in authority knew what to do. They took turns using the staff bathroom, and Cassie was feeling almost hopeful after she'd washed her face and eaten biscuits that Sami handed out from the kitchenette.

Everything was going to be okay.

"How are you doing?" Stephen asked quietly, finding her staring out the window. And she found it was the most natural thing in the world for him to thread his fingers through hers.

"I'm okay, I think. Hallie is where she needs to be, and we don't have to walk home. I was kind of dreading that."

"Yeah, I want to check on my parents, and it would have been driving me crazy the entire walk home. Any luck getting through to yours?"

"My cell is dead. I'll charge it when I get home and try again," she sighed, and turned into him, resting her cheek against his chest. "This is just all so crazy."

He didn't answer, just wrapped his arms tighter around her.

Everything is going to be okay.

CHAPTER FIVE

The streets of Sanford were quiet as Rachel drove Cassie and Stephen home. Cassie studied her own reflection in the car's window, ignoring the world outside. She would get home and call her parents. And then Mayor Townsend would tell them what to do.

It was going to be okay.

Her attention wandered to Stephen, sitting in the front passenger seat, chatting easily with Rachel. Cassie wished he were sitting in the back with her. They'd slipped into an easy intimacy where his touch didn't just offer comfort. It created a tingle of... *something*.

Was she developing *feelings* for him?

Rachel pulled into her driveway, and Cassie had to look twice.

"What's he doing here?" Stephen growled.

Jeremy was sitting on her front step.

Shit-shit-shit.

"Are your parents home?" Rachel asked, extending her arm along the passenger seat so she could turn her head to see Cassie.

"They're away on business, but I'm sure they're on their way back."

"What about your folks?" she asked Stephen.

"Home. But sick." His voice faded off as he stared over at his own house.

"Okay. Well, stay safe." Rachel raised her eyebrows when neither of them made a move.

"You can get out now," she prompted, shifting the gears into reverse.

They clambered out, and Rachel left without another glance.

"Why is he still here?" Stephen asked, his eyes intent on Jeremy.

"I have no idea." Cassie wasn't sure why she felt defensive. "Do you want me to come over to yours with you?" Having witnessed the sick at the hospital, she was loath to see how his parents were. But she also couldn't stomach the thought of him going alone.

"What about your boyfriend?"

"Really?" She gave him a withering look. "He's not my boyfriend, and you know it."

Jeremy had stood, and was twisting his ball cap in his hands.

She sighed.

"Give me a minute to see what he wants."

She approached Jeremy reluctantly. Last night in the hot tub seemed like it was a million years ago. So much had happened since, and she wasn't sure what her feelings were anymore. Not when it came to him, anyway.

"Have you been here all night?"

"No. I went home and came back this morning. Cass, I was a jerk," he said, shoving his cap back onto his head and reaching for her. "I shouldn't have let you go without me. Are you okay? How is Hallie?"

His brown eyes were brimming with remorse, and his hands were warm and firm on her arms. She breathed deep. It would be so easy to forget everything and fall into his embrace.

"I need to go next door with Stephen. Will you wait for me?"

"Of course. But don't be too long. Did you hear about the town meeting?"

"Yeah."

"I can take you."

"And Stephen."

He paused. "Okay."

"Okay."

Her feet were leaden walking next door, a heavy trepidation dogging her. What if they were... she couldn't even think the word.

Stepping inside, they were greeted by still, stale air. As though the house had stood empty for years. How could a sense of abandonment echo after just a few hours?

"Mom? Dad?" Stephen called out, his footsteps loud as he ran up the stairs to the bedrooms.

Cassie hesitated and then followed.

"Mom!" Stephen was kneeling at the door to the master bedroom, cradling his mother and using the sleeve of his sweatshirt to wipe blood from her face. Cassie exhaled a held breath when Mrs Worthington's eyes fluttered open.

"Cassie, help me get her to the bed," he yelled, already gathering her in his arms.

"No, don't," Mrs Worthington choked through a fit of coughing, bloodshot eyes streaming with tears. "Not in there."

"Mom?"

But Cassie had looked beyond and seen the prone form of Mr Worthington laying on the bed. Dead.

She realised with an alarming degree of detachment, that his was the first dead body she'd ever seen in real life. And she wasn't even sure how she knew from this distance that he *was* dead. Just that he was.

Rushing to help lift Mrs Worthington, she ushered them into the adjoining guest bedroom as Stephen struggled to comprehend the situation. He suddenly resembled the small boy she'd first met, all those years ago.

"Mom, is..." his voice was small, and he couldn't look his mother in the face.

"I'm sorry, Stephen." Lying on the bed, she raised a weak hand to his cheek. "He died earlier this morning."

Stephen bowed his head. His hands fisted the bed linen as his body shook with silent sobs.

Muffling her own cries, Cassie wavered, undecided. Would he want her comfort? Her sympathy? Or was she an intruder, witnessing the magnitude of their loss?

What could she do?

And then she recalled the many small touches from Stephen over the last twenty-four hours. The way he'd cared and supported and encouraged her. She dropped to her knees beside him, throwing her arms around his waist and hugging him. Hard.

This is what she would want, if it were her father who had died. Stephen, with his arms around her.

They cried together as Mrs Worthington lapsed back into a semi-conscious state, until Stephen pulled away.

"I need to look after her," he said, voice hoarse.

"I can call 911?" Cassie knew instinctively it would be

hopeless to call for an ambulance, but she didn't know what else to do.

The call failed to connect.

"She's burning up..." Stephen mumbled.

"I'll get a cold washer, you–"

"Cass, you need to leave," Stephen demanded.

"What? No." She turned to him, confused. "I can help–"

"No. You can't be here. She's infected, I'm probably infected. If you stay, you'll get sick."

Cassie recoiled, eyes widening in shock, and then narrowing.

"I'm not leaving you here alone," she insisted. "If you're infected, then I am, too. You can't make me go."

Mrs Worthington groaned and jerked restlessly, but didn't wake.

"Cassie!" Stephen hissed, dragging her from the room. "You. Can. Not. Stay. Here. Do you understand? Go!" He shoved her, and she spun, off balance.

"Stephen!" Shock turned to outrage, and she swung at him, the flat of her palm slapping across his face with stinging force.

Panting heavily, they faced each other.

Her heart was pumping furiously, raw and heavy with hurt.

"I need you," she whispered.

"I don't need you."

He was steely. Resolute.

Turning back to his dying mother, he shut the door in her face.

CHAPTER SIX

Face wet with tears, Cassie ran up her front steps and straight into Jeremy's arms. There was a jagged hole in her chest at being forced away, and it *hurt*. So damn much.

"What's wrong?" Jeremy hugged her close, but he didn't smell like Stephen, and that made her tears come faster.

"He's not coming." She hiccoughed around her answer. "Let's just go."

She wanted Jeremy to drive her away from her heartbreak—from the pieces of shattered heart lying in Stephen's hallway.

He led her to the passenger seat and helped her in, leaning across to do up her seatbelt. Yesterday she would have been *delirious* at such a gesture.

Yesterday seemed like a long time ago.

"My Dad said Mayor Townsend is creating a Safe Zone in the town, and evacuating everyone from the outer edges of the town into it," Jeremy said, starting the engine.

"Mmmmm."

"He's going to quarantine anyone who's sick at the

hospital. I saw school buses lined up at the Town Hall on my way here, ready to take anyone with symptoms straight there."

Cassie didn't mention the hospital was already over-crowded.

She said nothing at all. What was there to say?

"Did you end up talking to your parents?" he asked. "You know all the telecommunications are down now, right?"

A fierce longing gripped her. She wanted her parents. She should be waiting at home for them. How would they know where she was?

"Jeremy, stop—"

"Holy shit!"

Jeremy slammed on the brakes, mouth hanging open. Ahead of them, the church on the corner had burst into flames, fire licking through the two visible doors. In seconds, an explosion rocked the structure, the sound reverberating through their vehicle, as the structure erupted with flames. A man—Mr Jefferies?—ran onto the sidewalk and jumped into a truck, tearing away.

"What the hell?" Jeremy breathed, unable to take his eyes from the inferno.

"Do you think anyone was in there?" Cassie wanted to unsee all the vehicles in the church's parking lot. "I mean, there can't have been, right?"

"No one could have lived through that, so I sure hope not. Do you think we should call the fire department?"

"No telecommunications, remember?"

"Fuuuuuck. This is so screwed up," Jeremy cursed, pulling back onto the road.

The town square was already packed with vehicles, and

people were making their way to the Town Hall. Preoccupied with the blast they'd just witnessed, it took Cassie a moment to catch up with what Jeremy was pointing at.

"See? They're taking the sick to be quarantined."

Everyone was being funnelled into a line, and townsfolk wearing high-vis vests were corralling anyone sick onto waiting buses.

"Are they... armed?" Cassie asked, cold trepidation settling in her gut. "Jeremy, I think I want to go home."

"You what?" Jeremy paused as he exited, looking back at her over his shoulder. "Cass, don't be an idiot." He slammed his door behind him, coming around to her side. "I'm not taking you home again."

"I want to go home. I'm sorry, I know we just got here–"

"Cassie, I'm not taking you home. The meeting is going to start soon. Come on."

He opened her door and tugged on her arm.

"No, really." She crossed her arms stubbornly. "I don't feel good about this. I want to wait at home for my parents."

"Fine, do whatever you want." He huffed. "But I'm going inside. I'll drive you home after."

"Don't bother, I'll walk." Disappointment causing her throat to close in. She fumbled to unstrap herself, the metal buckle of the seatbelt flicking against her shoulder painfully. Her eyes pricked, but she swiped at them angrily, climbing from the car only to see Jeremy's back as he strode away.

What had she ever seen in him?

A scuffle broke out in the line ahead, with Mr and Mrs Hegertey insisting they quarantine with their sick kids. Cassie flinched as Mr Hegertey was hit between the shoulder blades with the butt of a shotgun, and his kids forcibly removed.

Cassie spun around and ran.

Having run track since she was a freshman, it wasn't a big deal to cover the distance back home. Feet pounding the pavement, she let her mind go blissfully blank. Concentrating on breathing in and breathing out.

Until the acrid weight of smoke filled her lungs, causing her to cut through a park and down a side lane to miss the church.

She was breathing hard when she rounded the corner to her street, slowing to a walk and then stopping completely when she saw Lucas, Jimmy and Sami sitting on her front lawn. With Stephen.

The sight of her best friend, his shoulders hunched with grief, kick-started her until she was sprinting, propelling herself into his arms. He received her with a grunt and, off balance, they tumbled to the ground, landing in a tangle of limbs.

"You don't get to send me away," she said fiercely, laying on his chest and gripping his face between both her hands. "Do you hear me? We are in this *together*."

She didn't care she was sweaty. She didn't care she was practically straddling him, or that they had an audience. She just needed *him*.

There was a beat. Two. And then he nodded.

"I lied. I do need you," he whispered.

She swallowed, tears of relief streaming down her cheeks.

"Guys? Can we go inside? It's cold out here," Sami interrupted them.

"Not my house." Stephen looked away. "Mom is... gone."

"Oh, Stephen."

He dislodged her gently and got to his feet, reaching down to help her to hers.

"Did you get through to your parents yet?" he asked.

"Cells aren't working," she replied, opening the front door and ushering them. "What about everyone else?"

They settled on the stools around the island bench in the kitchen, Cassie opening the refrigerator to get them soda.

"Power is out," she observed, closing the door quickly to conserve the cold air.

"I can't find my parents, they're not at home," Sami said. "And Jimmy's...."

"My brother and sister, they..." Jimmy choked up. "They're dead. And Mom and Dad aren't taking it well. They're... well, it's just better I got out of the house."

"I'm so sorry," Cassie murmured, not sure what else she could say. "And you, Lucas?"

Lucas looked down, his long hair flopping into his face and covering his eyes.

"Dead."

In the silence, they could hear a clock ticking.

"Should we go to the Town Hall?" Stephen asked, running his fingers over the condensation on the outside of his soda bottle.

"No!"

Sami's vehemence shocked them.

"Why?" Stephen traded confused glances with Cassie.

"I agree. There's something not quite right about what's happening there," Cassie admitted.

"That's an understatement," Sami retorted. "Mayor Townsend had men set fire to the church, and I don't know that everyone got out."

"What? Why?" Stephen cried.

266

"I saw it," Cassie said. "But I didn't know..."

"The congregation wouldn't leave to go to the town meeting. They wanted to stay at the church. So Townsend told them to burn it down," Sami said grimly. "Everything is *not* okay."

CHAPTER SEVEN

It had been two days now without electricity, and with no contact from the world outside of Sanford. With no cell service or internet, Cassie was losing hope her parents would make it home, while Stephen had given up waiting for a response to the letter he'd left on the front door of Perry's Funeral Home, and had started digging a hole in his backyard.

Sami still had expectations of the Army arriving with some kind of solution, and Jimmy and Lucas were furtively keeping tabs on the town's council, who appeared to be running the Safe Zone they'd set up in the middle of town.

Bunkered down in Cassie's house, they were in what had been termed the Evac Area, apparently alone now that everyone had either complied with Mayor Townsend's dictates to move into the Safe Zone or quarantine at the hospital.

Their neighborhood was disturbingly quiet—no cars, no planes overhead, and no people. Cassie was growing tired of hosting everyone, and worried about their dwindling food supplies.

Unlatching the shared gate between her backyard and Stephen's, she paused before walking through. Stephen had told her what he was doing, but she hadn't yet seen the grave he was digging for his parents.

She was afraid of how real this was going to make everything.

Stephen was leaning against a shovel, surveying his work. He was shirtless in the chill October air, his skin streaked with sweat and dirt. And tears. There were definite tear tracks down his face that he didn't bother to wipe away when Cassie approached.

"I just can't believe..." he trailed off. "How is it okay to bury your parents like this?"

Wordlessly, she wrapped her arms around him, the shovel thumping to the ground as he hugged her back. She breathed him in, still a little dumbfounded at how essential he had become to her. Essential in a fundamental way.

They'd been sharing her bed, taking comfort from the warmth of their spooning bodies. And she yearned for more, wanting the press of his mouth against hers, the rub of their skin moving together. But how could she ask for that? The world had ended, and they were grieving for everything they'd lost.

It was inconceivable she could have fallen in love at this moment in time. With this boy.

But she had.

Pulling away, she took his hands in hers.

"Is it... ready?"

Her gaze flicked to the hole in the grass that Stephen had been toiling over.

"Yeah. Lucas and Jimmy will be back soon. They're going to help me move..."

"I'll help, too."

"Thanks, Cass."

He led her to the side of the house where he washed up quickly with the garden hose.

"How long do you think we'll have running water?" she asked absently, watching the water sluice over the definition of his forearms.

"No idea." He used the t-shirt hanging from his back pocket to dry off. "Probably something to think about, though. How did you and Sami go finding bicycles?"

She and Sami had gone on a mission to find bicycles for them all, as an inconspicuous way of getting around—they didn't want to attract any attention from the town's council.

They were undecided about whether they should go back to the hospital and, even though Cassie was adamant she needed to check on Hallie, she understood the others' hesitation to be further exposed to the virus.

"As long as you're okay riding a purple unicorn bike, we're good."

He chuckled, and Cassie's chest eased some. Even in the depth of his sorrow, he was still here. With her.

They ended up in her backyard, on the swing set again.

Was it just a couple of days ago they'd been here in this very spot?

She saw the moment Stephen had the same realisation.

"Feels like a million years ago," he observed. "You know, I wanted to tell you something that night, before Hallie got here."

Cassie tensed. Was he about to admit he had feelings for Hallie?

"You did?"

Shit-shit-shit. Why was she playing dumb?

"You know I did," he admonished with a grin. "There

just hasn't really been the right time since then to finish our conversation."

"I guess not. That was the beginning of the end, wasn't it?"

"I was kind of hoping it was going to be the beginning of *us*."

Cassie's eyes jumped to his, her heartbeat quickening. "Not Hallie?"

"Hallie? What does she have to do with my feelings for you?"

"Nothing? I hope..."

"I hope, too," he murmured, reaching out to snag the chain of her swing, drawing her close enough that their breath became one. "Remember our first kiss?"

"Yeah, I do."

"Why didn't we...?"

"Do it again?"

"No. Yes. I mean, why didn't we become something then?" His eyes searched hers. "Why has it taken us two years to get to this point?"

Cassie flashed back to that rainy afternoon, watching re-runs of *The Gilmore Girls* on the laptop in his bedroom. They'd been on the floor, leaning against his bed, mouths numb from finishing a tub of choc mint ice-cream. She still wasn't sure how it had happened, just that she'd seen something on his face, something he'd seen reflected on hers, and then they were leaning into each other and parting their lips and... kissing.

It had been brief, and sweet, and they'd never spoken of it again.

"We're here now," she replied, giving in to the urge to run her fingertip over his lush bottom lip. She gasped when he opened and sucked her inside, his tongue warm and tempting. Pulling free, she grabbed both sides of his face and held him, maintaining eye contact as she nipped at his lips, licking and nibbling.

His groan shivered through her, tugging hot between her thighs. She clenched them, moving her lips more urgently. His smile curved against her lips before he titled her chin and *claimed* her. There was no other word for it. His mouth took possession of hers, moulding and teasing, and *when did he get so good at this?*

She was lightheaded and grounded, at the same time. Stephen's earthy, masculine scent was intoxicating, and she thrilled at his capable hands that were stroking beneath her sweater.

She was melting and molten and... she squeaked as he pulled them from the swings to the damp ground beneath, rolling so he was braced above her. Squirming, she stilled when she registered the hard length of him pressed between her legs, instinctively widening her thighs for him to settle against her hips.

He brushed his lips down the bridge of her nose, feathering them across her closed eyelids, and then to her parted, panting mouth.

"More," she demanded.

He smiled, capturing her lips, and her heart, and her future.

Because no matter what the future held, they would face it together.

THE END.

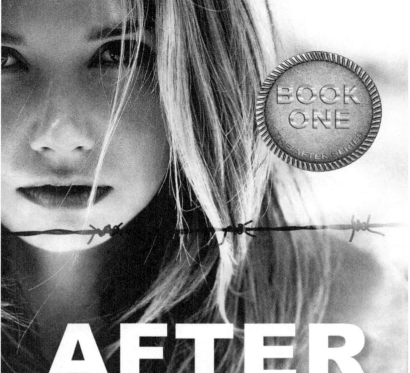

AFTER
today

JACQUELINE HAYLEY

BOOK
ONE
THE AFTER SERIES

Can love survive an apocalypse?

After a deadly virus ravages Chicago and destroys Mackenzie Lyons' carefully curated world, Mac escapes the devastation and horror to her childhood hometown with the help of her best-friend's little brother, Jake. But the small-minded community of Sanford isn't exactly welcoming, and the virus isn't the only battle brewing.

Jake Brent has secretly loved Mac forever, and while this isn't the way he'd dreamed of their relationship beginning, with the uncertainty of the outbreak he'll take every opportunity with Mac he can and hope—pray—for a better future.

But when Sanford's misogynistic council torment the survivors with horrifying demands and a lawless motorcycle gang threatens their fragile sanctuary, somehow Jake and Mackenzie must form new alliances and face down dangerous enemies in a struggle far worse than the outbreak.

Surviving the virus was one thing, surviving humanity after is another.

Printed in Great Britain
by Amazon

87872138R00163